Praise for Denis

"Hunter's latest is a healing and empo... Hunter's classic style, *The Summer of Yo... long after the end."

—Rachel Hauck, *New York Times* bestselling author

"Yummy romance with a dash of mystery, this friends-to-lovers novel, *The Summer of You and Me*, is wonderful! Hunter's deft hand mixes grief with new beginnings to make a delicious read that has Hallmark movie written all over it. Highly recommend!"

—Colleen Coble, *USA TODAY* and *Publishers Weekly* bestselling author

"Poignant and powerful, *The Summer of You and Me* is an exquisite 'out-of-the-box' romance that will rack your mind and ratchet your pulse! The amazing Denise Hunter has done it again with a truly riveting read that's short on sleep but long on hope."

—Julie Lessman, award-winning author of *The Daughters of Boston*, *Winds of Change*, and the Isle of Hope series

"This story pulled at my heartstrings from the first chapter right through to the last. I longed for Maggie and Josh to find their happily-ever-after, despite the emotional roller coaster they were on. Denise Hunter has written a beautiful story filled with the complexities that come with loving others, especially members of our own families."

—Robin Lee Hatcher, Christy Award–winning author of *Wishing for Mistletoe* and *To Capture a Mountain Man*

"Denise Hunter made me cry again. Wow—what a breathtaking, heart-tugging story! *The Summer of You and Me* has so many great surprises, twists, and turns that my head is reeling and I could not stop reading. You will not be sorry you read this book."

—Hannah Alexander, author of *A Woman Worth Knowing* and *One Strong Man*

"*Love, Unscripted* has it all—the funniest meet-cute ever, unique characters, and a charming beach town setting. If you love sweet romance with a lot of heart, this one has 'Hallmark movie' written all over it. Highly recommended!"

—Colleen Coble, *USA TODAY* and
Publishers Weekly bestselling author

"Hunter (*Bookshop by the Sea*) opens this heartwarming romance with Queens, N.Y., western writer Sadie Goodwin learning that her publisher wants her to switch genres to romance . . . Hunter's charismatic and complex characters effortlessly propel the story. Readers won't want to put this down."

—*Publishers Weekly* for *A Novel Proposal*

"A heartwarming tale written by an undisputed queen of the genre, *A Novel Proposal* is a love letter to readers, to writers, and, above all, to romance. As Sadie and Sam were forced out of their comfort zones, I sank deeper and deeper into my reading happy place. This cozy, clever, captivating love story is the perfect beach read and an absolute must for fans of happily ever afters. Denise Hunter charmed my socks right off with this one!"

—Bethany Turner, author of *Plot Twist* and *The Do-Over*

"A tragic accident gives a divorced couple a second chance at love in the warmhearted third installment of Hunter's Riverbend Romance series (after *Mulberry Hollow*) . . . Readers looking for an uplifting Christian romance will appreciate how Laurel and Gavin's faith helps dispel their deep-rooted fears so they can find a way to love again. Inspirational fans will find this hard to resist."

—*Publishers Weekly* for *Harvest Moon*

"Denise Hunter has a way of bringing depth and an aching beauty into her stories, and *Harvest Moon* is no different. *Harvest Moon* is a beautiful tale of second chances, self-sacrifice, and renewed romance that addresses hard topics such as child death and dissolved marriages. In a beautiful turn of events, Hunter brings unexpected healing out of a devastating situation, subtly reminding the reader that God can create beauty out of the most painful of circumstances and love from the most broken stories."

—Pepper Basham, author of *The Heart of the Mountains* and *Authentically, Izzy*

"A poignant romance that's perfect for fans of emotional love stories that capture your heart from the very first page. With her signature style, Denise Hunter whisks readers into a world where broken hearts are mended, lives are changed, and love really does conquer all!"

—Courtney Walsh, *New York Times* bestselling author, for *Mulberry Hollow*

"Hunter delivers a touching story of how family dynamics and personal priorities shift when love takes precedence. Hunter's fans will love this."

—*Publishers Weekly* for *Riverbend Gap*

"Denise Hunter has never failed to pen a novel that whispers messages of hope and brings a smile to my face. *Bookshop by the Sea* is no different! With a warmhearted community, a small beachside town, a second-chance romance worth rooting for, and cozy bookshop vibes, this is a story you'll want to snuggle into like a warm blanket."

—Melissa Ferguson, author of *Meet Me in the Margins*

"Sophie and Aiden had me hooked from page one, and I was holding my breath until the very end. Denise nails second-chance romance in *Bookshop by the Sea*. I adored this story! Five giant stars!"

—Jenny Hale, *USA TODAY* bestselling author

"*Autumn Skies* is the perfect roundup to the Bluebell Inn series. The tension and attraction between Grace and Wyatt is done so well, and the mystery kept me wondering what was going to happen next. Prepare to be swept away to the beautiful Blue Ridge Mountains in a flurry of turning pages."

—Nancy Naigle, *USA TODAY* bestselling author of *Christmas Angelss*

The Summer of You and Me

Also by Denise Hunter

The Summer of You and Me

DENISE HUNTER

THOMAS NELSON
Since 1798

The Summer of You and Me

Copyright © 2025 by Denise Hunter

Published in Nashville, Tennessee, by Thomas Nelson. Thomas Nelson is a registered trademark of HarperCollins Christian Publishing, Inc.

Thomas Nelson titles may be purchased in bulk for educational, business, fundraising, or sales promotional use. For information, please email SpecialMarkets@ThomasNelson.com.

Publisher's Note: This novel is a work of fiction. Names, characters, places, and incidents are either products of the author's imagination or used fictitiously. All characters are fictional, and any similarity to people living or dead is purely coincidental.

Any internet addresses (websites, blogs, etc.) in this book are offered as a resource. They are not intended in any way to be or imply an endorsement by Thomas Nelson, nor does Thomas Nelson vouch for the content of these sites for the life of this book.

Library of Congress Cataloging-in-Publication Data

Names: Hunter, Denise, 1968- author.
Title: The summer of you and me / Denise Hunter.
Description: Nashville, Tennessee: Thomas Nelson, 2025. | Summary: "Maggie Reynolds is finally ready for love again—until the past shows up in the form of someone who may or may not be the late husband she thought she'd lost"—Provided by publisher.
Identifiers: LCCN 2024045743 (print) | LCCN 2024045744 (ebook) | ISBN 9781400348558 (paperback) | ISBN 9781400348664 (library binding) | ISBN 9781400348671 (epub) | ISBN 9781400348688
Subjects: LCGFT: Christian fiction. | Romance fiction. | Novels.
Classification: LCC PS3608.U5925 S865 2025 (print) | LCC PS3608.U5925 (ebook) | DDC 813/.6—dc23/eng/20241001
LC record available at https://lccn.loc.gov/2024045743
LC ebook record available at https://lccn.loc.gov/2024045744
Printed in the United States of America

25 26 27 28 29 LBC 5 4 3 2 1

Chapter 1

*I*f Maggie Reynolds could just make it past August 7, she would finally be able to breathe again. But nearly two months of bittersweet memories stood between now and then like an emotional minefield. She hoped returning to Seabrook, North Carolina, for the summer wasn't a colossal mistake. Too late now.

At least she had her four-year-old in tow to distract her from all of the above.

As if on cue Zoey tugged Maggie's hand. "That one next, Mommy."

The canopied carnival ride spun in a slow circle, its young riders seated in sporty cars. "That looks fun, but we only have enough tickets for one of us. I guess you'll just have to watch me ride."

"*Mommy.*" Zoey rolled her eyes. "I should ride and you can watch. I can do it by myself. I'm a big girl now."

"That's right, I keep forgetting."

Hand in hand they headed for the short line, pressing through the crush. Evenings on the beach boardwalk were the thing of legends in Seabrook, a sleepy seaside town poised between the more popular Outer Banks and Myrtle Beach. Here the stilt houses lining the beach passed from previous generations and were revered for the memories they held rather than each square foot of beach frontage.

But come summer, the island, separated from the mainland by a bridge, would be overrun with sunseekers and golf carts. Each morning the tourists took advantage of the generous ocean treasures—numerous shells, driftwood, even shark teeth—that washed ashore at high tide. The ocean currents favored the stretch of beach along Seabrook's coast.

And each night the popular boardwalk would come alive with the sounds of blaring music, squeals of glee, calling carnies, and the mechanical whir of spinning rides.

Maggie absorbed the happy sounds, though the accompanying memories provoked a sense of melancholy: holding hands for the first time as they navigated the game alley, the two of them strolling the boardwalk, completely lost in each other, eating cotton candy from each other's sticky fingers.

The cloying scent of funnel cakes wafted by on a breeze, turning her stomach. She and Zoey had indulged in the treat just before boarding the swing ride. Zoey's young stomach seemed just fine— Maggie's not so much. At thirty-five she was no longer an impervious teenager.

Parents stood outside the barricades, waving and capturing photos of their excited children. Beyond the ride the town's iconic Ferris wheel lifted slowly overhead, its spokes sparkling with rainbow lights. Riders ascended high into the night sky, taking in the aerial view of the carnival, the boardwalk, and the beach beyond. At this hour the sea would be black and brooding, its white surf crashing the shoreline, rhythmic and relentless.

Maggie had wanted to share the view with Zoey, but her daughter had taken one glimpse of the soaring wheel and shaken her head.

As they settled in line, Zoey curled her small hands around the barrier's top rail, watching riders go around under the twinkling lights. Her hair, the same chocolate brown as Maggie's, was woven into two braids that hung over her shoulders. By the end of summer she'd have the kind of natural highlights Maggie paid good money for.

"This one's my favorite, Mommy," Zoey called over the cacophony.

Favorite was her new favorite word. "I thought the carousel was your favorite." They'd ridden it twice, Zoey choosing the white pony wreathed in pink roses both times.

"It was. But this will be my new favorite."

"Oh, I see. I like your optimism."

Wide brown eyes met Maggie's. "What's optism?"

Her daughter was a little sponge. "Opti*mis*m means having hope about how things will turn out. Like . . . I'm very optimistic this will be a wonderful summer." She smiled through the lie. Tried to believe it, for Zoey's sake if not for her own. She was ready to move on with her life. Desperate to do so.

Zoey's brows furrowed. "I'm very optimistic . . . I'll get to stay up late tonight."

Maggie laughed. "Good guess since it's already past your bedtime." Tomorrow they'd get back on a regular schedule. They'd left Fayetteville only yesterday and were just now settled into her in-laws' beautiful beach cottage. Brad and Becky had left last week for their long-awaited, extended trip to Europe.

When they'd offered Maggie their place for the whole summer, she turned them down. Wasn't sure she was ready to return to Seabrook. Then she'd given it some thought. Maybe it would be good for her. Good for Zoey. It would soon be five years, after all. Time to say good-bye.

Maggie's phone vibrated in her pocket and she checked the screen. *Save me!*

A photo accompanied Erin's text. Her best friend and sister-in-law stood alone in the gathering, looking adorable in a little black dress. She'd styled her sassy blonde bob in beach waves that complemented her pixie face. Erin wasn't a fan of large crowds or small talk.

That's what you get when you marry a pastor.

Another text appeared. *You're no help!*

Chin up. You can tell me all about it tomorrow.

"Almost my turn, Mommy!"

"It sure is." Maggie pocketed her phone as the ride crawled to a stop and a teenage girl helped the children disembark. Moments later the line inched forward and Maggie handed over the ticket.

"That one!" Zoey pointed to an old-fashioned red sports car. "I'll bet it's the fastest one."

"Mommy." The face she made as she clambered into the car was a preview of teenaged Zoey. "They all go the same speed."

"Are you sure?" Maggie buckled the belt. "Yours looks so much faster."

Zoey rolled her eyes.

Her daughter was growing up too fast. Too smart for her own good. "I'll be right over there."

"Okay."

Maggie exited the area and moved outside the stanchions. She took her phone from her shorts pocket and snapped a couple of pictures before Zoey noticed and treated her to a cheesy smile.

A few minutes later the ride began its slow, circular journey. "Have fun!"

Zoey waved, smiling as the wind ruffled her flutter sleeves. Her daughter would enjoy the ride, but she wasn't one to squeal or scream. She was so poised for her young age. So grown-up. A fun summer away from the daily routines back home would be good for her. She could use some time with her cousins and Uncle Josh, who could make her belly-laugh like no one else.

Maggie lifted the phone and stepped back to capture the entire ride. Camera in place, she waited for Zoey to glance over, but her daughter was busy working the car's steering wheel. When the ride circled back around, Zoey glanced up and flashed a smile.

But a passerby blocked the shot. Maggie's gaze homed in on the screen. On the man.

A tsunami slammed into her heart.

She gaped at his face even as he exited the frame. *It couldn't be.* She lowered the phone and searched the crowd. There he was, disappearing into the fray.

She charged that way, her attention pinned to the spot where she'd last seen him. *There.* Just a car's length away, striding in the other direction. She followed, her body surging with adrenaline, her eyes wide, afraid to blink. She laser focused on the white ball cap, bobbing in the sea of people.

She crashed into somebody, glanced down as a young boy caught his balance. "Sorry, honey." Breathless words scraped from her throat, barely audible.

She glanced around, frantically seeking. In that brief moment she'd lost sight of him. Where was he? *Where was he?* She scrambled toward the spot where she'd last seen him, the juncture where the walkway split in three directions.

She turned in circles. No sign of him. The white hat was nowhere to be seen. Her breath hitched. Her heart shriveled. She had to return to Zoey before the ride ended.

Still she searched, growing dizzy with the motion, the spinning rides, the blaring music. With the soul-crushing realization that he was gone. The unbelievable realization of who she'd just seen.

Ethan.

Impossible. She gave her head a shake. Her mind was playing tricks on her again. It couldn't be Ethan. It absolutely couldn't be her high school sweetheart, the only man she'd ever loved, the man she'd married and conceived a child with.

Because he was killed five years ago at his military post in Pakistan.

Chapter 2

C rew members, please prepare for mooring." With the ease born from years on the river, Josh Reynolds maneuvered the *Carolina Dream* into its berth. Minutes later the sixty-five-foot riverboat crawled into place, and Josh turned on his headset. "All right, folks, we're now safe to disembark. We hope you've enjoyed the beautiful Seabrook sunset. Thank you for choosing Island Tours."

As the passengers filed out, he exited the pilothouse, descended the stairs, and stepped onto the dock to see them off. "Have a wonderful night, y'all . . . Thank you for touring with us . . . Hope to see you next time."

"Bye, Cap'n Josh!"

"Bye, Caleb. Nice job steering the vessel. Come back when you're ready to be my first mate."

"Hey now!" Josh's mate, Darius, complained with flair. "That's not cool."

The boy snickered and gave a final wave as he trailed his parents down the dock.

Big D's chuckle rumbled in his barrel chest. "I love kids, man." A college football injury had stolen all hopes of a pro career as a lineman, and eventually Big D decided to pursue his captain's license.

He'd been Josh's first mate for ten months, accruing the necessary days at sea.

Josh nodded good-bye to an older couple. "When are you and Mila gonna have a few of your own?"

"Oh, I'm working on it, don't you worry." He winked.

When the passengers finished disembarking, the crew got busy, prepping the boat for the morning tour. It seemed a popcorn fight had ensued on the top deck. And one of the toilets was stopped up. Josh handled that one and by the time he washed up, the vessel was clean and ready to be put to bed.

"Coming to Boone's?" Conner asked. The twenty-year-old worked the snack bar and was new to the crew this summer. His surfer-boy looks and youthful energy made Josh feel every one of his thirty-three years.

"Addison and Big D are going," he added when Josh paused.

"Yeah, maybe for a while." He had yet to see Maggie and Zoey, who'd arrived in town yesterday. Part of him was stalling.

"We don't wanna keep you up past your bedtime, old-timer," Conner teased as they joined Big D and Addison on the dock.

"That's *Captain* to you, buddy," Josh said with a grin.

"You coming with?" Addison asked Josh.

"Sure thing. Lead the way."

"All right," Big D said. "That's what I'm talking about. We can catch the end of the Braves game."

"How exciting," Addison deadpanned.

Conner edged in beside her. "Don't worry. I'll keep you company." He'd been flirting with her since day one. They'd make a cute couple with their matching blond locks and wide-eyed innocence. But Josh hoped it wouldn't mess up his crew when things went awry—as they were apt to at their young age.

8

Conversation flowed among the group as they headed across the marina parking lot and caught the sidewalk. The tavern was only a short walk away and the June evening was balmy. The sun, which had adorned the sky in vibrant pinks, now slipped beneath the horizon, absconding with its brilliant show. The street was lined with towering palm trees, the medians blooming with pink azaleas.

As they walked, Josh's thoughts wandered to Maggie. She'd taken Zoey to the carnival tonight—had texted a picture of his niece earlier. But they were probably home by now, Zoey curled up with Bunny, the stuffie he'd gifted her at the hospital the night she was born.

It seemed so long ago. Maggie's pregnancy had been disrupted by waves of grief that came and went at will, each one shattering Josh's heart. He tried to be there for her—his whole family had. God knew she couldn't count on her own mom, and it was what Ethan would've wanted.

She'd been six months along when she asked Josh to serve as her birthing partner. Perhaps as Ethan's brother he was the next best thing. Maybe saying yes had been ill-advised, but after everything she'd been through, he could hardly turn her down.

Then Zoey was born, a red, wrinkled, squalling bundle that was somehow the most beautiful thing he'd ever seen. He felt like so much more than just her uncle. He'd already filled that role two times over, after all. It was the birthing experience, he told himself.

But it was more than that.

He'd carried a torch for Maggie since the day Erin brought her home her freshman year of high school. His thirteen-year-old self had walked through the back door and there she was, sitting at the island with Erin, eating grapes.

She was the prettiest girl he'd ever seen, with doe-brown eyes and a wide, contagious smile. She was tall and long-legged with swimmer's shoulders. She had sun-kissed skin and lush pink lips. And her laughter was like a song he never wanted to end. He'd fallen in an instant, head over heels.

Later he grew to admire less superficial things: her unrelenting loyalty, indomitable spirit, and dry sense of humor. Erin had brought her around a lot, and Josh made a real nuisance of himself, as teenage boys tend to do when they're smitten. He did his best to hide his feelings even as he dreamed of the day she'd see him in a different light.

But the two years between them might as well have been the Grand Canyon. He shouldn't have been surprised when she fell for Ethan instead. But he sure was heartbroken.

Big D's boisterous laughter diverted his thoughts. But seconds later Josh was once again thinking about Maggie and all the years he'd been on the fringes of her life. These past five years their shared grief had pulled them closer than ever. But her unrelenting love for Ethan held him back.

He hadn't gotten up the courage to tell her she was the sun his heart orbited. He'd tried so hard to change that. To root her from his heart like a pernicious weed. No man chose to be in love with his brother's wife. It was a torturous, guilt-inducing quagmire he wouldn't wish on his worst enemy.

He was scum. A lowlife. The bottom of the barrel.

But he'd loved her first. Also, hadn't he tried everything over the years? Avoiding her, focusing on her flaws, dating other women and lots of them. Shoot, he'd *married* another woman—he really thought he could make it work. But his stubborn love for Maggie had ruined all his relationships, including his marriage, because none of them were *her*. Hiding his feelings felt like a boulder on his chest that only grew heavier with each passing year.

But soon he would change all that. First of all, Maggie was back in Seabrook for the summer to say good-bye to Ethan, to move on. In August they would mark five years without him. Together the family would spread his ashes on the water.

Second, Maggie was officially ready to date again. On his recent visit to Fayetteville, she'd asked Josh for help in that arena. The thought of lining up dates for her hit him like a wrecking ball.

No way.

Never happening.

Instead he would finally put his heart on the line. Tell Maggie how he felt about her. In his dreams she drew him into her arms and kissed him. In his nightmares she recoiled in horror.

Telling her was a huge risk, but the status quo was killing him. He'd finally reached a breaking point, and so he'd tell her the truth. Either she'd be open to exploring a relationship with him . . . or he'd lose her forever.

If the latter happened, he was putting some distance between them. She might live two hours away, but now that she was braving Seabrook again, she'd come around more often. She'd bring Zoey for holidays and birthdays and summer vacations. And if she turned him down, there was no way he was putting his tattered heart through those visits. He'd already set a plan in motion—just in case. He didn't see how he'd ever get over her otherwise.

When they reached the building's entrance, Josh's phone vibrated with a call. Maggie's picture flashed on the screen—the one he'd snapped a few years ago at the beach. Her hair was still damp, the natural curls coming out to play. The sun lightened her eyes to creamy caramel, and a few freckles had popped out on her nose.

He hung back as the others entered. "I'll be right in, you guys."

He tapped the Accept button as he crossed the dinky porch, and carnival sounds carried through the phone. "Hey, Mags. You there?"

"Can you come over here?"

He tensed at the strain in her voice. "What's wrong? Are you okay? Zoey?"

"We're fine. I just— You have to come."

"What is it?"

"You're gonna think I'm crazy. I-I saw someone a few minutes ago. He looked just like—e-t-h-a-n. I lost him in the crowd and I need you to come help me search for him."

His heart gave a sharp crack. "Maggie . . ." In the months following Ethan's death, she'd regularly seen Ethan at the grocery store, the park, the mall. She'd seen a therapist for a while.

"I know it sounds crazy, but it's not like those other times. I saw his face. I saw the way he walked. Please just come and help me, Josh. *Please.*"

"Of course, honey. I'm on my way."

Chapter 3

*M*aggie had never been so glad to see anyone. Just the sight of Josh striding through the crowd lifted a weight from her shoulders. An Island Tours tee hugged his athletic frame and a pair of khaki shorts completed his outfit. The wind ruffled his wavy dark hair as he made a beeline toward her.

She met him by the arcade door, Zoey in tow, and grabbed him in a heartfelt hug. "He looked just like him," she said into his ear. *"Just like him."*

"Where'd you last see him?"

"Heading up the main walkway toward the boardwalk. I lost him where it splits off. We've already been around the whole place. He just disappeared."

He gave her a squeeze before he pulled back and tugged one of Zoey's braids. "How's my girl? Having fun at the carnival?"

"I rode the carousel and the spinny ride and the red-car ride—that was my favorite. And I ate a funnel cake with Mommy and it made her tummy hurt after the spinny ride."

"Is that so."

"It's past my bedtime and we're out of tickets so we can't ride any more rides. I don't wanna ride the big wheel, though, 'cause it goes too high. Did you find your friend?"

Josh sent Maggie a questioning glance. "I told her we were looking for someone you know."

His gaze toggled back to Zoey. "Not yet, Cupcake. We'll keep searching, though, all right?" He took her hand and they started down the walkway.

"He's wearing a white ball cap and he's tall." Maggie gave him a pointed stare. "I didn't imagine him, Josh."

He squeezed her hand. "Okay, honey. Let's keep searching. Two sets of eyes are better than one."

They scanned the area, staying close as they navigated the crowd. It took almost an hour to cover the two blocks of walkways. They searched every ride, every souvenir store. They checked Tully's Pizza, Scoops, and the Seascore Arcade.

Now they nearly reached the end of the boardwalk fronting the carnival, and Ethan's look-alike was nowhere to be seen.

"I'm tired," Zoey whined. It was way past her bedtime and she'd been a trouper.

Josh scooped her up. "We're almost done, sweetheart."

Zoey's arms noodled around his neck as she sagged against his shoulder.

The crowd was thin on the boardwalk, and Maggie could easily see the man wasn't up ahead. Her stomach filled with lead even as her steps slowed. "He must've left." She glanced down at Zoey, whose eyes were already closed. "I should get her home and to bed."

"I'll come over so we can talk."

"All right."

Maggie poured two glasses of lemonade in the kitchen while Josh put Zoey to bed in the room Brad and Becky had fixed up for her.

They'd purchased the cottage two years ago, and now that Zoey was old enough, she occasionally spent the night. Maggie was so lonely when she was gone, but it was important that Zoey had time with her grandparents. They loved her so much and she was the only piece of Ethan they had left.

Maggie returned the pitcher to the stainless-steel refrigerator. The home, an original ranch, was built on stilts and offered free (at least for her) beach views and sunrises. Her in-laws had spent nearly a year renovating the place, and Maggie loved the cheerful décor they'd chosen. Lots of white, accented with coastal colors: blue subway tiles, aqua throw pillows, sea-green rugs. The overall effect was calming and happy.

Maggie could use a little of both right now.

As she moved into the living room, the floor creaked on the other side of the house. Zoey had been asleep before they made it to the car. Her eyelids hadn't so much as fluttered as Josh carried her in.

Josh. It had been sweet of him to rush right over when she called. But that was Josh. She'd always been able to count on him. And after tonight he probably thought she was crazy. Maybe she was. A few years ago her therapist, Miss Allison, had assured her that seeing a lost loved one in a crowd wasn't unusual.

But August 7 would mark five years since Ethan's passing. Surely she hadn't conjured up his twin after all this time. She'd come such a long way from that pathetic puddle on her kitchen floor. She was stronger now. She'd come here to spend the summer, to spread her husband's ashes, to get on with her life—not to resurrect the past.

But she had to make sense of this. She had to believe she hadn't simply imagined Ethan's face. She'd gotten a good, if quick, glimpse of the man. She reviewed that moment in her mind for the dozenth time, and once again her memory presented Ethan's look-alike. Maybe a younger version of him, now that she thought about it.

Josh entered the room and sank beside her on the sofa. "She's out like a light."

"She was tuckered. It's been a long day."

He took a sip of lemonade and settled against the sofa back, his eyes trained on her.

She shifted under his steady appraisal. The funnel cake she'd eaten earlier sat in her stomach like an anchor, and her nerves were shot from an emotional roller coaster she hadn't purchased tickets for.

With that long, quiet perusal Josh was no doubt seeing much deeper than the surface. She glowered at him. "I wasn't imagining it."

"I didn't say you were."

"He looked just like Ethan."

"I believe you."

"Do you? Because the way you're staring at me right now says otherwise."

"I'm just concerned about you. I don't like seeing you so shaken."

"Well, how am I supposed to feel when I spy my dead husband and then he completely disappears?" *Again.* Tears sprang up and she didn't want to cry. Tears felt helpless. She wanted to be mad. Mad felt like control and darn it, she wanted some control.

He faced her, setting one arm across the sofa back. His hand dropped onto her shoulder. "Let's talk about this. Tell me about when you first saw him."

More of the anger faded as she fell into his denim-blue eyes. Josh wasn't her enemy. He was the furthest thing from that. "Zoey was on the kiddie-car ride and I was trying to take a picture of her. Just as she glanced up, he walked into the frame. I did a double take. It was Ethan. His high cheekbones, his deep-set eyes, his chiseled jawline. He was thinner, maybe . . . more like how he was built when he was younger before he filled in some. And maybe younger-looking in the face too, but it happened so fast."

"They say everyone has a twin. Maybe you just saw Ethan's?"

"Right here in Seabrook? Where he grew up? What are the chances of that?"

Josh was quiet for a beat. "Not very good, I guess. He had a hat on, you said?"

"Yeah, I couldn't see his hair. But his face . . ." She turned her eyes to Josh as a tear slipped down her cheek. "It was *Ethan*. I wasn't imagining it. I don't believe in ghosts, and I can't explain it, but it was Ethan." After a moment she ripped her gaze away and raked her hands through her hair, squeezing until her scalp stung. She was entertaining a crazy thought. "I know that's not possible."

"Hey." He thumbed away the tear. "I know this is unsettling, but you're gonna be all right. We'll get to the bottom of this."

"How? He's gone and we have no clue where he went."

"You saw him at the carnival—maybe he'll come back. We can search tomorrow night and the next and the next if you—" His brow furrowed. "Wait. You said you spotted him when you were taking photos of Zoey. Is it possible you caught him in a picture?"

She couldn't remember if she'd taken that shot. She'd been so rattled. She reached for her phone. Josh leaned close as she opened the photo app and tapped on the last picture she'd taken.

She gasped. There he was. *Ethan*.

It was a profile view and a woman partially blocked him. But Maggie's phone was set for Live photos, so she opened the feature and dragged her thumb across the bottom of the screen until the woman passed and Ethan's twin turned toward the camera. For the second time tonight the image stole her breath. Set off a jackhammer in her chest.

Her gaze shot to Josh, who stared at the screen as if he'd just seen a ghost.

A shiver passed through Josh. He grabbed the phone and pulled it closer. He could hardly believe his eyes. The photo was a little blurry. But it *was* Ethan. There were his bright blue eyes, set deep beneath the slashes of dark brows. His aristocratic nose, high cheekbones, square jaw.

"You weren't kidding. He's a dead ringer." Appropriate choice of words since his brother was, in fact, *dead*. And dead men didn't go walking around the town carnival. Josh peered at the photo. "He's thinner than Ethan."

"People can lose weight."

Not dead people. He didn't have the heart—or even the conviction— to say it aloud. Because they'd never actually seen his destroyed body. And suddenly that little detail opened up a cavern of doubt. Josh homed in on the man in the picture, permitting the impossible thought to emerge from the shadows of his brain.

Still. There had to be some other explanation.

Maggie gave her head a shake. "I know it can't be true. He's gone. It's not possible he's still alive."

"There has to be a rational explanation. Maybe he's a long-lost cousin or something."

Her attention returned to the man on the screen. "He seems

younger. Younger than he looked even at thirty-two. But he'd be thirty-seven now. This guy can't be that old."

"I agree." But Maggie was right—if they'd seen the guy in Wichita or Tampa or Houston, maybe they could write it off as a fluke.

But he was *here* in Seabrook.

For a while they studied the photo, noting every similarity. Zoomed in until his face was hazy, trying to find a hint to his identity.

After a few minutes Maggie sagged against the couch. "I know it can't be Ethan. But I need answers. I can't live with not knowing."

"Me either. We'll go back tomorrow night and look again."

"What are the chances he'd return to the carnival?"

"Probably small, but it's all we've got. We can show his picture around. Maybe someone will recognize him."

"Good idea." She took the phone and woke it up. Ethan's twin stared back at them. "We're going to Erin's tomorrow to swim and hang out. What should I say?"

His family had been through so much. It would be cruel to get their hopes up when they had no answers. Cruel enough that it was happening to Maggie and him. Because it was impossible to extinguish that tiny possibility. That impossible glimmer of hope. "Why don't we keep this between us for now—until we have some answers."

She nodded slowly. "No sense upsetting everyone." Maggie returned her attention to the photo for a long quiet minute. The phone trembled in her hands. She turned tear-filled eyes up at him. "It can't be him, right?"

It was hard to reconcile the facts. Tonight she'd seen Ethan's double. And yet almost five years ago, a uniformed officer and a chaplain had delivered news of his death. Both of these were true.

If Josh was reeling, he could only imagine how she was feeling. Maggie, who'd clawed her way back from the pit of grief to single-handedly raise her daughter. He took the phone from her hands, set it aside, and opened his arms to her. "Come here."

She came eagerly, settling against his chest, clutching his shirt in her fist. He palmed the back of her head, relishing the weight of her against him. The slight rise and fall of her shoulders. The sweet scent of her shampoo. He could hold her like this forever. Two hours ago he'd hoped to do just that. But everything had changed now.

Even so, he'd give anything if the impossible could be true. If his brother had somehow come back from the dead, he'd find it in his heart to let Maggie go once again.

"Thank you for coming tonight," she said softly. "For not thinking I'm crazy."

He pressed a kiss to the top of her head. "Anytime, honey. It'll be all right. I don't have any answers for you, but there's one person who does, and we'll just have to find him."

Chapter 4

*M*aggie's sister-in-law, Erin Gibbs, lived in a modest ranch about a mile from the beach. There wasn't much to recommend the house with its older white siding, outdated kitchen, and modest furnishings. But the backyard was a summer-lover's dream.

A large deck hugged the back of the home, complete with a built-in grill and a two-sided fireplace. Beyond it, a large kidney-shaped in-ground pool dominated the yard. Around the periphery of the pool, Erin's green thumb was on display. Palm trees, flowering bushes, and rubber tree plants burgeoned under her care.

Maggie reclined on a chaise lounge, eyes peeled for Zoey and her five-year-old cousin, Mia, who sat on the steps of the pool's shallow end. Erin's eleven-year-old son, Owen, was at a friend's house, leaving the young cousins to themselves today.

In her teal two-piece, Erin joined Maggie by the pool and offered her a glass of iced tea. "Mine's not as good as yours."

"Well, I was just thinking how unfair it is that you can sprout the garden of Eden while I can't grow a simple houseplant."

"I guess we all have our gifts." Erin sank onto the chair beside Maggie. Her chin-length flaxen hair glinted in the afternoon sun. "I could never teach English to a roomful of bored fifteen-year-olds. You deserve a medal."

"They're not all bored, thankfully. And I couldn't advise them on the traumas some of them face." Erin had a big heart, a wise spirit—and a doctorate in psychology.

"There's some of that, unfortunately, but there's plenty of plain ol' high school drama in there too."

"Always. All that and summers off too." Maggie loved her students, but she was glad for the reprieve from lesson plans, grading, and school politics. She raised her glass. "To a well-deserved summer vacation."

"Hear, hear." Erin clinked her glass with Maggie's.

Maggie stretched her lips into a smile she didn't quite feel. She'd been all set to be brave this summer. To face the memories she and Ethan had made here, where they'd fallen in love. To let go of him and start moving forward in a meaningful way.

But last night had changed all that.

Now she battled the ridiculous hope that Ethan wasn't dead at all and had to somehow hide it from Erin. How was she supposed to carry on as if her whole world hadn't been turned upside down?

"You okay? You seem a little quiet today."

Maggie slipped on her sunglasses. "Just tired. Didn't get much sleep last night."

"It must be hard being back here, huh?"

"It is." She'd been to Seabrook many times since Ethan had died. But only day trips, avoiding certain places, not wanting to dredge up memories. "But it was high time. It'll be a great summer for Zoey. She's been asking about her daddy more lately, and I can share my memories with her. We all can. Give her little pieces of him to carry with her."

As her daughter made friends at church and preschool, becoming exposed to other families, she'd also begun asking if she could get another daddy. But Maggie didn't mention that. It was yet another sign that she needed to let go of the grief and focus on their future.

"Mommy, can I get in now?" Zoey called.

"Sure, honey." At three feet, eight inches tall, her daughter could reach the shallow bottom now. She was tall for her age, as tall as Mia, which was no surprise given Ethan's height and Maggie's own five-foot-seven frame.

Zoey moved into the water with the confidence of a fish and began swimming freestyle across the width of the pool.

"Wow, look at her go."

"We've been swimming at the Y. She loves the water."

"She's a natural—but I guess that's no surprise since she has your genes. Are you still swimming?"

"At least once a week." Maggie had swum competitively in high school and college. When she swam it was just her and the water. Sometimes it felt as if she *was* the water, when her body moved in harmony with the flow. Swimming was her escape, her refuge. She wasn't sure she could've maintained her sanity all these years without it.

"Do you ever regret not going further with it?"

Once upon a time the Olympics had been her dream. "Nah. I needed a few more inches of height to really get where I wanted to go. Besides, I'd never regret settling down with Ethan." Even more so because they'd had so few years together.

"It seems you might have a little prodigy on your hands."

Zoey had just attempted a flip turn at the wall.

"We just added that to our practices. Good job, Chickadee!" Maggie called when Zoey came up for air. "Have you heard from your mom and dad? Becky messaged me yesterday from Barcelona."

"Dad sent me a picture of Mom in some bakery. She looked pretty happy."

"It's good to know they're having a great time. They've waited so long for this trip."

"I love the idea of them gallivanting all over Europe, Mom dragging Dad to all the tourist attractions, Dad complaining about the price of entrance."

Maggie chuckled. "Sounds about right. When's their cruise?"

"Not for a couple weeks. Dad's worried Mom won't do well with the cramped quarters." Erin gave her a wry look. "He even paid extra for the balcony."

"He must've been really concerned to dole out that kind of money."

"Mom says his wallet squeals every time he opens it."

Zoey wiped water from her eyes and joined Mia by the steps. The girl was adorable with long blonde locks and green eyes—Erin's mini-me, though she had Patrick's dimpled smile.

Zoey tried to get her cousin to join her in the shallow end. But the girl wouldn't leave the safety of the steps. That dimpled smile was nowhere to be seen right now.

"Is Mia okay? She's always liked the water."

"Late last summer a wave got her at the beach. She took in some water and it scared her pretty good. I was hoping by the time we opened the pool in the spring she'd have forgotten. She was just learning to swim."

Mia watched from her post as Zoey tried a handstand several feet away.

"She just needs to build her confidence in the water. I can work with her this summer if you'd like."

"Really? You wouldn't mind?"

"You kidding me? I'd love to help her. It'll give me a chance to get in the water."

"You're welcome to use the pool anytime—you know that. But it would be great if you could help Mia. I haven't been able to get her off that step."

"Leave it to me. We'll have her swimming by summer's end. You'll see."

Maggie's phone vibrated with a text. Her mother. *How's your trip going, honey? I haven't heard from you since you left.*

The words caused a prick of guilt—Maggie had been distracted with settling in. And ever since she'd seen Ethan's look-alike, she'd been consumed with thoughts of him.

Another text appeared. *And something terrible has happened.*

As her mom had no doubt intended, the words set off a cascade of concerns and questions. Was it her heart? Did something happen at work? Had the smarmy guy she'd recently started dating hurt her in some way?

"It's my mom." Maggie checked on the girls, then tapped out a quick reply. *Sorry I haven't checked in. Everything's going well here. What happened? Are you okay?* She sent the text, electing not to mention where she was—her mom was jealous of the Reynolds family, and Maggie didn't feel like dealing with a passive-aggressive response.

"How's she doing?" Erin asked.

"Something's wrong but she didn't say what." Maggie and Ethan had moved to Fayetteville after her mom's heart attack. She didn't have any other family. Maggie's dad had left them years ago—she barely remembered him.

"Try not to let it bother you. You know how she likes to bait you."

"You're right." Maggie had been attempting to navigate her mother's narcissism for as long as she could remember. Developing her life around it was a real challenge because her mom viewed Maggie as an extension of herself. She'd shown interest in her granddaughter only to the extent that she usurped Maggie's attention. Yet she demanded that Zoey comply with and respect her.

Maggie tried to shield her daughter from her mother as much as possible, but it was hard when they lived in the same town. And truthfully, since Ethan had died, Maggie had let her boundaries slip where her mother was concerned. She hadn't had the emotional reserves to keep her in her place.

She confided in Erin more than anyone about her mom. Not only because she was her best friend, but because she was great with advice. Maggie set down her phone and attempted to put her anxious thoughts aside. "So how did last night turn out? You seem to have survived what looked like the social event of the season."

"It was fine, really. It was for a good cause at least." Erin caught her up on the event, putting a humorous spin on the whole thing until Maggie was laughing so hard that she nearly wet her pants.

By the time the girls were ready to go inside, Maggie was thoroughly glad for the reprieve from her heavy thoughts. As she slipped through the sliding glass door, she checked her phone and saw that her mother hadn't responded.

They got into dry clothes and had a late lunch. Afterward, the girls watched *Moana* while Erin and Maggie chatted at the kitchen table. When Erin got up to refill their drinks, Maggie sent another text. *Mom? Is everything okay?*

She sent another text when the movie ended, and at four thirty, when they headed home, she still hadn't heard back. Zoey fell asleep on the way home and Maggie carried her inside and laid her on her bed. The sun had worn her daughter out and a nap was probably best since they might be out late at the carnival again.

Maggie headed to the living room where she grabbed her phone and placed a call to her mom. She tried not to worry that something had happened, but she couldn't seem to help it. It was her mom—the only one she'd ever have. And with Maggie now two hours away, Mom really didn't have a support system of any kind. The new boyfriend hardly counted.

The call rang through to voice mail. No surprise. A moment later the beep sounded.

"Hi, Mom. Just making sure you're all right. Give me a call, okay?" She tapped the End button and wished she could quell the useless anxiety fraying her nerves. Maggie had hoped a little distance would provide a reprieve from the emotional exhaustion that came from her relationship with her mom. But she should've known her mother would never let that happen.

Chapter 5

The carnival crowd was dwindling, and they'd been here so long that even Zoey was ready to leave. The blaring music, arcade sounds, and giddy squeals were giving Maggie a headache. She gave the boardwalk one last searching glance before heading back to the bumper cars where she was meeting Josh and Zoey.

Hours earlier he'd bought a truckload of tickets, and the two of them had been switching off between riding with Zoey and searching the crowd.

But so far no sign of the man.

Maggie stopped by a couple who were sharing a dish of mint chocolate ice cream. "Excuse me, have you seen this man?" She held up her phone.

The woman shook her head. "Sure haven't. Sorry."

"Have you tried the arcade? There's a ton of people in there."

She'd been in there at least five times. "Thank you."

A knot pressed her windpipe as she moved on. The tang of pizza carried from the open-doored shop, turning her stomach. They'd been searching almost six hours and nothing. Not a single sighting. Not even a hint. No one recognized the man who'd been here only the night before.

What if they never found him? How would she ever live with that kind of uncertainty?

The bumper cars were emptying as she approached the ride. As Josh and Zoey skirted the barricades and headed her way, he sent Maggie a questioning look.

She shook her head.

"Uncle Josh hit the blue car, Mommy!" Zoey grabbed Maggie's hand. "The one with a little boy, and he laughed. He hit us, too, and we banged against the wall, then another car hit us. Uncle Josh said we only have one ticket left and I get to ride the carousel."

"Is that right? Well, it's almost closing time. We'd better head that way so you can get your favorite horse."

"The one with the pink roses!"

"That's right."

"Well, there he is, Cupcake," Josh said as they approached the ride. "There's no line and your favorite horse is looking for you."

"It's a *she*, and it's not a real horse, silly. Only pretend."

"Oh, I see." Josh handed over the ticket, and he and Maggie followed Zoey, who stepped onto the carousel base and scurried over to the horse.

Josh lifted her up and secured the belt. "Hold on tight. I hear this one likes to buck pretty little girls."

"You're silly, Uncle Josh."

"He sure is." Maggie stepped away. "We'll be right over there."

Josh and Maggie moved outside the barricades while the ride filled. By habit now, she searched the shrinking crowd. "I know running into him again was a long shot, but I was hoping someone would recognize him."

"Me too. I feel like we've been here for a week."

"How will we find him?"

"We could post his picture around town."

"What if Erin saw it? I don't want to bring her into this. It's awful—this uncertainty and fear we might never have answers." Hopelessness swept over Maggie, making her eyes burn.

Josh wrapped an arm around her shoulders, pulling her close. "Hey. We won't give up. It's only been one night."

The familiar woodsy smell of his aftershave comforted her. "I know it can't be him. But at the same time I'm so afraid of finding out for sure it's not."

"I'm right there with you, honey. I've stared at that photo till I'm cross-eyed."

"Did you know the chances of a stranger looking just like you is one in one trillion?" Finding that statistic had only buoyed her hope that this man could actually be Ethan even when reason told her it couldn't be.

"Maybe he's not a stranger, per se. He could be some long-lost relative. Someone could've donated sperm, or, God forbid—" He pressed his lips together.

"What?"

"My dad could've had an affair."

Maggie shook her head. "No way. Your mom and dad are so in love. Plus, he'd never do that."

"I know. I'm just tossing every possible idea out there."

"Maybe your mom had twins."

"And didn't realize it?"

"I guess that is a little outlandish. All I know is we have to find him. I have to know for sure." She scanned the crowd. "But it's like the tide washed him up onshore, then took him right back out to sea."

"I was thinking earlier . . . Maybe we could approach this from a different angle."

She looked up at him. "Such as . . . ?"

"Let's just suspend all disbelief here and say that man really is Ethan. What possible scenario would have him here in North Carolina and not knocking down your door? Why would he be here if not to reunite with his family?"

It seemed too ridiculous to even consider. But they needed to cover all their bases. "I'm not in Fayetteville at the moment and your parents sold their old house. You and Erin have moved."

"He could've called us, though. And he knows where I work."

True. She'd actually mulled this over all afternoon, in between calls to her mother—whom she still hadn't heard from. "He could have amnesia." She felt silly saying it out loud.

Josh gave her a wry grin. "Does that actually happen outside of rom-coms?"

"I know, I know. You're the one who said to suspend disbelief."

He nudged her. "You gotta stop reading those romances."

"I did." For three whole years after she'd lost Ethan. It was too depressing to remember what it was like to have a lover. "But come on, a girl's gotta have hope."

"More like a fantasy."

She smacked the back of his head. "Hey, you liked the one I made you read."

"I *tolerated* it."

"You said *liked*. I have it right here in a text if you'd like to fact-check me."

"Fine, fine. I didn't hate it. But back to the subject at hand—you have to admit it's highly unlikely Ethan's alive and wandering around Seabrook with amnesia."

"You hear about it on the news sometimes—someone turns up with no idea who they are. And I actually looked it up—1 percent of men get amnesia from things ranging from strokes to traumatic or stressful experiences. And Ethan was in an explosion."

"Okay . . . Are you saying maybe he was just knocked on the head instead of . . . ?"

Being blown up. She winced. "Is it possible? An event like that would've created a lot of chaos and confusion on the base. Maybe they couldn't find him and only assumed he'd died in the explosion. They didn't give us any details." She couldn't believe she was allowing herself to go there.

"And then what? He wandered off base to the nearest airport and flew back here, to Seabrook?"

The words released a gush of air from her balloon. "I guess that doesn't make much sense." And if he'd lost his memory, how would he even know where to go? "But he's here in Seabrook, not Fayetteville. What if he didn't have his recent memories but only his very old ones? Then he'd just remember living here."

"That's true."

It would also mean he might not remember her. "That doesn't solve the issue of how he got off the base without the military knowing he was alive."

He glanced her way. Then he fixed his gaze on the whirling carousel, his brows furrowing.

"What?"

"Nothing."

"It's not nothing. And while we're throwing out far-fetched ideas, you might as well add to it."

He returned Zoey's wave. Then his expression sobered again. "What if they know he's not dead?"

Maggie frowned. Why would the military tell them he'd died if he hadn't? She shook her head. "That doesn't make sense."

"I'm not a conspiracy theorist, but the military is government run, and who really trusts the government? Maybe there's more going on than we know."

"Like what?"

"No idea. I'm talking nonsense at this point."

"Did Ethan say something to you? Did you sense something was off?"

"No, not at all. He seemed completely normal the last time I spoke with him."

"Me too." She thought back to the last video call. She'd reviewed those moments a thousand times: the low rumble of his voice, the new fine lines at the corners of his eyes, the smile that tipped slightly crooked. He'd told her he loved her like crazy. Reminded her she was growing a human being and to make sure she was getting proper rest. Being a medic, he wanted to review every word her OB had said at her last visit.

"He got to see the baby move. He was so excited to be a daddy." Her throat tightened. He'd never even gotten to see Zoey's precious face or touch her delicate newborn skin.

Josh gave her shoulder a squeeze. "We'll get to the bottom of this."

The ride began to slow. Maggie checked her watch. It was closing time and the carny wasn't sticking around one extra minute. But her feet hurt and she'd kill for a glass of sweet tea.

However, she wasn't finished discussing the topic at hand. She hated to ask. Josh had a sunrise cruise tomorrow with a youth group. But neither of them would get much sleep tonight without some kind of plan. "Can you come over?"

He nodded. "We'll both feel better if we have some kind of strategy in place."

Josh reclined next to Zoey, reading *Alexander and the Terrible, Horrible, No Good, Very Bad Day* for the fourth time. Two songs and three books. Her eyes were now closed, she clutched Bunny in her arms, and her chest rose and fell slowly beneath her Elsa blanket.

He closed the book and eased off the bed. She resembled a little angel in the soft lamplight, her lashes touching the tops of her cheeks. She had her mommy's brown hair and doe eyes, but he glimpsed Ethan in her olive skin tone and facial expressions.

He pressed a kiss to the top of her head and shut off the light on his way out. He pulled the door until there was only a slight gap, as she didn't like it completely closed.

When he reached the living room, a breeze cut through the open French doors. He joined Maggie on the elevated deck where she was texting someone. Two glasses of iced tea sat on the small circular table between the chairs.

A million stars twinkled on the sky's onyx canvas, which melted into a sea as dark as the Black River. The white-crested waves rolled landward, bombarding the shore with a continuous roar. The scent of burning wood carried on the breeze. Someone was enjoying a campfire at Freeman Park—fires were illegal on every other beach.

He took the chair beside Maggie. "She's down for the count."

"How many stories?"

"Three and a half."

"You got off easy."

"No doubt. Ever hear back from your mom?"

"That's who I'm texting. She's not answering or picking up my calls."

"I'm sure it's nothing to worry about."

"You're probably right."

This was hardly the first time Nora had left Maggie hanging. He couldn't fathom why the woman enjoyed causing her daughter anxiety—especially when Maggie had already suffered so much. But it sure seemed like she did it maliciously. It was hard to watch.

Maggie was a kindhearted, generous person. He'd never understand how she'd turned out so wonderfully with Nora for a mom. Must've been the good influence of her aunt. Plus the teachers and swim coaches at school, where she'd been well accepted and had success, both academically and athletically.

She pocketed her phone and turned a chagrined smile his way. "I haven't even asked how your business is going or how you're doing. I just arrived in town and demanded your time and energy, and as always, you gave it. I'm sorry."

"I think we can give you a little grace here since you ran into your deceased husband's doppelganger at a carnival."

Her husky laughter sent a thrill through him. "I mean, come on. You have to admit it's completely absurd."

His lips twitched. "Ridiculous."

Still laughing, she wiped her eyes. "Leave it to Ethan to cook up a mystery for us."

"He always did like to mess with me." When Josh was little, Ethan had convinced him he was adopted. Erin exposed his lie, but not before Josh put a dead jellyfish in Ethan's bed. And so it went.

"He sure did love you, though."

At Maggie's wistful tone, Josh's expression wilted. "The feeling was mutual." As they'd grown older, Ethan had become more the protective big brother. But even with his height, Ethan was more cerebral than physical. And Josh, who'd begun to bulk up for football, could easily hold his own.

He glanced through the doorway to the fireplace mantel where two urns sat—his parents' and Maggie's. They would release them at sea in August on the fifth anniversary of Ethan's death. His brother had loved the ocean.

But were those actually Ethan's ashes? He shook away the absurd thought.

"I was thinking while you were putting Zoey down . . . Just to get some closure here, why don't we reach out to one of his friends who was there on base? I remember him mentioning Rocky a lot. That was his best friend over there and he worked at the field hospital too. I met him once on a video call. Surely he'd be able to give us answers or at least direct us to someone who could. Maybe even someone who was there when the explosion happened."

"Ethan mentioned him to me too. Do you remember his last name? Or have any idea where he'd be now?"

"I don't remember a last name, but he was from South Carolina. His tour would be up by now, though."

"Yeah, he's probably been discharged."

"Maybe there's something in Ethan's letters. I lost the emails somehow when my computer bit the dust, but I have the copies I printed—back at the house, of course. I could ask one of my friends to send them . . . or maybe I should drive back myself. I don't want to risk losing them."

"I still have his emails too. Let me pore over them and see if I can find anything first. Maybe save you the drive."

"Okay." Her tone was full of resolution. She crossed her arms over her chest, seeming to sink in on herself.

"What's wrong?"

"I guess I was just hoping for a quicker answer. This sounds like it might take a while."

"Maybe not. I'll look over the letters when I get home."

"It's late—and you probably didn't get much sleep last night either. This can wait till tomorrow."

Maybe it could. But he didn't like seeing Maggie so hopeless. He'd get through those letters if it took all night. He hoped he could find the answers they needed. He didn't want Maggie to have to wade through Ethan's emails and stir up the loss just as she was starting to move on.

But that ship had probably already sailed.

Chapter 6

"Thank you for coming along," Maggie said to Josh, whose promise to nap in the car had gone unkept. Zoey, on the other hand, was sound asleep in her car seat.

"Didn't have any plans beyond watching the Braves game."

"How was the sunrise cruise?"

"The kids were fun. The youth leader did a devotion after the sun rose, then I narrated the rest of the tour."

"It was nice of you to do it on your day off."

She wasn't sure he'd gotten any sleep last night. He'd texted early this morning saying he'd found no clues about Rocky in Ethan's emails. So they were headed back to Fayetteville. Maggie wasn't looking forward to reading the letters again.

She turned into her neighborhood, an older subdivision containing modest brick ranches with small, well-kept yards.

"Do you want to read them here or take them back to Seabrook?"

"Might as well do it here." If they both read, it would go twice as fast. She wouldn't mind Josh reading the messages, though of course there was a fair share of flirtatious banter and innuendos. She'd leave that up to him.

A minute later they pulled into the paved drive. She and Ethan had bought the house prior to his deployment. She was well established at Fayetteville High School by then and able to afford the mortgage even without Ethan's pay. The plan was for him to pursue a medical degree after he was discharged. From the Army to med school, Ethan seemed determined to follow in his father's footsteps. He'd been raised with a great sense of patriotism. A strong sense of gratitude for this country's freedoms. From the time she'd begun dating him, she'd known he planned to serve, but that hadn't made it any easier to let him go.

When she shut off the ignition, Zoey stirred in the back seat.

"We're home, sweetheart."

Dazed, Zoey glanced out the window. "Can I visit Pokey?"

The next-door neighbor's schnauzer was Zoey's favorite plaything. "If he's outside."

Inside the house Maggie went straight for the thermostat. "Let's get some air going in here."

"Uncle Josh, come see my room."

He'd seen it a hundred times already but he followed Zoey anyway. "I'll keep her company while you read."

Maggie watched him go. He was such a good uncle. He doted on both of his nieces and his nephew. Probably at least in part because he was unable to have children himself. And that was a shame because Josh would've made such a wonderful dad.

AN HOUR LATER, Maggie was sprawled on the sofa with a stack of emails. The threads continued for pages and pages. She'd initially tried skimming them for Rocky's name, but she soon got caught up in Ethan's words. She blinked back tears and made two discreet trips to the restroom to blow her nose. She'd found nothing helpful yet.

Josh entertained Zoey with a puppet show. Then they went outside for a while, making use of the swing set. Judging by the happy barking that followed, Pokey had come outside to chase Zoey around the yard. Now Zoey and Josh watched *Frozen II* on the Disney+ app.

Maggie read for what seemed like hours as Josh came and went with Zoey. Sometimes Maggie forgot she was even looking for clues. She got so caught up in Ethan's world. But unlike the last time she'd read them, his words didn't drag her deep into a vortex of suffering. Instead she smiled wistfully at his familiar phrases and tired jokes. She warmed at his declarations of love and blushed at his innuendos. She missed him so much and couldn't keep her mind from straying into dangerous territory, because having him back again would be the kind of miracle she'd dreamed of.

She read on. Her husband was a good storyteller. He never mentioned anything grisly in his letters or calls. He mostly just told her about the pranks the guys played on each other or funny anecdotes about things that happened on base.

And in the more recent letters he talked about the baby. She remembered the video call when she'd told him they were having a girl. He was so happy that his eyes teared up and a big goofy grin spread across his face. In the email she was now reading, he suggested the name *Zoey*. Maggie had loved it but later they'd tossed other ideas back and forth. She didn't decide to use his favorite until after she'd gotten word of his death.

"Hey, Mags . . ." Josh said from across the room. "How about if I order pizza? The cupboards are pretty bare."

"Great idea."

"Cheese for Zoey, deluxe for us?"

"Perfect."

She resumed reading, getting caught up once again in Ethan's words. Before she knew it, the pizza arrived and she took a break for the first time since she'd begun reading. Zoey chattered endlessly and insisted Uncle Josh cut her pizza, not Mommy. Maggie was so grateful they had him in their lives. Besides Zoey's papaw, he was her only male role model.

After Maggie finished her second slice, she stretched her neck, feeling a pull on her tight shoulder muscles. Josh turned from helping Zoey wash up at the sink. Seconds later his large hands kneaded her shoulders.

She gave a low moan. "That feels so good."

"You've been hunched over those letters for hours."

Zoey sang as she played in the kitchen sink, probably making a mess. But Maggie couldn't bring herself to care, what with Josh's hands working magic.

"How are you holding up?" He wasn't referring to her muscles.

"Reading those letters makes me miss him more. I'd forgotten about his expansive vocabulary."

Josh chuckled. "He did know how to throw around those fancy words."

"He was so smart."

"But he read the most boring books."

Maggie laughed because Josh was right. Ethan hadn't read fiction like she and Josh did. He fancied hefty nonfiction tomes he found in secondhand bookstores. The remembered detail opened up an ache in her chest. What else had she forgotten about him? She wanted to remember everything so she could relay every detail to Zoey as she grew older.

Then again, was there any chance at all Zoey could know him personally? Dare Maggie even hope for that? She glanced over her shoulder at Josh. "Is there any way it could be him?"

His hands stilled and a silent pause followed. "I honestly don't know what to think. No matter how many times I work it around in my brain, I can't make sense of it."

"I don't want to hope." Her eyes stung. "Losing him hurt so much the first time. I'm not sure I could bear that kind of disappointment."

He gave her shoulders a squeeze. "You're stronger than you think. You're the strongest person I know. And I'm right here with you, honey. Whatever happens, we'll get through it together. I promise you that."

The words comforted her, as did his gentle touch. At the thought she eased away from him, grabbed her plate, and stood. "Thanks, Josh. I should get back to the letters."

She joined Zoey at the sink and helped her with the words to "Show Yourself" as she soaped up her own hands. When they heard Pokey barking outside, Maggie helped her dry off so Josh could take her outside to play.

Maggie retired to the living room and dug back into the letters. But she had trouble focusing on the words. She could still feel Josh's hands kneading her shoulders with such care. He'd been such a comfort to her. A warm, steady presence in her life.

He was such a good guy. But so different from Ethan. Not as handsome in the traditional sense. Though Josh had nice thick dark hair and a physique he worked at, his face was rather average with its symmetrical features. There was nothing particularly memorable about his eyes or nose or mouth. But when his face broke into a grin, his left eyebrow did this little involuntary bounce. Something was so alluring and mesmerizing about that quirk. Something so endearing.

But it wasn't his looks that had women beating down his doors—and they did. It was his irrefutable charm. And with so much attention from the ladies, who could blame the guy for moving from woman to woman the way he always had? The bigger surprise was that he'd ever settled down at all.

Of course, his marriage to Samantha had eventually gone down in flames. Maggie had never faulted him for that failure, though. Not Josh, who was so devoted to those he loved. So good at making everyone feel special.

But the truth was, Josh was the special one.

Maggie gave her head a shake and redoubled her efforts to concentrate on the words before her. Because if she wasn't careful, her thoughts just might veer back to that night two and a half years ago when Josh had kissed her.

Chapter 7

*M*aggie hadn't been particularly sorry when Samantha divorced Josh. That was a terrible thing to admit, given how distraught Josh was over the demise of his marriage. But Maggie never felt the woman was good enough for her brother-in-law. And the fact that she served him divorce papers barely a year after he'd lost his brother said it all.

Josh had initially tried to reason with Samantha, but in the end he didn't contest the divorce. Didn't dispute her demand for their Seabrook home. Didn't even object to her request for spousal support. It drove Maggie crazy that he rolled over to Samantha's every demand, though she tried to hold her tongue since he was so despondent.

When Ethan had died, Josh made the trip to Fayetteville every other week to visit Maggie and later to help with Zoey, who even as a baby lit up at the sight of her uncle. But his trips soon dwindled to once a month or less, punctuated by phone calls. Josh never said so, but Maggie suspected Samantha put a stop to his frequent visits.

Upon succumbing to the divorce, he resumed his frequent trips, but he was not at all his charming self. Oh, he put up a good front. But his smiles were forced, his laughter absent. He obviously missed Samantha terribly, though he didn't confide much in Maggie. He resisted her attempts to pry him open, and eventually she stopped trying. Put her efforts into trying to cheer him up instead.

North Carolina required that a separated couple live apart for a year before obtaining a divorce decree, which took another sixty days. By the time it was all finalized, Josh was more his old self. Though his eyes had lost their twinkle, and Maggie hadn't seen that little brow hitch in months. As far as she knew he wasn't dating again. Maybe that was what he needed—another woman in his life.

A few months after the divorce had been final, the holidays were upon them, and Josh arrived with plans to do his shopping in Fayetteville with Maggie and Zoey. In a few weeks, Christmas would find them gathered in Seabrook at Brad and Becky's house for the last time as they'd just purchased a seaside cottage.

Josh arrived on Saturday morning, and Zoey ran to him all smiles, yelling, "Yosh! Yosh is here, Mommy!" They'd just celebrated her second birthday and her vocabulary was increasing by the day.

Maggie had done most of her shopping, but Josh was on a mission to complete his list in one day. So they hit what seemed like every store in Fayetteville. Zoey napped in her stroller while Josh picked through jewelry displays for his mom and coatracks for his dad. The toy store was next. Josh purchased enough gifts to spoil his nieces and nephew rotten, despite Maggie's admonishments that Zoey didn't really need a backyard swing set just yet.

She didn't fight too hard as he charged up his credit card, but only because she hadn't seen him so happy in months. He had such a generous heart. His business was profitable, and if spending his hard-earned money on his family made him happy, who was Maggie to deny him?

They grabbed dinner out and returned home by Zoey's bedtime. She'd fallen asleep in the car, so Josh carried her inside and laid her on the bed. Maggie covered her with her Winnie the Pooh blanket and pressed a kiss to her forehead.

"We wore her out," Josh whispered as they left the room.

"You wore *me* out. Who does all their Christmas shopping in one day?"

"Smart people, that's who."

Maggie pulled Zoey's door almost closed. "I'd offer you some eggnog, but you think it's gross."

"It is gross. But I'll pour you a glass." He nodded toward the living room. "Go relax. You've earned it."

"I'll take you up on that." In the living room she turned on the Christmas tree lights along with the garland and candles on the mantel. This was their third Christmas without Ethan and the first she'd gone all out with decorations. Zoey was old enough to enjoy the lights and hopefully stay away from the ornaments.

Maggie sank onto the sofa, her back loosening painfully. Even though teaching kept her on her feet most of the day, it hadn't prepared her for a full day's shopping with Josh. She smiled at the memory of him tackling the toy store aisles like Santa on a Christmas mission.

"I can't stay long." Josh returned, handed her a glass of eggnog. "I have a part in my church's Christmas program tomorrow."

"Do tell." She took a sip. "Are you playing a wise man?"

He cut her a wry grin. "There are better men for those roles." He took a gulp of water, looking a little sheepish. "I'm actually singing 'O Holy Night.'"

She did a double take. "Wait. You can sing? That's a hard song!"

"Tell me about it. I've been kicking myself ever since Jeff Watkins talked me into this."

"How did I not know you can sing? Does your family know? Ethan never said a word."

"I've been careful to avoid letting anyone know. And if Jeff hadn't caught me belting out a tune when I thought no one was around, my plan would be working just fine."

"I can't believe I didn't know. Sing me something."

"*No.*"

"Oh, come on. It's just me." Even in the dim lights she could see the mottled red suffusing his neck. "Are you blushing? That's so cute."

"It's not cute. I don't like singing in front of people."

A laugh burst from her chest. "It's a little late for that, my friend. Come on, just one line. It'll be good practice. Please? I won't laugh."

He pulled a face. "You think it's gonna be funny?"

"I don't know what to think as *I've never heard you sing.*"

He pressed his lips together. Stared her down. "Look the other way."

"What?"

"I'll do it, but you have to look the other way. I can't sing with you staring at me."

"You're being ridicu— " Josh started to get up. "Okay, okay, I'll look the other way. Jeez. You'd think I was asking you to pick your nose."

"That would be less embarrassing."

She pivoted away from him, staring at the Christmas tree. "Is this good enough, or should I step outside?"

"That would be better actually."

"Just get on with it already."

He muttered something, but she only made out the word *bossy*.

She huffed, waiting. She couldn't believe he was so self-conscious about this. He'd played several sports in high school. If quarterbacking a team in front of peers didn't give a guy stage fright, she couldn't imagine why singing would. She'd always wished she had a—

The first tentative notes of "O Holy Night" rang out. She stilled, ears perked. The notes were clear and bright and finished off with a rich and warm vibrato. He finished the first verse flawlessly, then he was moving into the chorus, his voice ringing out strong and vibrant. The vocals swelled, sending chills up her arms. The words, his skillful dynamics, carried her away, making her want to fall on her knees right then and there.

Before she knew it, the last note of the chorus rang out into a shocked silence. She slowly turned and met Josh's gaze, her view blurry from tears she didn't realize had gathered. "That was beautiful."

He scratched his neck. "You don't have to say that."

"*Josh*. You're really good."

He gave an awkward chuckle. "Well, don't worry, I won't quit my day job."

She put a hand on his arm. "You're going to wow them tomorrow. You have nothing to be nervous about. I want to come and hear you sing."

"What? No, it's two hours away."

"I don't care."

"*No*. That'll only make me more nervous."

"But I've already heard you sing."

"I don't care. You're not coming."

She poked him in his ticklish spot. "Now who's bossy?"

Lightning fast, he grabbed her foot.

"Not the foot!" she said through her laughter, trying to pull away. When that didn't work, she went on the offense.

"Hey!" He jerked away. Dropped her foot. Leaned in, going for her ribs this time.

"Stop!" She fell back onto the sofa as his weight crashed down on her. "I'm too old for this!"

"You're never too old to be tickled."

"You're so right." She went for his ticklish spot again and found purchase.

He caught her arm and redoubled his efforts, making her laugh harder. His deep chuckle rumbled against her chest.

"We're gonna wake Zoey!"

"Promise me you won't go."

She squirmed, breathless, batting his hands away even as he did the same. All the while laughing so hard she felt giddy.

He hit his target, making her squeal. "Promise, and I'll stop."

"All right, all right, I promise. Jeez."

Instantly his hands paused. His eyes narrowed with suspicion as their breaths clashed in the space between them.

She was about to reissue her promise when something shifted almost imperceptibly in his eyes. His smile wilted slowly as his eyes fastened on hers.

He was inches away and suddenly the mingling of their breaths seemed very intimate. The way he stared at her even more so. Her eyes locked on his as if held by some imaginary force. The air crackled between them. Her heart threatened to burst from her chest.

His gaze lowered to her mouth, making her lips tingle. He closed the gap between them slowly, eyes seeking permission.

Please, please, please was all she could think before her lids fluttered shut and her lips welcomed his. The soft brush of his kiss set off an earthquake inside her. All focused on the epicenter of their lips. Moving in a way that gave rise to a tidal wave of sensations. The gentle sweep of his touch. The sweet taste of his mouth. The low hum of her skin.

His fingers slid into her hair as his lips wreaked havoc on hers.

Feelings of affection bubbled to the surface. She palmed his neck and felt the racing thrum of his pulse. Even as want coursed through her veins, unwelcome thoughts surged to the surface.

This was Josh. Her brother-in-law.

He was *kissing* her.

She was *kissing* him!

As if reading her mind he eased back, only inches away. Their eyes locked, ragged breaths tangling in the space between them. The dimness hid his thoughts from her.

What had just happened?

Coolness rushed over her skin as he eased off her, moving to the far side of the love seat. Numb, she sat up and rested against the sofa's arm. How had that happened? One minute they were laughing and being their usual platonic selves, and the next . . .

Josh had been so sad lately. He'd just come through a traumatic divorce. It was normal to seek relief from that kind of heartache.

What was *her* excuse?

Josh cleared his throat, a crack of gunfire in the unsettling quiet. "We should, ah, probably talk about that."

The low scrape of his voice made something flutter in her belly. She met his gaze across the length of the sofa. At once sorry and relieved he was so far away. What was wrong with her?

"It's okay," she said. "I understand. You've been sad a long time, and this is your first Christmas without her. You're lonely. It's completely natural you'd want to feel something else—anything else."

Josh stared at the Christmas tree as if mesmerized by the sight. The warm, sweet memory of that kiss played back in her head. But she couldn't let her thoughts go there. The reasons for it were too confusing, too awful to contemplate. "And I—I miss Ethan."

She'd just used Ethan's death to justify a kiss with his brother. At the realization, her hands flash froze to blocks of ice. What kind of person did that? The fairy lights took on a halo as tears filled her eyes.

Maggie's last words sliced through Josh like a razor blade. All these years of self-control and he'd lost it over a tickle match. How many times had he imagined what kissing Maggie might feel like? That's what he got for entertaining the thought.

Maggie wasn't ready to move on. He'd known that.

But he hadn't imagined that come-hither look in her eyes, had he? Hadn't imagined the way her lips responded so readily to his. The way she'd rested her warm hand against his neck as if she wanted to jump right inside him.

She was thinking of Ethan, you idiot.

A fist tightened in his gut. He'd never been more jealous of his brother than he was right this minute—and that was saying something. Sometimes it amazed him that he could hurt this much and still go on breathing.

But there was no time to deliberate the realities of heartbreak. He had to get it together and quick if he was going to salvage his relationship with Maggie. He couldn't let one impulsive moment ruin things between them. At least she'd attributed his motive to loneliness. To longing for his ex-wife.

Oh, the irony.

But she still loved Ethan and was missing him. She was probably feeling guilty about kissing Josh. And that was on him. Bolstering his courage, he turned and offered a smile.

The sight of a tear slipping down her cheek wiped the smile from his mouth. He reached across the sofa and took her hand. "Hey, hey. This was all my fault. I'm sorry. You're right. I'm lonely and it—it just happened. But it won't happen again. Please forgive me. You know what a dolt I am."

She huffed a laugh. Then her chin quivered.

He scooted the length of the sofa and pulled her into his chest like he'd done a hundred times over the past two and a half years. "Don't, honey. You're making me feel like a colossal jerk."

"You are a jerk."

He smiled against the top of her head. "Something we can both agree on." He rubbed her arm. Wondered if she could feel his heart wobbling painfully in his chest.

"I don't want anything to change between us," she whispered.

He closed his eyes, wishing he could shut out those words. Because he wanted everything to change between them. But if he wanted Maggie to be happy, if he wanted her in his life at all, he had to jump on board this friends-only train. "Let's just forget it ever happened."

"Agreed," she said so quickly he flinched. But as she pulled back and peered up at him, she looked more like her usual self. She set her palm against his cheek. "Someday you'll find someone who makes you forget all about Samantha."

He lifted his lips in a smile. "I know."

He already had. Too bad she didn't feel the same way.

Chapter 8

$\mathcal{J}$osh wasn't the settling-down type. Hadn't Maggie watched him move through woman after woman all his life? And his marriage had lasted all of four years. She wasn't sure how a man who'd been raised by such a loving couple ended up with major commitment issues.

But then again, given her background, it defied reason that she'd found herself in a loving, committed marriage to a wonderful man. A miracle if ever there'd been one.

The sound of the back door slamming jarred Maggie from her reverie.

"Mommy, Pokey licked my mouth! And then he jumped on Uncle Josh and got mud on his pants and he barked and barked at him." She barreled into Maggie smelling of outdoors and sunshine.

"Is that so?"

"Miss Laura said Pokey loves me. She's not sure about Uncle Josh, though."

Speaking of . . . Josh leaned against the wall at the room's threshold, grinning affectionately at Zoey. His hair was wind tousled and those broad shoulders hadn't happened by accident.

The memory of his kiss washed over her, making heat flush her limbs.

"Huh, Mommy, can they?"

Maggie gave her head a shake. "What, honey?"

"Can doggies love people? Or can only people love people?"

Josh's lips tipped in humor as he quirked a brow at Maggie.

Because yes, her daughter asked great questions. "I think doggies are capable of love too."

"That's good. 'Cause I love Pokey and I want him to love me too."

Maggie kissed Zoey on the cheek. "How could he not?"

And just like that, Zoey whirled, made a beeline for Josh, and grabbed his hand, pulling him toward the hall. "Let's play princess, Uncle Josh! You can be the prince 'cause you're a boy."

"Do I get to wear a crown?"

"I only have tiaras, but I get the one with the pink jewels 'cause it's my favorite."

Their voices faded as they entered Zoey's room.

Maggie glanced down at the letter she'd been reading. Or at least staring at while her mind strayed into forbidden territory. She shook off the memory of that kiss—and the guilt it induced—and began reading. She had a crucial mystery to solve and needed to focus if she hoped to find answers.

MAGGIE WASN'T SURE how long she'd been reading, but she was down to the last few letters. Hope drained like water from an unplugged bathtub. If they didn't find more to go on, how would they ever find Ethan's friend? And if they never found his friend, how would they find closure?

She was midway through the second to last letter when Rocky's name caught her eye. She devoured the words like a starving woman. Her heart leapt in her chest. "Josh," she called. "Come here."

She read the passage a second time while she waited for him to extract himself from her daughter.

"What'd you find?" Josh entered the room wearing a golden tiara atop his head and a mint-green baby blanket draped around his shoulders and secured with a hair clip.

Maggie was too excited to give him a hard time. "Listen to this. 'We spend an inordinate amount of time complaining about the food. I dream about your meatloaf and lasagna every day. I never realized what a glutton I was until I joined up. Rocky's family has a diner in Rock Hill and he describes the food in meticulous detail. He has us all salivating by the time he's finished describing the cuisine they serve up.'"

Josh beamed at her. "They own a diner in Rock Hill, South Carolina."

"How many diners can there possibly be in the town?"

He was already on his phone. "He didn't give the diner's name later?"

"No, that's all he says about it. But that really narrows it down. Surely we can find his family."

"There are only two restaurant names containing the word *diner*. But there are quite a few that seem like they might be actual diners."

"Let me get through the last letter and see if there's anything else. If not, we can start calling." She grinned widely, her body buzzing with excitement at the thought.

Josh joined her on the love seat as she read the last letter. It was hard to concentrate when they were so close to finding Rocky.

Eventually she reached the end. "Nothing else here. But we have what we need." She pulled out her phone. "We should start with the ones with *diner* in the name."

"Wait. Supposing we find the right restaurant . . . have you thought about what you'll say?"

"I don't know. I guess something like 'My husband knew your son in the Army, and could I get his phone number so I could ask some questions?'"

"You think his family would give out his contact information so easily?"

She hadn't thought that far ahead. "I could just ask them to give him my contact info. They'd know Rocky was his nickname so they'd know I'm telling the truth."

"That only proves you know someone who knew him over there."

She huffed. "Stop being such a downer. We're *this* close."

"I know, but . . . I was just sitting over here thinking this is too big to mess up. What if we make them suspicious and get their guard up? We might never find him then."

"You think we should drive over there?"

His gaze locked on hers for a long moment. "They're more likely to take us seriously and believe us. Plus, provided we do actually get to talk with Rocky, this won't exactly be an easy conversation. A lot of vets avoid talking about this stuff. And depending on what he says, it might not be so easy to hear either. Seeing you in person might compel him to talk—and to tell the truth, whatever that is."

Her spirits flagged. He had some good points, but she was so eager to get answers.

He was tapping the keyboard on his phone. "Rock Hill's only four hours away. We could leave Sunday morning."

"Are diners even open on Sundays?"

"Let me check."

She entertained the idea of calling. Surely his family, once they found them, would be willing to pass her name and number to Rocky.

"Some of them are open Sundays and some aren't. If we don't find Rocky's family on Sunday, we could hit the other diners early on Monday and still have time to drive home that night."

That seemed like a logical plan. But it also meant waiting a whole week. Not knowing was going to drive her crazy.

Josh took her hand. "What are you thinking?"

"That I can hardly bear the thought of waiting a whole week to figure this out." To put this behind her.

"Tell you what. In the meantime we'll keep searching for the guy, showing his picture around. Not just at the carnival but all over town, at the beaches and restaurants."

"But not to anyone who knows your family."

"Yeah, we have to be careful about that. Sound like a plan?"

She mulled it over for a long moment. "All right."

Maggie checked her watch. It was going on seven o'clock. "Would you mind if we stopped at my mom's on the way out of town? I still haven't heard back and I want to check on her."

"No problem. I'll go help Zoey clean her room."

"Good luck with that."

Chapter 9

*M*aggie pulled into her mother's drive, eyeing the two-story brick home situated on a large wooded lot in a prestigious neighborhood. Mom had bought the property shortly after being promoted at work. Maggie found the size and grandeur of the home off-putting.

She put the car in Park. It was hard to tell if Mom was home since she parked her car in the three-car garage.

The click of Zoey's car-seat buckle sounded as Maggie shut off the engine. "Stay in your seat, honey. Let me see if Grandma's home first."

"I wanna see Cleo."

The cat was usually the main attraction for Zoey. "If Grandma's home."

"I'll wait with Zoey," Josh said.

"Thanks." Maggie exited the car and followed the walkway's arc to the brick porch steps. If her mom wasn't home, Maggie would have to use the hide-a-key to enter. After that last cryptic text, she needed to make sure Mom wasn't unconscious on the floor or worse.

She knocked on the storm door, anxiety buzzing through her. There were no lights or movement through the sidelight. She should've had one of her friends check on her yesterday.

She knocked again. Or at the very least she should've come

straight over when she'd arrived in town. She'd convinced herself this was just another of her mother's antics, but if something was really wrong, Maggie would never forgive herself.

The door swept open and her mother appeared, blue eyes widening. Every dark hair on her head was in place, and her makeup was done to perfection. "Maggie, what are you doing here? I thought you'd run off to the beach for the summer."

She didn't seem to realize Maggie had been trying to reach her since yesterday afternoon. "Mom, didn't you get my texts? I've been worried about you."

Her drawn-on brows arched as she opened the storm door. "Well, whatever for?"

Maggie's blood pressure shot into the danger zone. "Mom, your last text said something terrible had happened and then you didn't answer my calls or texts."

"Something terrible . . ." Her head tipped back. "Oh, that. It was nothing. Just an issue with Cleo, but it turns out she's fine. Are you just doing a drive-by or are you going to come in? And where's Zoey? You didn't leave her out in that hot car, did you?"

Still flustered, Maggie turned and waved Josh over. "Why in the world didn't you answer my calls and texts? I've been worried sick."

"Oh, for heaven's sake. You're such an overreactor. My phone's just been glitchy lately, that's all. Come in. I wasn't expecting company, but I might have some tea left."

Heat flushed Maggie's entire body as she entered. She'd left for Seabrook only four days ago, but she'd forgotten how terrible being around her mother felt. The thought brought an instant pinch of guilt.

She slipped off her sandals in deference to the pristine hardwood floors and welcomed the cool breeze of the overhead fan.

"I didn't realize you'd brought company." Mom reopened the storm door for Josh and Zoey.

She was still very attractive at sixty with thick hair and long legs. Maggie had inherited her mother's dark hair and tall, lean physique. She hoped that was all she'd inherited.

As Josh entered, Mom greeted him in such a way as to maintain civility while still making him feel unwelcome. It was a special gift.

Maggie gave her head a sharp shake. That was so unkind. Why did she let her mother bring out the worst in her?

"Where's Cleo?" Zoey glanced around the room.

"Well, that's a fine how-do-you-do," Mom said to her grand-daughter. "Haven't you got a hug for your grandma?"

Zoey wrapped an arm around her grandmother's waist while the woman patted her shoulder. "Why don't the three of you have a seat? I was just heading out, but since you're here, I can offer you a glass of tea."

"Don't worry yourself on my account." Josh took a seat on the sofa.

Maggie sat beside him. "We're fine, Mom."

"Nonsense! I'm nothing if not hospitable."

As Mom swept off to the kitchen, Cleo entered the room from the hall, heading straight to Zoey. The tabby wound between Zoey's legs. "She missed me, Mommy."

"She sure did." The cat was unusually affectionate, especially with Zoey, who treated her with great care.

Josh tugged at Maggie's hand, and only then did she realize she'd been chewing her nails. Old habits.

"Did she say what happened?" Josh whispered.

"Some mini crisis with Cleo. And her phone has been *glitchy* so she didn't get my messages."

His lips tightened.

"I know, I know. What can I do?"

"If I didn't think that was a rhetorical question, I'd have a whole list for you."

"It's complicated." When her mom was left as a struggling single mother, she'd done her best by Maggie. At least, that was what Maggie told herself.

Maggie hadn't exactly escaped her father's abandonment unscathed. She'd missed having a dad in her life. Had wondered what was so wrong with her that made her father take off and never look back. Her mother had also planted plenty of doubts in Maggie's mind. Doubts that had led to deep-rooted insecurity.

That insecurity had caused problems between Ethan and her. It took a lot for Ethan to get past her defenses. A lot of patience, a lot of reassurance. Every change in their relationship felt to Maggie like a threat: when he left for college, when they began talking marriage, when he left for the military. All of it scared her. Loving him scared her. Losing him scared her.

And ultimately, she'd done just that. Her fears had come to fruition, and losing him had been even more awful than she'd imagined.

Now Maggie was a single mom—something she'd been so determined to avoid. Her daughter was supposed to have a mother *and* a father. She was supposed to experience the safety net of two loving parents. So much for that dream. It had died right along with Ethan.

If Ethan had died at all.

She quickly squashed the thought. Couldn't go hoping that. She wished she could open up to her mom about the mystery man. But where her mother was concerned, she'd learned to keep her thoughts to herself.

"I had to use my small glasses since I'm almost out of tea." Mom handed the glasses to Josh and Maggie, who each took a sip.

Her mother did have a way with sweet tea. "It's very good, Mom."

"Delicious," Josh added.

Mom hadn't brought Zoey anything to drink, but Maggie let it go. Her daughter was entertaining herself with Cleo and didn't notice.

"I'm surprised you were able to get away, Joshua. Weekends must be busy in your line of work." The blue-collar kind, her tone implied. Never mind that Josh had put in two years of maritime school, passed a rigorous fifty-ton license exam, put in 180 days aboard a ship, and now owned his own business.

"We're actually closed on Sundays."

"Oh. Okay . . ."

Whereas Maggie would've explained herself, Josh simply gave Mom a polite smile.

Her mother turned her steady blue gaze on Maggie. "Have you been swimming in the ocean yet?"

"Not yet. We haven't had time."

"It seems you have all the time in the world with all these summers off. You don't know how good you've got it."

Maggie bit her tongue. Between staying after school to help students, serving on committees, coaching the girls' swim team, making lesson plans, and grading papers, she worked a ton of hours during the school year. But she resisted the urge to go on the defense. "How's your job going, Mom?" She was president of a well-known business consulting organization, having worked her way to the top over the past fifteen years.

"Very well, thank you. I just secured a contract with the new hospital. It'll be a multimillion-dollar project."

"That's wonderful. I'm glad to hear it's going well."

"It's all a matter of attitude and hard work. It starts at the top, you know." She went on, regaling them with her recent accomplishments and complaining about the dreary chairman of the board. Her mother was gifted at her job—that much was obvious by the position she'd attained. Even before the promotion she'd been a workaholic.

Growing up, Maggie had been closer to her aunt Clara than her mother. She'd stayed with Maggie while her mother worked, given her the nurturing a little girl needed, and loved her unconditionally. Sometimes Maggie had pretended her aunt was her mother. Who knew where she'd be if not for Aunt Clara's warm and nurturing presence in her life?

It boggled her mind that the sisters were so different. They'd both come from the same tragic background. Their father had deserted them and their mother had neglected them until they were finally shuffled off to Seabrook to live with their cold grandmother. Maggie had gotten most of the story from her aunt. Her mother only ever brought it up when Maggie dared to complain about her own childhood.

"You're so ungrateful, Maggie. You have no idea how lucky you are. My mother didn't even know I was alive."

Aunt Clara had passed away shortly before Maggie's mother's heart attack. Maggie still missed her terribly.

As her mother's monologue droned on, Maggie nodded and *hmm*ed in all the appropriate places while watching her daughter play with the cat.

Much later when her mother checked her watch, Maggie gathered the empty glasses and stood. "Well, it's getting late. We should probably be heading back to Seabrook."

"I've hardly even had a chance to talk to my granddaughter. She's been playing with Cleo the entire time."

Maggie forced a smile. "You can call anytime and talk to her." Though she knew that would never happen. She went to the kitchen and put the empty glasses in the dishwasher, rushing so she wouldn't leave Josh alone with her mother for too long.

When she returned to the living room, Josh and Zoey were already waiting by the door.

Mom swept Cleo into her arms and joined them in the foyer, offering Maggie and Zoey limp one-armed hugs. "Drive carefully now."

"Of course. Chat with you soon, Mom."

"Bye, Grandma." As soon as the door was open, Zoey took off for the car and Maggie and Josh followed.

After they were all buckled up, Maggie started the car and caught Josh's raised brow as she turned to back from the drive. "Don't even start."

Chapter 10

*F*rom her spot on the pool steps, little Mia bit her bottom lip.

She and Maggie had started out playing with squirt toys, then progressed to a breath-holding contest. Maggie had just demonstrated putting her face in the water while holding her breath, then asked Mia to give it a try.

Mia's wide green eyes flickered with fear. "I can't."

"Why not?"

"It's too scary."

"What do you think might happen?"

Her niece smoothed her hands over the surface of the water. "I could drown."

"But I'm right here. I'm an expert swimmer and I'd never let that happen. I wonder if you could hold your breath and put your face to the water just for a quick second. I'll be right here the whole time."

"You won't let me drown?"

"Of course not."

"You teach big kids to swim?"

"I do. They're already very good swimmers and I teach them how to get even better."

"Owen can swim real good. He says I'm a baby."

"You're not a baby. Lots of people get nervous in the water. It's okay to feel scared. But the important thing is to overcome that fear. Because learning to stay safe in the water is very important."

"'Cause what if I fell in?"

"That's right. It's all about safety. Once you learn to swim, you won't have to be afraid of the water anymore."

Mia stared into the pool. That familiar pattern danced through the water as light refracted against the ripples. "Can I hold my nose?"

"Of course."

She seemed to deliberate for a full ten seconds. "Okay, I'll try. Just for a quick second."

Maggie bit back a smile. "Whenever you're ready, take a big breath and hold it."

Mia grabbed the railing. A moment later her cute little face took on a battle-like expression. Then she sucked in a breath, held her nose, and went face down in the water.

She was back up in a flash, water streaming down her cheeks. Her spiky lashes opened to gleaming eyes as her face broke into a dimpled smile. "I did it!"

Maggie hugged her. "You did great! You held your breath and put your whole face in, just like an old pro."

"It was easy."

"That's only because you're so brave."

"How's it going out here?" Erin called through the French doors.

Mia jumped up from her stoop and water dripped at her feet as she dashed toward her mom. "I'm an old pro, Mommy."

"Is that so? You'll have to tell me all about it." Erin beamed at her daughter. She'd been inside making cookies with Zoey while Maggie worked with Mia.

This was a good place to stop. Maggie eased from the water.

"Oh no you don't," Erin called. "You stay and enjoy a nice long swim while the girls and I finish up the cookies."

"Are you sure?"

"Positive."

Mia was still rambling about her accomplishment when the door closed.

Maggie walked around to the deep end. She and Erin had agreed on twice a week for lessons, and Maggie was pleased with the progress Mia had made with this first one. Each small step would go a long way toward building her confidence.

As Maggie reached the end of the pool, she pulled down her goggles. It was hard to believe it was only Wednesday. The week was passing like a kidney stone as she awaited the trip to Rock Hill. She and Josh had looked for Ethan's twin at the beach, at several of his favorite restaurants, and down at the pier. A couple of people on the pier thought he seemed familiar but couldn't provide any practical help.

She glanced back at the house. She felt guilty for hiding this monumental secret from her best friend. But it would be unkind to raise Erin's hopes unnecessarily.

At the other end of the pool, Maggie lined her toes up on the curved edge. It had been a few weeks since she'd been in the water for a real swim. The end of a school year was hectic, and when she'd managed to make it to the Y, she always had Zoey along. But now with her daughter in Erin's capable hands, the thought of diving into that liquid heaven brought a smile to her face.

She bent her knees, aligned her hands, tucked her head, and sprang from the edge. She sliced into the pool hands first, barely aware of the coolness as the water sluiced over her skin. She completed her pullout and began swimming freestyle, falling into an easy rhythm, a little slow as her body awakened.

Swimming was as easy, as natural, as breathing for her. The water was like home. A place where she was always welcome. A place where she felt safe and free, at peace. Cocooned from the world and all its troubles.

Her legs fluttered fluidly and her arms windmilled through the water. *Catch and pull. Catch and pull. Catch and pull. Breathe.*

When she reached the wall, she did a flip, placed her feet on the wall, and got a good push—an arrow shot from a quiver. Her body glided effortlessly through the water, aerodynamic.

At the surface she lifted an arm, kicked a leg, her face in the water, her lungs still full of oxygen. She was reborn. Her mind, now fully engaged, focused on the physical. She found her rhythm with the water and her speed increased. She could swim to Aruba.

It may have been weeks but her muscles knew what to do. Once again her body cruised through the water, taking her to that mindless place, that dreamlike space where she was free from worry and fear and grief.

Chapter 11

*W*hile Josh drove to Rock Hill, Maggie kept Zoey occupied in the back seat. They drew pictures, assembled puzzles, and played tic-tac-toe and I Spy. Maggie had packed an entertainment arsenal fit for a little princess. She was such a good mom.

It was Maggie who fidgeted, at turns biting her nails and checking her watch. He understood her nerves. As much as he'd wished the whole week away, now that the day had arrived, his anxiety swelled like a wave.

He'd given a lot of thought to this field trip. It could go one of four ways: They wouldn't find Rocky and would go home empty-handed; they would locate Rocky and he'd have no definitive answers; they'd track down Rocky only to confirm Ethan really had died five years ago; or they'd find Rocky and learn Ethan was still alive.

The first and second would end with no answers and disappointment. The third would dash hopes that had swelled over the past nine days despite their best intentions. The fourth and least likely scenario would be a miracle of epic proportions.

At most, there was a one-quarter chance this trip would end well. He didn't love those odds. They needed to resolve this perplexing mystery, but he didn't relish the thought of dragging Maggie back into that vortex of grief—or going there himself. Part of him wished she'd never seen that man at the carnival. But the slim hope that Ethan might still be alive carried him past that fleeting regret.

Come what may, he was glad he was here for her. Having Zoey along might prove tricky. They'd told the girl they were visiting a friend.

Josh turned and caught Maggie's gaze in the rearview mirror. Hope battled fear in the depths of her eyes. He knew just how she felt. He wished he could wrap his arm around her and tell her it was going to be okay. He settled for a wink.

"Your destination is on the right," the GPS announced. "Fourteen forty-four Cherry Road."

Maggie checked the visor mirror as Josh pulled the rental car into a parking lot. She smoothed her hair and added a bit of lip gloss. She'd worn a comfortable pair of jeans and a nice summer top with flutter sleeves. She was probably thinking too hard, but she wanted to appear decent and trustworthy.

Josh turned into the one open parking spot at the front of the building. Cindy's House Diner was aptly named since the restaurant was located in an old brick house.

Only two diners were open today, and they'd started here because it closed at one. "This place must be popular with the church crowd."

"Apparently so."

Maggie checked the back seat and her spirits flagged. "She fell asleep."

"Want me to carry her in?"

"She'll likely wake up and then she'll be grumpy all afternoon."

"I can go in alone then."

Maggie stared at the neon Open sign in the window. "I'll go." She opened the door and stepped out into the southern heat. "Wish me luck."

"You've got this."

She didn't feel like she had it. Her legs trembled as she approached the door. A man in farmer's apparel exited, holding the door for her. "Thank you."

As she stepped inside, the smell of frying bacon and stiff coffee assaulted her. A diner-style bar extended the length of the wood-paneled room, seating at least a dozen customers on swivel stools. Two middle-aged servers bustled behind the bar, pouring coffee, swiping empty plates, and hanging orders as if their movements were choreographed.

Maggie moved straight to the register and within seconds one of the servers called over, "Just grab a seat wherever you can find one, hon. Someone'll be with you in a minute."

"Oh, I'm not staying. I was wondering if I could talk to the owner real quick."

The server leaned into the kitchen. "Cindy, you're wanted up front." She grabbed two full plates from under the heat lamp. "She'll be right with ya."

"Thank you." Maggie reviewed the script in her head and prayed for the hundredth time that they'd get the answers they needed.

Moments later a woman swept through the kitchen door. She was a bit older than Maggie and wore her blonde hair in a low ponytail. A smile lit her face with warmth as she approached the register. "Hi, I'm Cindy. What can I do for you?"

"Sorry to bother you in the middle of your lunch rush."

"No worries."

"My name's Maggie Reynolds. I'm looking for an Army friend of my husband's—he went by the name of Rocky. His parents own a diner here in town—"

Cindy shook her head. "That's not us, if that's what you're asking. Sorry. My husband and I own this place and our kids are only in high school."

Maggie propped up her smile. "Would you happen to know the family I'm looking for? It's really important that we find Rocky."

Lines formed between Cindy's brows. "I mean, it's a small town, but it's not that small. Can't be the Roswells—they own the Breakfast Bunch south of town. They only have two daughters. Beyond that I really couldn't say."

One of the servers passed by. "Cindy, can you make some more decaf when you get a chance?"

"Sure thing." The owner stepped back with a parting smile. "Sorry I couldn't be of more help."

"That's okay. Thank you for taking the time." Maggie's hopes flagged as she exited the restaurant. The Breakfast Bunch wasn't open today anyway, and now they could cross that off their list. That was a little progress at least.

Chapter 12

*T*he savory scents of breakfast meats filled Maggie's nose as they entered the small diner the next morning. They hadn't found Rocky's family yet, but they'd crossed three diners off their list yesterday. Then because the other diners were closed, they'd taken Zoey to the local children's museum.

Maggie had been up early with her daughter, but they'd delayed their visit to the Iron Skillet, hoping the early morning crowd would dwindle. She was glad to see only about half of the red vinyl booths were filled.

They stopped by a sign that read "Hostess will be with you shortly." A moment later the sign kept its promise. A middle-aged woman ushered the trio to a booth in the back corner and left them with menus. The restaurant was clean and comfortable, if lacking the old-fashioned diner appeal of the other restaurants they'd visited.

"I want two of whatever I'm smelling right now," Josh said.

"Can I have pancakes, Mommy?"

Maggie perused the menu. "How about the ones with strawberries?"

"Yummy."

She'd just closed her menu when Maggie and Josh got a group message from his mom. "They made it to Paris last night," Josh said.

"By train." They had tickets to go up the Eiffel Tower in a couple days.

"Mom'll love using her French." Before she'd retired she taught the foreign language to high schoolers. "And Dad's been talking about those baguettes since they planned the trip."

"Are they going to Italy next?"

"First they're going to Interlaken, Switzerland, then Italy via Monaco. Dad wants to see where the Grand Prix takes place, even though they missed the race by a few weeks."

"Sounds like fun."

He cut her a look. "If they knew what we were up to back home, they'd be on the first plane back."

"Which is why we can't say anything."

"Agreed, but with any luck, we'll strike gold here."

A friendly male server brought water, and they went ahead and ordered, wanting to expedite their day. They had three restaurants to visit and had to leave time to (hopefully) speak with Rocky before their drive back.

When the server left, Maggie studied Josh. He looked like he didn't get much more sleep than she did. His dark hair was tousled and his eyelids seemed puffy.

She didn't look much better. She hadn't bothered to bring makeup and had thrown her hair back in a ponytail.

Their server was pouring coffee a few tables down and Maggie flipped over her mug. "Why don't we ask him about the owners next time he comes around? That way once we're finished eating, we can move on if we don't learn anything."

"Sounds good."

"Are we gonna go to the museum again today?" Zoey asked.

"No, honey. But that sure was fun, wasn't it?"

"The pretend kangaroo had a baby in her pocket."

"I know. That was so cute."

Josh tugged at his T-shirt. "How about if I put you in my pocket? I can carry you with me wherever I go."

Zoey giggled. "I can't fit in there."

"Are you sure? I'll hold it open and you can just jump right in, like the little joey."

Zoey turned to Maggie. "Uncle Josh is silly."

"He sure is. Maybe you can fit in my purse instead."

"Mommy! I'm too big."

"Well, that's too bad. It would be fun to ride around in my purse all day."

"We have a long drive home today."

"That's right," Josh said. "We can play games again."

"But when are we gonna see your friend?"

Maggie met Josh's gaze. "Hopefully today, honey. We have to find him first."

Zoey opened the crayon box and began coloring the kids' menu that doubled as a place mat.

The server returned and filled Josh's and Maggie's mugs with steaming hot coffee.

"Thank you"—Maggie glanced at his name tag—"Grant."

"Can I get you anything else while you wait?"

"Well, actually, yes. We were wondering if the owner was here today."

"My family owns the place. How can I help you?"

Maggie's attention sharpened on the man, noting the high forehead. The familiar shape of his eyes. The hawkish nose.

75

She sucked in a breath. She hadn't recognized him because of his hair and bushy beard.

Rocky.

She must've said the name out loud. Because his eyes homed in on her face and his congenial smile wilted. "Maggie? What are you—? I can't believe you're here. I didn't recognize you at first. I think about you all the time."

Josh cleared his throat. "Hi, I'm Josh, Ethan's brother."

Rocky extended a hand, smiling once again. "Of course. Josh. I feel like I already know you. I've heard so many stories."

Josh's gaze darted toward Zoey. "We'd love a chance to chat. Maybe when the food gets here we could sit over there." He nodded toward a booth across the way.

The adrenaline that flooded Maggie left her in a state of heightened awareness. She'd been thinking about everything except how they might handle this with Zoey.

"Yeah, sure. I'd love to. Your food's probably coming up any minute now. Let me find someone to cover my tables." He strode toward the kitchen.

Josh grabbed Maggie's hand and she found in his expression the same excitement that bubbled up inside her. They were about to get their answers.

He squeezed her hand.

Despite her best efforts to remain realistic, hope expanded inside like helium, filling her until she thought she might float to the ceiling.

A few minutes later Grant returned and began unloading their plates from a circular tray. "Here we are."

When he set down Zoey's plate, Maggie automatically began cutting her pancakes and strawberries.

"I can do it, Mommy. Can I have syrup?"

"Jeez, I totally forgot." Grant seemed as flustered as Maggie felt. "You need refills too. And did you want gravy with your biscuits?" he asked Josh.

"No, thanks."

"Be right back."

When Grant returned, Maggie set the syrup by Zoey's plate. "Honey, this is our friend Grant. Grant, this is Zoey."

His gaze softened on her daughter. "It's sure nice to meet you, sweetheart."

"Uncle Josh and I are going to sit right over there with our friend while you eat."

Zoey stuffed a bite of pancake in her mouth and nodded.

One hurdle down. Maggie and Josh left the booth and joined Grant across the way. This was happening so fast. She hadn't expected to find Rocky in the restaurant, and she'd been so intent on how to extract information from his parents, she hadn't given much thought to what she'd say to Rocky himself.

Josh must've caught on to her panic. He leaned onto his elbows and lowered his voice. "Thank you for being willing to talk to us."

"You kidding? It's so nice to meet you guys. I feel like you're practically family."

He hasn't asked about Ethan. If he were still alive, Rocky would've asked where he was or how he was doing by now. The thought punctured a gaping hole in her hope.

"You must be wondering why we're here," Josh said. "I guess we need to hear what took place the day of the explosion. Were you there when it happened?"

Grant's face sobered, then he stared at his hands on the table. "I was. I've relived that day a million times. Still have nightmares about it. Sometimes dreams where I did something different. Something that changed the outcome. Then I wake up and realize all over again that it really did happen."

"I'm sorry for what you've been through," Josh said.

"It must be hard to talk about," Maggie said. "But it would be very helpful if you could tell us what happened."

"Of course." Rocky's Adam's apple bobbed. He glanced up at Maggie. "Least I could do. I should've contacted you sooner. I'm sorry I didn't."

"That's okay. What you're doing right now means the world to us."

Eyes fixed on his hands, Rocky seemed to travel back in time as he spoke. "It was just a normal day. All the routine things. We did our jobs, cut up, poked at each other. Then someone brought in this Iraqi woman. One of our guys found her on a road outside the base, passed out and bleeding. Hollywood was first on hand. He went over to assess her injuries." Rocky swallowed again. A mottled red stain climbed his neck and flushed his cheeks.

"That's when the explosion happened. I was lucky. It just threw me back into a bed. I didn't even lose consciousness. But when I gathered my wits, my ears were ringing and I just—I was like, *This isn't happening*, you know? We train for all sorts of terrible things. It felt so surreal. Like it was happening to somebody else."

Maggie's heart shriveled inside her chest. Her shallow breaths left her dizzy.

Josh leaned forward. "You said Ethan went to assess her. Where was he when the explosion took place?"

"He was—he was right there. Bedside. One second he was there and the next . . . It was quick. He didn't suffer. I hope you can find some comfort in knowing that."

Her eyes filled with tears. She tried to think of something to say.

But she couldn't think beyond the gut-wrenching sense of hopelessness spreading like poison through her veins.

Under the table, Josh took her hand. "So you're 100 percent certain Ethan couldn't have survived?"

Grant blinked. Opened his mouth. "No. I saw . . . He didn't survive." He looked back at Maggie, questions in his eyes.

"We—" She cleared the croak from her voice. "We just had to be certain. You know. They didn't tell us much."

"I wish so badly I could say otherwise . . ." His gaze fell to the table and the muscles in his jaw ticked as he seemed to go back in time. "I'm so sorry. I've wished a million times I could trade places with him. I'm not married, no kids." He glanced over at Zoey. "He should've been here to be a dad to her. He was so happy about becoming a father. He'd shown me the ultrasound the night before." Grant shook his head, his eyes glazing over, remnants of shock and horror in his expression.

She couldn't fathom what that room must've looked like following the explosion. It had left seven people dead and more injured. But Maggie could barely process the idea that the hope building relentlessly for ten days was false.

They were right back where they'd been before she'd seen Ethan's look-alike. No. It was much worse than that. That terrible news seemed to have stripped away all the progress she'd made over the past five years. Now grief rose inside, threatening to engulf her all over again. She stuffed it down.

"I wasn't sure how much they'd told you," Rocky said. "I hope I didn't—"

"You told us the truth." Josh's voice had a ragged edge. "That's what we came for."

She'd actually let herself believe, just a little, that Ethan might be out there somewhere. She swallowed against the boulder in her throat.

"I've wondered a hundred times how you're doing, Maggie. Hollywood was so smitten with you. He had your pictures by his bed and bragged so much when you got pregnant." He glanced over at Zoey, who sipped milk from a straw. "She smiles like him."

Maggie tried to lift her lips. Tried to find comfort in his words. But her heart felt like a barren wasteland. The emotions bubbled to the surface, threatening to erupt with the force of a volcano. "Excuse me. I need to use the restroom."

Chapter 13

*M*aggie hadn't said a word since they'd left the diner. She returned from the restroom with puffy, red-rimmed eyes, appearing ravaged by grief. Josh wanted to take her in his arms and comfort her—comfort them both. But Zoey looked on and Maggie wouldn't want to frighten and confuse her.

Somehow Josh held it together while Rocky told him stories about Ethan. When the man was called back to work, they exchanged heartfelt hugs and promises to keep in touch.

Now Josh glanced in the rearview mirror. Zoey talked to herself, her chatter barely filtering through his fog of disappointment. Yeah, he'd told himself they were only coming here to eliminate all doubt. But that seed of hope had sprouted in both of them. He could only imagine what Maggie was feeling, but they'd been unable to talk with Zoey nearby.

Following the guidance of the GPS, he turned into a residential neighborhood and spotted the destination ahead. He shut off the navigation, then pulled along the curb lined with two-story homes situated on small lots.

"Where are we?" As if awakening from a long slumber, Maggie glanced around, looking lost, and he felt a pinch in his chest.

"At a park. I thought we could let Zoey burn off some energy before the trip back." He shut off the engine.

"Okay." Maggie got out, moving slowly.

"Zoey, stay put a minute, okay? I'm gonna help your mom with something."

"Okay."

After turning up the playlist of her favorite songs, he exited the car and met Maggie at the back. Those big brown eyes were so sad. Her wet eyelashes clumped together. Pink bloomed on the tip of her nose.

He opened his arms to her, and she fell into him, clutching him tightly. His embrace seemed to unleash a torrent of sorrow, and the raw sound of her grief wrenched his heart. "I know, honey. I know."

"I . . . I let myself hope he was—" Her words broke off on a sob.

"I know. Me too." His eyes stung as he tightened his arms around her and buried his face in her hair. He wished he could absorb all her pain. That he could carry it for both of them. "I'm sorry this is happening."

The familiar smell of her hair, the warmth of her body, and the softness of her skin comforted him. For a while there he'd let himself hope he might have his big brother back. Hope his family might be whole again. But it had all been a ridiculous dream.

And now grief was wrecking them all over again. At least they hadn't told his parents and sister. They'd be spared this second wave of sorrow. He never should've let Maggie hope again.

Though he still couldn't conjure a rational explanation for the Ethan look-alike who roamed Seabrook.

Maggie shuddered as she brought her sobs under control. "He seemed pretty certain . . . didn't he?"

Josh hated to remove that last thread of hope, but it would be unkind to allow more false hope. "He did."

"And you—you believed he was telling the truth?"

"No doubt in my mind, honey. The whole thing left him pretty messed up." He kissed the top of her head. "We were wrong. We hoped for the best and we hunted down the answers we needed. We did what we had to do." And now it was over.

Her body shuddered reflexively. "I don't like the answers."

"I don't either."

She drew back, studying his face in a way that drew heat to his cheeks. She feathered away the dampness on his cheek. "Are you okay?"

He tried for a smile but it wobbled and gave way. "I'll get there."

"You always take such good care of me. But who's taking care of you?"

"We take care of each other. And we'll both be just fine."

"I don't like seeing you so sad."

"I don't like seeing you sad either."

They took each other in, time suspended in a way that sent Josh's mind back to a December evening when they'd shared that monumental kiss.

Just as quickly, guilt torpedoed the memory.

"We should get Zoey out before the car gets hot." She withdrew from his arms and wiped her face dry. "Do I look okay? Can you tell I've been crying?"

Mouth tipping in a mirthless grin, he plucked a wet strand from her temple and brushed it back behind her ear. "You're good to go."

Maggie went to open Zoey's door while Josh collected his phone. He shut off the rousing strains of "Let It Go" as Maggie helped Zoey from the car.

"Ready to play at the park, Chickadee?"

"Are there swings?"

"There sure are."

Josh checked both ways, and as they crossed the street, he caught Zoey studying her mom's face.

"Did your friend make you sad, Mommy?"

Josh traded a glance with Maggie. That daughter of hers missed nothing.

Maggie offered Zoey a smile. "Yeah, honey, I guess he did. But I'll be okay."

"That wasn't very nice of him."

"He didn't mean to make me sad. Sometimes it's nobody's fault."

Zoey's brows furrowed as they stepped up onto the curb and headed toward the playground. "Like when Swishy died? That made me very sad and it wasn't my fault."

"That's right. Goldfish die sometimes. It was nobody's fault."

Zoey tugged Maggie to a stop in the grass and held her arms up.

Maggie picked her up and Zoey wrapped her arms around Maggie, squeezing her in a hug. "Feel better now, Mommy?"

Josh met Maggie's gaze, finding her eyes wet with tears.

"So much better, honey. Thank you. I love your hugs."

A moment later Zoey wiggled free and Maggie set her down. The girl ran toward the playground, her little legs eating up the distance.

"Uncle Josh! Come push me high on the swings!"

Chapter 14

*M*aggie's heart was heavy after the trip to Rock Hill. It was difficult to act as if everything was okay. Finding out the truth had triggered those old feelings of loss and anger. A part of her felt abandoned by Ethan all over again. It didn't make sense, but there it was.

So over the next week and a half, Maggie focused on establishing a routine. Their arrival had been so disrupted by that random sighting of Ethan's twin that they hadn't had a chance to settle in.

In the mornings they ate a healthy breakfast, got ready, and took a walk on the beach. Zoey collected shells, asked a million questions, dodged waves, and petted every friendly dog they passed. During their walks Maggie also shared random facts about Zoey's father: his favorite childhood book (*The Foot Book*), his insatiable curiosity, his ability to remember just about everything he read. Sometimes Maggie shared a brief memory or two. After their walk they worked on Zoey's numbers and letters, then she played while Maggie piddled around the house. Then came lunch.

Afternoons were usually spent on the beach. Sometimes Erin and the kids joined them. Wednesday and Fridays were for swimming lessons with Mia and poolside chats while the cousins played.

But even as she went through the motions, she feared her joy would never be restored. That all her work toward healing had been in vain. But about a week after their return, Maggie found herself climbing out of that mire of despair and hopelessness. She still had her beautiful daughter and a summer at the beach. She wouldn't waste it rehashing her grief.

Josh checked in regularly via text. He came over the following Sunday and had dinner with them. His sidelong looks betrayed his concern. But they watched a movie with Zoey and shared some laughter, and by the time he left, Maggie was in a better place.

Then the Fourth of July was upon them. June seemed to have vanished like vapor. Early in the morning Maggie staked out a spot on the beach. Erin and her family were coming over later and so was Josh. The group would grill burgers, then they'd watch the fireworks from the beach. Zoey was beyond excited to see the "firelights" and hear the big booms.

Erin arrived first, juggling three sacks of groceries. "Figured I might as well shuck the corn over here."

"Come on in." Maggie helped her with the bags, then covered the pot of boiling eggs and set the timer.

"Aunt Erin!" Zoey threw her arms around her aunt's legs as if she hadn't seen her just two days ago. "Where's Mia?"

"She's coming later with Uncle Patrick and Owen. Wanna help me shuck corn?"

Zoey tilted her head, wrinkling her nose. *"What?"*

Erin laughed. "Oh, you're gonna love this. We'll do it on the deck so we can keep the mess outside."

"I'll join you while the eggs are cooking." Maggie grabbed the trash can and followed the two outside.

Erin set down the sack of corn and settled in one of the chairs. "I can't wait to have your deviled eggs again."

Maggie's eggs, topped with candied bacon, were a hit with the whole Reynolds family. "I'm more than happy to send you the recipe."

"I'd rather you keep making them for me." She handed Zoey a corncob and demonstrated how to peel away the layers.

Zoey took right to the task. When she got down to the corn silk, she held up the ear. "Look, Mommy, it has hair."

"It sure does. But we don't want to eat that part, so we have to pull it off like this." Maggie demonstrated.

Zoey followed suit but soon gave up on the tedious task, leaving the ear covered in corn silk when she set it in the finished pile.

The sun had long since passed overhead, leaving them in the shade. But the temperature, tipping into the nineties, made sweat bead on Maggie's skin. The beach, usually abandoned by sunbathers this time of day, teemed with people claiming spots for tonight's display.

They chatted as they shucked, and when the timer buzzed, Maggie transferred the eggs to a bowl of cold water and set it in the fridge. When she returned to the balcony, Zoey was gone.

"She got a little bored and decided she'd rather go play," Erin said.

"She's been playing with those finger puppets Mia loaned her. That was awfully sweet of her."

"She doesn't share with just anyone." Erin tossed her short blonde hair from her face and gave Maggie a sheepish look. "So . . . I may have mentioned Mia's swimming lessons at a ladies' luncheon this week."

Maggie turned a questioning look on Erin.

"It seems a couple of them were wondering if you might have time to work with their kids the rest of the summer."

"*Erin.*"

"Don't hit me. I know you're here for rest and relaxation, so no pressure, truly. I only mentioned it in passing. Ella has a daughter who's six and can't swim yet, despite her best efforts, and Kyra has a teenage son who's going out for the swim team this year . . . and one thing led to another."

Would it be so awful to have something besides the mystery man to occupy her mind? Because yes, the sighting was still haunting her. When she was at the beach or the grocery store or a restaurant, she searched the crowd for that familiar face. Couldn't seem to help herself.

She hadn't mentioned it to Josh. He'd suffered the same disappointment and she was reluctant to pull him into it again. He hadn't brought it up, so maybe he'd been able to move on with no real answers.

"I'll tell them you're not available," Erin said. "No big deal."

Maggie shook her thoughts away. "I don't know how it would even work. There's no pool here. And what would I do with Zoey?"

"I'm happy to watch Zoey anytime. The Johnsons have a pool—they're the ones with the teenage son. And you could use my pool to teach Ella's daughter. She's in the same class as Mia at church, and now that Mia's putting her face in water, you could probably teach them together." Erin threw her hands up, palms out. "Not that I'm pushing you on this. It's totally your call."

Maggie gave her a dubious look.

"There's money involved. Just saying. But that's it. No pressure from me."

Maggie tossed the shucked corncob into the pile and began removing silk from another. "I'll *think* about it."

"That's great. I'll let them know."

Maggie hadn't anticipated doing any kind of work this summer. But teaching swimming was a joy. Truth be told, she enjoyed coaching the swim team more than teaching expository writing to a class of restless students.

"You seem a little better today."

"What do you mean?"

"You've seemed a little sad and withdrawn the past week or so. I've been worried about you. Is your mom giving you grief?"

"No more than usual." And here she'd thought she'd done such a great job of hiding her feelings. "I've been struggling a bit. These waves of grief—you'd think I'd be over it by now."

"Hey, you don't have to explain. I still grieve him too. It can hit at the oddest times. One day back in February I saw butter pecan ice cream at the grocery store and it hit me so hard, remembering the way I teased him for liking such an old-man flavor. I barely made it out of the store before falling apart. I felt so stupid."

"You should've called." She'd had a million such moments, it seemed. "He sure did love his ice cream."

"Remember when he bought that three-gallon tub from Scoops?"

Maggie chuckled. "It took up half our freezer in that little apartment." Sometimes it seemed like yesterday. Other times it seemed he'd been gone a decade.

Erin grabbed her hand. "Don't ever feel you have to hide your grief from me, okay? I feel it too."

The warmth in her friend's eyes soothed Maggie's soul. "Thanks, Erin. You're the best friend a girl could ask for."

Erin squeezed her hand. "Sister. We'll always be sisters."

Daylight gave way to dusk, lifting the heat of the day. The smells of grilled burgers and gunpowder lingered in the air. Maggie snuggled with Zoey in one of the beach chairs and dug her toes in the sand. Josh sat beside them holding a sparkler while Zoey and Mia looked on. Erin lay on a beach towel reading a novel, and down at the shoreline Patrick and Owen tossed a Frisbee.

While Mia favored her mother, Owen resembled his dad. They shared a lean build, an olive complexion, and thick dark hair, though Patrick's hairline was already receding. He jokingly blamed his congregation.

Maggie's stomach was full of good food, and her heart was lighter from the pleasant company and conversation. Her mother had called to guilt her about being absent for the holiday weekend, but Maggie wouldn't focus on that.

"Wave it around, Uncle Josh," Zoey said.

Josh moved the sparkler in a figure-eight pattern. "Your daddy loved fireworks. We had a great time playing with them on the beach."

Maggie recalled them shooting bottle rockets at each other when they were teens. She gave Josh a stern look. "But fireworks are very dangerous, so we have to be careful."

Erin set her book aside. "Anyone wanna take a walk before we lose the light?"

"Me, me!" Zoey scrambled off Maggie's lap.

"Me too," Mia chimed in.

"I think I'll stay and keep Uncle Josh out of trouble," Maggie said.

"You know how he gets with fireworks." Erin followed the girls toward the shoreline. "You'll have your work cut out for you."

He held up his sizzling sparkler and called out to Erin, "I haven't even caught anything on fire yet."

"Is that where you've set the bar?"

The family never let Josh forget about setting their neighbor's bush on fire when he was eleven. The bush blaze had then spread to the house's overhang and the fire department got involved.

Josh's sparkler fizzled out and he stuck the stick in the sand under his chair. "Did you see the pictures Mom posted today?"

"The one of your dad holding up the Leaning Tower of Pisa is a keeper."

"I can't believe she convinced him to participate. He must be really relaxed."

Maggie was so glad they hadn't ruined his parents' trip with false hope of Ethan's survival. It would've devastated them.

"They're headed to the Greek isles next. Mom's been talking about Santorini and those blue rooftops for years. I'm not sure how it can live up to her expectations."

"I'm sure it'll be beautiful." She scanned the beach. It was getting darker and more difficult to make out facial features. Down at the waterline Patrick jumped for the Frisbee and missed, then got hit by a wave, soaking him up to the hips. Owen cackled.

"How was business this week?" she asked.

"Crazy busy. Every tour was full." He afforded her a humorless grin. "Conner quit."

"Oh no. He's your snack-bar guy, right?"

"He started seeing Addison a couple weeks ago and he was way more into her than she was into him. Saw it coming a mile away. Now he's off to greener pastures."

"Did he give you any notice?"

"Only a week. He got a job with a home-improvement company, making better money. Big D's gonna cover till I can find someone to take his place."

"I'm sorry. That's probably the last thing you needed during high season. I can pitch in some if you don't mind my having a four-year-old around to help."

"That's sweet, but I think we can manage until I find someone. Also, you might eat up all my profits in cotton candy."

"There's a good chance."

He gave her a sidelong glance. "You seem a little better today. I know it's been a rough patch."

"It's been hard for you too. How are you doing?"

"Staying busy has helped."

She was glad he had work to keep him occupied. Even as busy as he'd been this week, he'd still made time to check on her. She was blessed to have such a devoted brother-in-law. That kiss from two and a half years ago flashed in her mind, flushing her face with heat. She could hardly believe that had ever happened. And yet the memory only seemed sweeter with time.

Before guilt got a stronghold, she pushed the thought away. "Did I ever thank you properly for going to Rock Hill with me? I don't know how I would've handled the news alone."

"We're in this together. Grieving sure isn't for the faint of heart, is it?"

"Amen."

As they fell quiet, Maggie breathed deeply of the briny air, mixed with the metallic tang of fireworks. She hadn't celebrated the Fourth in Seabrook since Ethan was home on leave. They'd watched the display with his family from the town pier. Then they'd driven home to Fayetteville and made love late into the night. Would the memories ever stop haunting her? Then guilt nipped at her.

She should hold tightly to every single one. She just didn't want them to make her so sad. She'd been doing better before this whole doppelganger episode. Before she'd given hope a foothold. Now it seemed she'd lost some of her hard-won progress.

"You're still looking for him, aren't you?" Josh said.

Maggie's gaze snapped to him. "What?"

"You've been scanning the crowd all evening. You're still wondering about him. Trying to figure out who he is and why he looks so much like Ethan."

He was right. She'd been searching for him without thought. "I can't seem to help it."

He stared at her for a long moment. "Why didn't you say something?"

"I've already dragged you down this road once and it was painful for both of us. I don't want to see you hurt anymore."

"I can take care of myself—and I've been wondering about him too."

"You have?"

He offered a humorless grin. "It's been driving me crazy. There has to be a logical explanation."

"Why didn't *you* say something?"

"Same reason you didn't."

His concern warmed her heart. But she was relieved she wasn't the only one still working this puzzle around in her head. "I don't think we're going to figure it out—unless we find him." She turned her attention to him. Would he be willing to take this another step?

"I agree . . ."

"But?"

"But I'm reluctant to cause you more grief."

"Know what's causing me grief? Not knowing why there's a man roaming Seabrook who looks just like my husband."

He chuckled, his eyebrow doing that little involuntary bounce that upped his appeal 1,000 percent.

"There it is."

"There what is?"

"Nothing. Let's start looking for him again."

He studied her for a long moment, then something flared in his eyes. "Tomorrow night?"

"It's a date."

Chapter 15

*W*hen they arrived at the carnival, Josh's spirits sank. Throngs of people pressed one another between rides, already spinning and whirling. Kool & the Gang's "Celebration" blared from the speakers and the sweet scent of waffle cones carried on a sea breeze.

"It's packed," he called over the clamor.

"Holiday weekend and a Saturday night. It'll be hard to find anyone in this mess."

"But the more people, the more chances he'll actually be here." And it was only six o'clock, so the light was still good.

"Should we split up so we cover more ground?"

"Let's stick together."

"Okay. Maybe we should head for high ground and keep a lookout from there."

They were both tall enough to see over the crowd, but a lot of people were coming and going. "Good idea."

As they entered the crowd Maggie drew close, clutching his elbow. Even though the action was perfunctory, he relished the slight weight of her hand, the gentle press of her body against his.

He'd been glad that she wanted to keep searching for this guy. He tried to convince himself that finding answers was the only reason, but it didn't quite wash. Spending time with Maggie was exhilarating. And okay, also frustrating and depressing in ways he couldn't express to her. But the way she lit him up—that always seemed to override common sense or the reality that she was oblivious to his true feelings.

They reached the boardwalk and took the steps that would put them above the fray. Then they settled at the top along the railing and began scanning the crowd. Erin had invited Zoey to go bowling with a group of kids from church. Without her to keep track of, they'd be able to cover a lot of ground.

Forty minutes later he was less hopeful. It was too bad Ethan's look-alike had been wearing a hat in that picture. They had no idea of his hair color, which put them at a disadvantage.

He took out his phone and opened the photo for the zillionth time. Not a single hair showed beneath that ball cap. But something else caught his attention. "Maggie . . . look. He's wearing a red shirt."

"So?"

"Look at the carnies." Each one wore a similar tee with the carnival's logo on the back.

"We can't see the back. It could be just a red T-shirt." A smile spread across her face. "Or he could work here."

"He could work here." They'd been so busy surveying the tourists when the man could actually be working a game counter, a ticket booth, or a food stand.

"But we already showed his picture to some of the carnies."

"It's a big operation. Or maybe he's new."

"Good point." She grabbed his hand. "Let's go."

She was obviously as hopeful as he. Seeing her light up like the sun made him feel like a king. He only hoped she wouldn't be disappointed again.

They started with the rides since they were closest, showing the man's photo to each carny. Then they wove their way around the rides until, almost an hour later, they'd covered them all.

"Let's head to game alley," he said.

They jostled through the crowd and arrived a few minutes later, greeted by a medley of bells and whistles.

"You check that side," she said.

They passed the booths slowly, caught in the tide of the crowd. Stuffed animals of all sizes hung from the walls as carnies called out for more players. They passed the ring-toss game, Lucky Duck, Shoot Out the Star, and Whac-A-Mole.

The game carnies were young—college age at most. The ride operators were older and seemed a more likely option. Maybe the man worked the rides but it was his night off.

Maggie stopped in the middle of the fray, squeezing his hand. *"Josh."*

He followed her stunned gaze to the water-gun game. And there he was. The man they'd been searching for. The man who was the spitting image of his dead brother.

Chapter 16

*M*aggie's feet seemed rooted to the ground. Her breaths stuffed into iron lungs.

Ethan.

He took tickets from a boy who settled on a stool with the others. The guy spoke through his headset. "All right, folks. Squeeze the trigger and aim for the hole to make the minions rise. This is a race—first minion to the top wins a prize. Ready, set, and . . . go!"

A bell sounded. In her peripheral vision the minions quickly rose.

Seconds later the guy called out, "And seven is our lucky winner. Come claim your prize, young lady."

Someone bumped Maggie from behind, pushing her forward, but her attention never wavered from the guy.

Josh steered her from the crowd, stopping near the game as the players left their stools. The carny assisted the winner with her prize.

"We found him," Maggie said numbly.

"He's younger than Ethan would've been."

Maggie nodded. Her mind spun in dizzy circles like the swing ride, making her stomach churn.

The guy handed the girl a small furry turtle, then called through his headset, "Step right up! It's easy-breezy. Aim the gun and win a prize!"

"What should we do?" Maggie asked. "I can't think."

"Let's play the game so we can get a closer look."

As they headed over, Maggie was unable to tear her eyes from that familiar face. He looked so much like Ethan had at that age. Those deep-set blue eyes and strong jawline. His mouth was a little different. His lower lip thicker, his smile different—not tilted up more on one side like Ethan's had been. Not his twin, but close enough.

"Two?" the guy asked as Maggie and Josh approached.

"Yes, please."

"That'll be two tickets."

Maggie looked at Josh. They hadn't bought tickets tonight.

But Josh must've had some left over from last time because he pulled the tickets from his wallet and handed them over. "You look an awful lot like someone I used to know. Ethan Reynolds?"

The guy shook his head. "Doesn't ring a bell."

"The resemblance is uncanny."

"Really?" He flashed a smile. "Well, they say everyone has a twin out there somewhere."

Another customer approached and he diverted his attention to the newcomer.

Josh tugged Maggie to the stools farthest from the young man and they took their seats.

Maggie squeezed Josh's arm. "He even sounds like Ethan, don't you think?"

"He does. But there are some differences too, up close."

"I noticed." Her attention swung back to the boy. "How old do you think he is?"

"Eighteen to twenty-one maybe?"

"He looked older in the photo."

"It wasn't a clear shot. He's built lean like Ethan. Not as tall, though."

"We should talk to him after the game. Find out how old he is and where he's from. We have to figure this out. Maybe we can get his name and contact information, then we could just look him up."

His gaze locked on her. "Listen, Mags. We should probably tread carefully here. We don't know what we're stepping into."

His comment made that anchor sink a little deeper in her gut. What were they dealing with here? "You're right."

While the guy rallied more players, they studied his every move. He seemed more extroverted than Ethan, calling boldly, making conversation with folks who came over. But some of his mannerisms, like the way he gave his cap a sharp tug, reminded her of Ethan.

There was definitely something here.

THEY PLAYED THREE games in a row. Maggie, mind whirling with questions, could hardly hit the target. Josh, on the other hand, won the last two games.

After the winning bell sounded, he stood and Maggie followed suit. She hoped he had a plan because she hadn't thought this far ahead, and his warning about treading carefully buzzed in her ears.

Ethan's look-alike approached. "Congrats, man. You get to pick from these prizes since you won twice. The sea turtles are popular, but personally I think the monkey's pretty sweet."

Josh nudged Maggie. "Whatever the lady wants."

"Um, let's go with the monkey."

"Good choice. Plus, bonus, his hands Velcro together so he can hang on to you instead of the other way around."

Maggie accepted the little blue guy. "You do a nice job with the game. You must've been at this awhile."

"Actually, I've only worked here a few weeks."

"You're a natural then," Josh said.

"Well, thanks, guys." He stepped away, clearly needing to return to his job.

"Have a good evening now."

"Same to y'all." He turned on his headset. "All right, folks, step right up. Aim for the target, make the minion rise, and win a prize! It's just that easy!"

As she and Josh folded into the passing crowd, Maggie couldn't resist glancing over her shoulder. "We have to go back. We didn't even get his name."

"We know where to find him, though. We should talk this through a little. Plus Erin will be dropping Zoey off soon."

Maggie checked her watch. He was right. She'd completely lost track of time. But who could blame her when she'd just found the apparition of her dead husband?

It was too noisy to talk, so they kept their thoughts to themselves as they navigated the crowd. But the longer Maggie reflected, the more she realized Josh had been right about biding their time. They might've stumbled upon a tricky situation. The particular scenario she imagined made her wonder if they'd soon regret their curiosity.

Was he thinking the same thing?

Once inside the quiet of the cab, Josh started the vehicle and pulled from the lot. The glow of streetlights flickered on his face, revealing a furrowed brow and a downturned mouth.

Maggie didn't want to be the first to say it.

He glanced her way, holding her gaze for several full seconds before returning his focus to the road. "It can't be what we're thinking."

"I know."

"My parents are happily married. I mean, don't get me wrong, they fuss and fight sometimes, but they're completely devoted to one another."

"I agree."

"My dad is head over heels for my mom."

She twisted the situation every which way and couldn't come to any other reasonable alternatives. Marriages could go through difficult times. Case in point: her own parents, whose marriage had lasted only a handful of years. But it was hard to imagine Brad having an affair with another woman. Even good people could make terrible mistakes, though.

"And yet"—Josh's voice carried quietly through the cab—"there's a young man running around town who looks almost exactly like my brother."

"Maybe your dad donated sperm at some point."

He shook his head. "Say the guy's twenty years old—we would've been teenagers when he was conceived. He was making good money and Mom was also working—"

"What?" she asked a moment later when he remained silent.

"It could've been back when I was sick. I was too stuck in my own misery to give them a thought at the time, but imagine the stress they would've been under, having their son's life on the line."

Josh had had lymphoma when he was a young teen. He'd been in and out of the hospital a lot. And she remembered well the stress the family had been under while they prayed he'd survive the disease. "We don't know for sure how old he is."

"He wasn't around a lot when I was sick. I thought it was work. But could he have been under so much stress that he strayed?"

She wished she could say no. But it was a long time ago and his father, though wonderful, was only human. "I don't know, Josh. It doesn't seem like him at all. He's the most honest person I know."

Josh was quiet the rest of the drive and Maggie didn't want to press the sensitive issue. When they arrived at the cottage, he walked her to the door in silence.

On the porch he turned to her. "I'm going back down there."

"To the carnival? Now?"

"Yes."

Maggie wanted to go with him. She checked her watch. Erin had texted that they were on their way and it was already past Zoey's bedtime. She'd had a busy day and would be tired and possibly cranky. "What will you say to him?"

"I don't know yet. I don't want to make him suspicious. If an affair did happen—well, we don't know what his situation is. I don't want to make him question everything he might've been told about his paternity. Especially when we have no proof it even happened. I'll think of something."

"If you wait till tomorrow, I'll go with you."

"We don't know if he'll be working tomorrow. And I don't know about you, but if I don't get more answers, I won't be able to sleep tonight."

He seemed so despondent. The porch light illuminated creases above his brows. The thought of his dad having an affair seemed to be wrecking him. This was not the direction either of them had expected the situation to go.

She set her hand on his jaw, the bristles tickling the soft flesh of her palm. "It's gonna be okay. You'll see."

One side of his mouth lifted in a mirthless smile. "Hope you're right."

She wanted to ease his worry. Comfort him the way he'd comforted her in Rock Hill. But the memory of that kiss they'd shared all those years ago—the memory of that confusing connection—stopped her from drawing him into her arms.

She offered a smile instead as she let her hand fall. "Either way, we're in this together."

He squeezed her hand. "I'll call you later."

Chapter 17

*F*rom the game stool Josh watched the carny from the corner of his eye. He'd already dropped ten tickets on this game, but he'd drop a hundred more if it meant solving this mystery. He'd only made small talk since arriving, trying to warm the guy up. Trying to act naturally.

But all he could think was, *Could this guy be my brother?*

Josh didn't know what he'd do if that were the case. But he needed answers. Once he got them, he'd decide what to do with them. The last thing he wanted was to cause irreparable harm to his parents' relationship. But then, if his dad had stepped outside the marriage, he was technically the one who'd done that.

Had Josh's prolonged illness driven his dad to such a low? Josh tried to deflect the dart of guilt. Common sense said he was in no way responsible for falling ill. But sometimes emotions had little to do with reason.

A couple in the throes of helping their son fight for his life might cling to one another—or they might be driven apart by disagreements over critical health care decisions. Josh didn't remember any acrimony between them at the time. But maybe they'd put on a brave face for the family.

Had his dad sought comfort in the arms of another woman?

Josh knew all about falling for the wrong woman. He was practically an expert on the subject. Watching Maggie fall for his brother had been a cruel form of torture. It was a wonder he hadn't gone mad years ago.

In his younger days he'd practically made dating a sport. He could admit now that he'd made a show of it around Maggie, desperate to make her jealous. He'd eventually grown out of his stupidity. He still dated, of course, but it never took more than two or three dates to realize the woman could never compare to Maggie.

Eventually he gave up on ever finding another Maggie and just tried to find someone he could love. Someone who could replace her in his heart. For a time he'd thought that might be Samantha. But it turned out there was no room for anyone else in his stubborn heart.

And somehow he'd managed to hide it from everyone. Everyone but Samantha, that was. He'd devastated her and as a result she lashed out at him. She harangued him in those last months, filled him with shame, tortured him with insults. *"You're pathetic—sniffing after your brother's wife. Disgusting. You should be ashamed of yourself."*

And he was. He never should've married Samantha.

Stupid.

He remembered the way Maggie had palmed his face on the porch earlier. His heart raced at her touch. She had such a soft, gentle way about her. She was compassionate and caring. Sometimes she had a look in her eyes that made him think she might feel something for him. Something other than friendship. Something more than a familial bond. After all, she had returned his kiss on that long-ago night. Maybe it hadn't just been loneliness and grief.

He'd been determined to find out for certain this summer—but now all that had been put on hold.

The game started and Josh mechanically aimed the gun at the target, while his thoughts, already a million miles away, returned to his father.

Maybe his dad had believed some other woman might heal a broken part of himself—a part wrecked because his younger son's life hung in the balance. Maybe he sought relief from his own heartache. And that relief resulted in a pregnancy, another son. It was even possible Dad knew about this boy.

Josh shook the idea away. He couldn't bear the thought of it. It was somehow worse even than his potential infidelity. Contrary to everything he knew of his father. He hoped somehow none of this was true. That this guy's resemblance to Ethan was just some random fluke. But what were the odds?

The bell rang, ending the game.

"And number four is our lucky winner! Come claim your prize. And that's our last game of the night, folks. Y'all have a good evening and come back soon."

Josh lingered as the twentysomething winner picked out a prize for his girlfriend. When they wandered off, Josh approached the carny. "Guess my luck ran out early tonight."

"You had a couple close calls. The guy who won those three in a row—he's a regular. I'd avoid playing him if you're hoping to win."

"Thanks for the tip. Hey, I meant what I said earlier. You really have a way with people. I like your energy."

"Thank you." He slid behind the counter with a wide grin and went about the business of closing down. "I'm a people person, always have been."

"That much is obvious. I know you haven't been working here long, but I'm looking to hire someone to run concessions on my boat." He withdrew a business card and extended it to the guy. "Someone personable and able to manage the area independently. Is that something you might be interested in?"

"Island Tours. You're the owner?"

"Owner and captain, Josh Reynolds." He stuck out his hand.

"Will Jennings." They shook hands. "Nice to meet you."

"We could really use someone like you on board the *Carolina Dream*. It's a small crew, good people, fun environment. The pay's good." Josh paid his crew well, but he'd gladly pay even more for this kid. He'd do a nice job in the position, but more importantly it would give Josh a chance to get to know him. To feel out the situation so he could decide how to proceed. "No pressure, though, if you're happy here."

"Well, I'm saving for college and I don't mean to sound greedy, but when you say the pay's good . . ."

Josh named a dollar figure that was two bucks more an hour than he'd paid Conner.

Will's eyes popped wide. "You've got my attention. I've never worked around boats before, though."

"Well, listen, that's not a problem. The position is just selling food and drinks to our guests, keeping the snack bar stocked, running a register, taking credit cards, pitching in where needed."

"That sounds manageable. I worked the drive-thru at Wendy's last year."

"Perfect. That's great experience." The games around them were going dark, the carnies abandoning their posts. "Hey, if you think you might be interested, you're welcome to come aboard for one of our tours next week and observe, see what you think."

"Really?"

"Yeah, no problem. Just give me a call and I'll set it up."

Will pocketed the card and shut off the game lights. "Thanks, man. I just might do that."

"I think you'd like it. Well, hey, I'll let you close up. It's been nice meeting you, Will. Hope to hear from you."

"Yeah, you too, man. Thanks."

Chapter 18

*W*ill Jennings was scarfing down a bowl of Cheerios when his mom rushed through the kitchen on her way out the door.

She'd pulled her dark blonde hair away from her oval face, and her brows furrowed over harried blue eyes. A pair of teal scrubs hung more loosely from her five-foot frame than they had a few years ago. "Sure you don't want some eggs? Growing boys need protein."

"Haven't grown an inch since junior year, Ma."

She stopped her frenetic rush to work long enough to pat his cheek as she looked at him in that way of mothers everywhere. "My boy . . . so young and already being recruited for a job."

"It's just an entry-level position."

"With a considerable pay raise." Her gaze swept his attire—a collared shirt and navy shorts. "You look so handsome. Maybe you should take some Dramamine."

"It's just a one-hour tour." Will hadn't been on a boat in years, but his mom was prone to seasickness. She'd once gone on a two-day fishing trip and spent the entire time puking over the railing. "But maybe you're right."

Mom pecked him on the cheek, making him slosh a spoonful of cereal, then grabbed her purse. "I think there's some in the medicine cabinet. You're gonna do great, honey. Let me know how it goes."

"Will do."

"Have a good day. Love you."

"Love you too, Mom."

"Don't forget to call your dad."

"I won't." The door closed and Will slurped the milk from the bowl.

His mom's last words gave him that sinking feeling in his stomach. But he opted not to dwell on that right now. He had a job opportunity that would get him closer to paying for that degree he'd been aiming for since freshman year in high school, when Mr. Keating introduced the subject of neurobiology.

The brain was such a mystery even to scientists who spent a lifetime studying it. He couldn't think of anything more interesting, more fascinating. He'd gotten more serious about his grades, about those scholarships the guidance counselor had mentioned.

When his parents had separated the next year, then divorced, he added a job to the equation, part-time during the school year and full-time through the summer. Because theirs had become a single-mom household and college wasn't in the budget.

That was okay. He had his first year under his belt now. He'd managed a couple decent scholarships and there were loans for the rest. But he was practical and wouldn't borrow any more than he had to.

Sure, he'd made some sacrifices. He had to live at home with Mom instead of in a dorm with friends. And there was no time for partying when you had to squeeze in studying between job shifts. Also, he couldn't afford dating, much less an actual girlfriend. But he was motivated by his love of science.

Speaking of jobs . . . he checked the time. Then he slurped the last of his milk and got up from the stool. He had a promising position to acquire.

THE *CAROLINA DREAM* was a sixty-five-foot steel riverboat. Heat shimmered from the sidewalk as Will set eyes on the white vessel with blue and red trim. It boasted an enclosed main level, an open upper level, and a 600-horsepower engine. He'd learned all this from his online research.

What he hadn't learned from the website was that the young woman working the check-in booth was drop-dead gorgeous. He joined the line, keeping his cell phone with the QR code handy while he tried not to stare.

Her pale blonde hair was pulled into two thick braids that framed her pretty face and hung past her shoulders. She was tanned and natural looking, and when she smiled her eyes sparkled.

He stepped next in line, getting within feet of her.

Green. Her eyes were green. And there were faint freckles on her nose. His heart whipped against his rib cage. His mouth was suddenly dry, his tongue thick and heavy.

The couple in front of him moved away and he stepped forward.

"Hi there," she said.

Her smile disrupted his neurotransmission, rendering him momentarily mute. She was even prettier up close. The sun glinted off the golden tips of her lashes. "Uh, hi."

"You have a ticket?"

Idiot. You're staring. "Sorry." He held out his phone only to find his hand shaking.

"Um, you'll have to put in your passcode."

"Oh, right. Yeah. Sorry." It took three tries to get his thumbs to cooperate while the girl waited. His cheeks were hot and he was probably getting perspiration rings under his arms. Real sexy. He opened the email and enlarged the QR code. "Here you go."

"Perfect." She scanned the code, then handed him a laminated boarding pass, treating him to a dazzling smile. "Boarding is in ten minutes right over there."

"Great. Thanks." He walked away, fighting a strong urge to slap himself. Wow, what a charmer. A 4.2 and he couldn't manage a single complete sentence. Just as well. He was here for a job, not a girl.

He gave his head a shake, wondering if he had marbles in there instead of neurons, and joined the line already forming in front of the boat. He had to get his head on straight and focus on securing this position. Thank God the girl was only working the booth and wasn't part of the crew.

THE GIRL WAS part of the crew. She'd not only given out the boarding passes, but now she was collecting them, boat side, and telling guests she'd see them on board. When it was his turn, he managed to hand his over without making a complete idiot of himself, then he filed on board with the paying customers.

Josh Reynolds stood at the ready, greeting passengers. "Welcome aboard. Make yourselves comfortable." His eyes lit with recognition as they fell on Will. "Good to have you along today, Will. Stick around after the tour. I'll introduce you to the crew."

"Sounds good. Thank you."

"Snack bar is on the main level. Feel free to check it out and roam around all you like."

"Will do." Once on board Will followed the majority of the passengers up the steps to the upper level. As promised it was covered, providing a shady reprieve from the July sun. Bench seats, facing a door that read "Pilothouse," took up most of the space. But Will settled at the railing, enjoying the water view while the rest of the passengers boarded.

He'd never seen himself working on a boat, but he enjoyed new experiences and challenges. Plus there was the money. And the owner seemed like he'd be pretty cool to work for.

About ten minutes later Josh's voice came over the speaker, introducing himself as Captain Josh and welcoming them aboard. He stood in front of the pilothouse, delivering safety information and life jacket locations through a headset. "While you're aboard, feel free to move about the vessel. However, we would ask that you maintain a point of contact at all times, especially when going up and down the stairs.

"For those of you on the upper deck, please be aware we will have variable winds today, so be sure to hang on to your hats. If the wind does catch a hat and pull it into the water, we do have a hats-overboard procedure. We ask that everyone stand up and offer that hat a final salute because we will not be going back to retrieve it."

The crowd chuckled.

"Before we get underway, I'd like to introduce you to my first mate, Darius"—the stout guy offered a wave from a seat nearby—"and Addison, who handed out and collected your boarding passes, is filling in at the snack bar today."

Will fought the urge to run down for another peek even as he reminded himself why he was here.

After encouraging the group to sit back and enjoy the ride, Josh stepped into the pilothouse and began maneuvering the boat into the waterway.

A few minutes later the scent of popcorn mingled with the diesel fumes, and some of the passengers made their way below.

Once the boat was headed downriver, Josh settled on a bench and listened to Captain Josh's monologue. He told the history of the area, including Snow's Cut, the scenic waterway that bridged Wilmington and Seabrook. He explained that the Cape Fear River had gotten its name from the twenty-eight miles of shifting silt known as the Frying Pan Shoals, where more than 150 ships had met their demise.

Having been born and raised in Wilmington, Will knew the history, but Josh made it interesting and his sense of humor kept the passengers entertained. Along the route he used his headset to point out areas of interest and otherwise let the guests enjoy the scenery.

At the halfway point Will made his way belowdecks. The space was open down here with tables lining both sides. The snack bar was on the far end. Addison waited on a family of four. He took a seat nearby to observe as she made small talk with the couple visiting from Ohio. After they received their sacks of popcorn and drinks, the family moved to a table across the deck and she waited on the next person in line.

The job seemed simple enough. Certainly no more difficult than the carnival game. He made a list of questions for Josh while he quietly observed and idly wondered if Addison was actually part of the crew or if she was merely filling in. He found himself hoping for the former, despite his uninspired first impression on her. And despite the fact that the last thing he needed was a distraction—no matter how beautiful—from his goals.

Chapter 19

*M*aggie and Zoey were headed out to the beach when Maggie's phone vibrated from her cover-up pocket. She'd been waiting for Josh's call—Will Jennings had ridden along on this morning's tour, and she was eager to hear what he'd discovered. But the ringtone was her mother's.

Maggie was currently loaded down with two chairs, a soft-sided cooler, and a beach bag, trudging through the thick Carolina sand. But Mom had called while Maggie was in the shower, and if she didn't answer, it would set off another round of silent treatment, long-distance edition.

Almost to their spot, she quickened her steps and, once there, dropped her burden as Zoey, beach pail and shovels in hand, rushed toward the wet sand.

"That's far enough," Maggie called.

Zoey dropped at the shoreline and Maggie, out of breath and prickling with sweat, grabbed her phone just in time. "Hi, Mom."

"Well, it's about time. For someone on summer break you seem awfully busy."

"Sorry I missed your call earlier. I was in the shower."

"That was three hours ago. Lucky for you I haven't forgotten why I called."

Maggie unfolded a beach chair, then plopped down and took the bait. "What is it, Mom?"

Her mother waited a full five seconds before answering. "I wanted to pass along the good news that Derrick will be getting in touch with you soon."

Maggie searched the archives of her brain and came up empty. "Derrick?"

"*Derrick Morgan.* Honestly, Maggie, your memory is appalling for such a young woman. Maybe you should get that checked out."

Maggie was only youthful until they discussed her single/widow status, and then she "wasn't getting any younger." The thought tweaked a memory. Derrick Morgan . . .

Oh no, she did not.

"The son of our most esteemed board member, Maggie, for heaven's sake. I ran into him at a fundraising gala last night. He's quite charming. It's a good thing I called. I can't imagine how insulted he'd have been when you didn't even recognize his name!"

Maggie gritted her teeth. "What do you mean he'll be getting in touch, Mom? Whatever for?"

"Why, he's interested in meeting you, of course. We discussed this in the spring."

"Yes, we did, and I told you I wasn't ready to—"

"Oh, enough already. It's been five years and you're not getting any younger. How long will you play the widow card? Do you want to be single the rest of your life?"

Like you? She bit back the words. Mom and her smarmy boyfriend had broken up last weekend. Her decision, or so she'd claimed.

"Derrick is successful and attractive. He's a renowned pediatrician and keeps excellent company. You're lucky he's interested in you at all. If you can't bring yourself to do this one simple thing, maybe you should think of Zoey."

"Zoey already has a stellar pediatrician."

"Yes, Maggie, make jokes even though humor is not your strength. Meanwhile your daughter will grow up fatherless."

"Just like me." The filter kicked in late this time and she winced as her pulse raced with regret.

"Well, excuse me if I was too busy supporting you on a single mom's salary to find you a father. But you don't have that excuse, do you? Ethan's life insurance left you quite secure and you have half the year off work."

"Summers, Mom. I have summers off."

"And fall and Christmas and spring . . . I didn't call to quibble. Just be ready for Derrick's call."

A call—great. Couldn't just be a text. She'd never even met the man and now she'd have to make polite conversation over the phone. Maggie massaged her temple and hoped a migraine wasn't coming on.

He was probably a perfectly nice man, but Maggie hardly trusted her mother's judgment. Likely she didn't give a flying fig about his character. He was the son of a board member whom she wanted in her back pocket. She probably expected Maggie to not only date the man but marry him just so she could maintain the upper hand at work.

"Did you hear me, Maggie? Please put your best foot forward. I built you up quite a bit. He's probably expecting nothing short of a saint. What was I thinking? You'll have to pull it together."

She couldn't even fathom what positive traits her mother might have extolled. She must've dug deep. "I realize you want me to go out with this man. But maybe it can wait till fall. The timing is unfortunate since I'll be two hours away for the rest of the summer."

"Two whole hours? Then maybe you can send missives on the stagecoach and later he can hitch up his horse and buggy and meet you at the train depot."

"Okay, Mother, you've made your point."

Mom gave a weighty sigh. "Oh, for heaven's sake. I try to set my daughter up with a virtual paragon, and this is the grief I get for my trouble."

"I said I'd do it."

"You're welcome." A click came through the receiver, then silence.

"No, *you're* welcome," Maggie muttered as she dropped her phone into the beach bag.

She checked on Zoey, who was making limited progress on her sandcastle. Maggie shrugged out of the cover-up and made her way toward the shoreline. The beach wasn't very crowded as it was a weekday and the sky was overcast.

She sank in the sand across from Zoey. "Need some help with your castle?"

"It's not a castle, it's a carousel. See? Here's my favorite horse."

"Oh yes, I see. Very nice. Did you know your daddy and I used to make sandcastles when we were teenagers? He was very good at it."

"Were they big?"

"Not so much big as very detailed. He'd make the moat and fill it with water and even have a drawbridge."

"Like Cinderella's castle!"

"Exactly. I teased him that he should become an architect—that's someone who designs buildings."

"But he was a medic."

"Yes, and a very good one."

Zoey worked in silence for a minute. "Can you fill the bucket with sand, Mommy? It's heavy."

"Of course." As Maggie went to work, the sun came out, hot and bright, making her glad for the cool, wet sand beneath her.

Zoey pressed her small hands into the sand, molding the carousel. Her delicate brows drew into a straight line as she focused. A few freckles had popped out on her nose, and her skin was bronzing up despite the sunscreen Maggie applied religiously.

Her thoughts returned to her conversation with her mother. Zoey was already four but would likely have only a few memories from these early years. If Maggie found a good man relatively soon, it would seem to Zoey as if she'd always had a father. She wouldn't feel that prick of jealousy when a friend's dad gave his daughter a piggy-back ride or miss daddy-daughter dances at school. She wouldn't wish for a father who'd hold her tight when she had a nightmare or sometimes pretend her daddy was just at work.

Maggie had gone into this summer with the goal of laying down the past and moving forward. She'd expressed to Erin and Josh her desire to begin dating. And while the random sighting of that young man—Will Jennings—had distracted her from those goals, there was no reason not to move forward now.

She didn't relish her mother's connection with Derrick Morgan. But he'd apparently weathered years of college, internships, and residencies. Surely he wouldn't be a man easily pushed around by her mother. Maybe he'd even stand up to her. Wouldn't that be fun?

"Well, there's a wily smile if ever I saw one."

"Uncle Josh! Come help me with my carousel."

All smiles, he approached in his work uniform—khakis and a white polo sporting the Island Tours logo—carrying his tennis shoes in one hand.

"Hey," Maggie said, then addressed her daughter. "You forgot the magic word."

"Please, Uncle Josh?"

He squatted beside them. "Wish I could help you, Cupcake, but I only have a few minutes, and I need to talk to your mom."

"Aww . . ."

"Tell you what. Maybe I can stop by tonight after my sunset tour." He glanced at Maggie and mouthed, *Pizza?*

She nodded.

"I'll bring pizza and you can show me pictures of your carousel. I'll bet it's gonna turn out great."

"Can I get cheese?"

"Yes, ma'am. Cheese it is." With a jerk of his head to Maggie, he gestured up the beach, then stood and reached out to help her up.

As he drew her effortlessly to her feet, he quickly eyed her form, making Maggie hyperaware of the skin exposed by her tank suit.

Once she was standing, he dropped her hands and followed her up the beach.

Maggie was blessed in the physical department. She'd always been tall and slim, and years of swimming had left her with strong shoulders. But her tummy was no longer perfectly taut and her hips had widened a bit with age. Did Josh find her attractive? Just because a man's gaze swept a woman's form didn't necessarily mean he did. She was in a bathing suit, after all. Probably just a reflex.

Josh stopped beside the beach chairs.

Maggie slipped into her cover-up and crossed her arms. He wasn't here to ogle her in her swimsuit but to tell her about the tour with Will. "So? How'd it go?"

Josh flashed a smile at her. "He took the job."

"Really?"

"And he filled out an application. I have his birthday, address, you name it. He lives in Wilmington, which explains why we've never seen him around here before."

The city was thirty minutes away. "We can run a search, maybe discover who his mom is, what his home situation is like."

"That's right. Thought maybe we'd do that tonight after Zoey's in bed." He cocked a brow. "If you can wait that long."

It wouldn't be easy. Now that they had such easy access, she wanted answers. But this was about Josh's parents now and he deserved to run point on this.

"I'll be waiting for you."

Chapter 20

*M*ommy, Mommy, help me!" Zoey flung herself against Maggie's legs. "The tickle monster's gonna get me!"

Maggie set the plates in the sink and swept her daughter into her arms just as Josh appeared in the doorway, crouched, fingers wiggling menacingly. "I have come to tickle the girl child!"

Zoey let out an ear-piercing scream and buried her head in Maggie's shoulder. "Run, Mommy!"

Maggie sent Josh a mock scowl. "This is how you get her ready for bed?"

"The girl child is in her sleep clothes," he growled.

When Zoey peeked at Josh, he wiggled his fingers and snarled, inducing another squeal.

"She'll never get to sleep after you've wound her up, you know."

"I'm not winding her up. I'm wearing her out."

"We'll see about that. How about you put the tickle fingers away and find a nice quiet book to read her."

Zoey scrambled down. "I want the giraffe book!" she called as she ran toward her room.

"How many pages does it have?" he called after her.

"Two million fourteen hundred zillion!"

He met Maggie's gaze. "Seems excessive."

"Yeah. Good luck with that." She snapped a dish towel at him.

A threatening expression came over his face as he wielded his tickle fingers and let out a snarl.

Maggie pointed a finger at him. "Don't you dare."

He lifted a brow, inching closer.

"Josh."

"That schoolteacher tone doesn't work on me."

"We have work to do and it's getting late. Plus, I'll tell your mom you sneaked out of the house for that Nickelback concert senior year."

He leaned back. "You wouldn't."

"Try me."

"You'd ruin a mother's perception of her perfect angel-child?"

"In a heartbeat."

"Uncle Josh, I found the giraffe book! Come read to me and turn on my princess light."

"Magic word," Maggie called.

"Please!"

Josh studied Maggie, narrowing his eyes. "You're just lucky I have a date with a cute little four-year-old right now." He turned to go.

She snapped him in the seat with the towel.

He whipped around, fingers wiggling.

She screamed, leaped behind a chair.

But he was already heading toward Zoey's room, laughter ringing out.

Josh leaned over Maggie's shoulder as he homed in on the laptop. Will's job application sat on her lap. A list of articles and social media accounts dominated the screen. "It's hard to tell which ones are him and which ones might be some other Will Jennings."

"Also, there are multiple entries for William Jennings."

"He put Will on his application, but I guess that doesn't mean that's his full name. Try enclosing his name and location in quotation marks." They'd already found his Facebook account, but he'd only posted two pictures and hadn't filled in any information on his About page. He didn't seem to be on any other social media sites.

Maggie ran another search. "There, that's better. This one has a picture." She clicked on it and a photo of Will wearing a basketball uniform appeared.

"Wow, he was all-state."

"And he attended John T. Hoggard High School."

"That might be helpful."

She opened more web pages, but either they were dead ends or they couldn't be certain if it was the right Will. "I'd love to find his mother's name. You might recognize it."

"Maybe we can get access to his senior yearbook. His parents' names might be in there."

"Do they put yearbooks online these days?"

"Only one way to find out."

As she typed into the search window, Josh became aware of the way his arm pressed against hers. She smelled like sunshine and coconut—she always had. The image of her in that modest red suit flared in his mind. He'd seen her in a swimsuit a million times before—at swim meets, at the beach, at Erin's—and managed to keep his eyes and thoughts where they belonged. Mostly.

But she wasn't married to his brother anymore and he was *this* close to telling her how he felt. The sweet recollection of that kiss they'd shared washed over him, bringing every cell to life. He'd relived every second of that kiss a thousand times. Dissected each glance, each touch, each sweep of her lips. The memory was as worn as a well-read love letter and just as treasured. There had to be something here, didn't there, for her to have kissed him that way?

Except she'd probably been pretending he was Ethan.

The thought sluiced him like a bucket of cold water.

"Not finding it," she said. "I don't think they have them online. We could always try the school later."

He forced his thoughts back to the task at hand. "What about those sites that find people?"

"We can try, but I think you have to pay for a membership."

Maggie put Will's information into one of those sites and waited as the search engine took its time downloading its findings. "So what's he like? Did you talk to him much?"

"He's nice. Ambitious. He'll be a good addition to my crew—and it'll give me a chance to know him better."

"If we come up empty here, you can always fish for information."

"I'd rather learn as much as we can online, even if it does make me feel like a stalker. I don't want to be weird with him and make him suspicious."

"Sure." The downloading finally stopped and a box came up. "They want money. Let's try a different one."

"I can always pay for a membership and cancel it later."

"Let's see if we can get around it first."

A few minutes later she found a site that gave away a bit of information for free. "Look, this is definitely the right Will. It lists his phone number and there's a woman's name associated with him."

"Robyn Jennings. She's about the right age to be his mother."

Maggie clicked on her name. "It's her. Same address. Does the name sound familiar?"

Robyn Jennings. His dad had done his fair share of work talk around the house when he was growing up. But the name didn't ring a bell. He shook his head. "Not at all. Let's run a search on her."

"Maybe there'll be more information on her. She'll have lived a little more life than a nineteen-year-old kid."

"Plus her name's not as common."

"Let's see what we can find out." Maggie keyed in her name and city, then hit Return, and a page of sources turned up. "There's a Robyn Jennings who works at Novant." She clicked on the link and they scanned the hospital's article.

The one sentence including her name made Josh's heart sink. "She's an RN. That would put her in the same field as my dad. They might've worked together."

"We don't even know for sure this is her. Look, there's another Robyn Jennings who works for a gallery downtown." Maggie clicked on the link and a photo appeared with a caption listing the women pictured.

Josh pointed at the woman in the middle. "Can't be the right Robyn. She looks younger than us."

"You're right." Maggie went back to the source page and began scrolling as they scanned the links. "Most of these refer to the nurse."

"Well, let's click on them one by one and see what we can glean."

It was a long, tedious process. Most of the articles were from the hospital's website or medical newsletters and brochures. She'd attended NC State and worked for at least two hospitals and an OB practice. Finally, the Novant Health directory turned up a photo.

"There she is," Maggie said.

Josh leaned closer. Robyn Jennings's straight blonde hair framed a smiling face. She possessed deep-set blue eyes and an inviting expression.

"Recognize her?"

"No." He frowned. "If this is a current photo, she's a lot younger than Dad. Maybe midforties?"

"It lists her as on staff so the photo is probably current. Would she have even been in medicine that long ago?"

"Let's say she's forty-three. Will is nineteen so she would've had him at twenty-four. Old enough to have completed her schooling and have her license."

"Will's got her blue eyes."

He cut her a look. "Or my dad's. When I was interviewing Will, we got off topic for a bit and he laughed. Maggie, it sounded so much like my dad's laugh, it was eerie."

Maggie pressed a hand to his. "This must be so hard."

"I don't want to believe it. But the evidence is stacking up." Josh returned to the photo. When he'd learned Will's age, he'd done some math. At the time of Will's birth, Josh would've been fourteen and finished with his treatment for lymphoma. But nine months earlier, at the time of Will's conception, Josh would've been in the throes of treatment. Could his dad, in the midst of that ordeal, have turned to a colleague for comfort?

Maggie shook her head. "Your dad just turned sixty-five. That would've made him forty-six when Will was born. I can't imagine him hooking up with anyone, much less a woman twenty years his junior."

Neither could Josh. But every time he saw Will, he was taken aback by his resemblance to Ethan. "And yet that scenario happens so often it's a cliché." And the more he thought about it, the more it bugged him that his dad was so absent during his sickness. And a little distant even when he was present. Why hadn't Josh noticed that before?

Maggie's cell phone buzzed. She dug for it and checked the screen. "Sorry, I have to take this."

"Sure."

She handed him the laptop and headed toward the French doors. "Hello?"

"Yes, hi . . ." Her melodic laughter sounded as she opened the door and slipped out into the night. "Sounds about right."

She was talking to a man—he could tell by the soft quality in her voice. She hadn't closed the door but the roar of the surf made her words unintelligible.

As far as Josh knew, she hadn't been seeing anyone back home. Had she met someone here in Seabrook? She hadn't even been here a month, but Maggie was an attractive woman. She'd never had trouble drawing male attention.

Or maybe she'd reconnected with an old friend from high school. She didn't have an old boyfriend—Ethan had been her one and only—but that didn't mean some of her male friends hadn't been interested. It wasn't hard to believe she'd made contact with one of them. Would she have mentioned it to Josh?

As she continued her conversation, she leaned on the deck railing, her hair fluttering in the breeze.

He was letting his imagination run away from him. For all he knew the caller was a colleague or something.

On summer break?

Maggie was a friendly person. She had male friends.

Her laughter carried over the sound of the surf and jealousy pricked.

She straightened and wandered back inside. "All right, sounds good." Another laugh. "No, I won't . . . All right. Talk to you later then." She pocketed her phone, closed the door, and returned to the couch.

Was it his imagination, or were her cheeks flushed?

He tried for a neutral expression. "Who was that?"

"Oh, just someone my mom knows. You know how she is."

He arched a brow and went for playful. "She's setting you up with a man?"

Maggie rubbed her neck. "Well . . . she's trying to. I'm just humoring her."

"Sounds like he is too." The strain had crept into his voice.

Maggie's gaze sharpened on him.

Even though jealousy now spread through his veins, he flashed a sardonic grin. "Mother knows best?"

"Hardly. But Derrick seems nice enough. We agreed to chat again, that's all. Believe me, having my mother's recommendation is an automatic red flag. He has an uphill battle and doesn't even know it." Maggie reclaimed the laptop and typed something into the search engine. "Find anything else?"

"Um, no." Hopefully she wouldn't notice the screen still displayed the same page as when she'd stepped away.

She hit Enter and a new search popped up.

Why was he so caught off guard by the call? She'd told him she was ready to date again. That's why he'd decided it was time to tell her how he felt. Ask for a chance. If he didn't do it soon, some other guy would swoop in and win her heart—and no way was he going through that again. He'd wanted to put all this stuff with Will to rest first, but he wouldn't risk losing Maggie for good.

Either he'd get a chance with her or he'd sell his business and take that job at the Charleston Yacht Club. The manager had given him till August 1 to decide. Big D would be happy to take over Island Tours and he could keep his crew intact. The new job was good money and would put plenty of distance between him and Maggie. It would also put more miles between him and his family. It wasn't the option he was rooting for.

He watched her in his peripheral vision, his heart thumping in his chest as he tried to form the words. He'd planned a million times what he'd say, but he couldn't seem to pull up a thing at the moment. He just had to say it. Get it out there.

He placed a hand over hers on the keyboard.

She looked at him, a question in her eyes.

"Maggie, there's something I—"

"Mommy!" Zoey called from her bedroom. "I don't feel good!"

Maggie smiled at him. "Hold that thought."

His breath escaped in a huff as Maggie went to check on her daughter.

He used the distraction to construct a few meaningful sentences. He wouldn't tell her he'd been in love with her for years. It made him seem pathetic and the shame of it still ate at him. Besides, there was no sense in scaring her off. She'd likely be distressed enough at the thought of dating her former brother-in-law. Of what his parents might think. One thing at a time. He'd just ask if she was open to the idea of giving them a chance.

But a few minutes later the unmistakable sound of retching came up the hall, putting all thoughts of the conversation on hold.

Chapter 21

*H*is parents are divorced," Josh said on the phone a week later.

Maggie had just finished a swim lesson in Erin's pool and stood dripping on the deck. Olivia, Mia's church friend, had turned out to be a great encouragement for Mia. She seemed to forget her fear of the water with her brave little friend cheering her on.

Maggie wrapped a towel around her waist and perched on the low brick wall. "He said his 'parents'?"

"He said his 'mom and dad.' I didn't even have to ask the question. We were hanging around today after the tour, making small talk, and Big D asked him about his family."

"That's good. But just because he mentioned his 'dad' doesn't necessarily mean it's his biological father. He could simply view the man as his father if he raised Will. Or he could be unaware. Parents don't always tell their kids the truth about their biological parents."

"I know. It gets tricky from here. How are we supposed to find out if Will is my dad's kid?"

"If he is, there are two people who know."

"Only one person for sure. It's possible Robyn never told my dad."

"So what . . . We show up on her doorstep and ask point-blank?"

A pause sounded over the distance. "I'm reluctant to do anything that might blow up his family. What if Will's father doesn't know the truth? If this comes out, it could devastate Will. He doesn't deserve that."

"He could already know his dad isn't his biological father."

"Or he might not. We need to find out when they got married."

"Even if we found out they didn't marry till after Will was born, that doesn't prove he and Robyn weren't in a relationship at the time of conception."

"That's true," he said.

Maggie understood his reservations. Josh was a compassionate person. But could he let this mystery go? Could he just write off the idea that he might have another brother—one he now employed?

The afternoon sun beat down on her skin and she slid over into the shade of a palm tree. "So what do you want to do? The ball's in your court."

"Even if we confronted Robyn, she could simply lie. If she's been hiding the truth from Will or her ex-husband, she'd likely do just that. We need to do more research. See if we can find a common workplace. We know Dad's work history. If we find a clinic or hospital that puts them in the same place at the same time, that'll have to be more than coincidence. Right?"

"That's still not definitive proof."

"It would be enough to confront my dad, though."

"Is that what you're planning to do? Confront your dad?"

Josh's sigh sounded over the phone. "I don't know. I guess I'll cross that bridge when I come to it."

Of course, it was possible his parents already knew—but Maggie doubted it. She couldn't imagine either of them being okay with Brad not acknowledging a son.

If Will *was* his son, that knowledge put Josh in an untenable situation. "I'm sorry this is happening, Josh. When we started looking for Ethan's look-alike, I never dreamed we'd end up going down this road. I feel responsible."

"It's not your fault, Mags. And I'm trying to hang on to the positive here. It's possible I have a brother again—and he seems like a pretty great kid."

"He really does." Another thought had been on Maggie's mind this week. "Have you considered doing a DNA test?"

"I'd have to get DNA from both Will and my dad, wouldn't I?"

"I'm sure there'd be something of your dad's at the house we could use. And as for Will . . ."

"What? Should I yank a hair out by the root as he passes by?"

She laughed at the absurdity, the bit of levity relaxing the tight muscles at the base of her neck. "I was thinking more like a utensil or used glass."

"That's no fun." A long pause drew out between them before Josh continued. "I think we should go the research route for now. I don't want to do anything that invasive or . . . sneaky."

"Fair enough." Maggie glanced at the house. She needed to get Zoey home. Ever since that twenty-four-hour bug she'd had last week, she needed an afternoon nap. "Well, I should—"

"Maggie, can we meet up sometime? Just you and me?"

Maggie blinked. What could Josh want to talk about that they couldn't address on the phone—or with Zoey present? "Uh, sure. Yeah. Text me and we'll set it up."

"All right. Will do."

They ended the call. But as Maggie said good-bye to Erin and her kids, as she put Zoey in her car seat, and all the way home, a sense of nervous anticipation fueled a release of adrenaline.

Chapter 22

*W*ill finished cleaning the popcorn machine, then washed the grease from his arms, all the while observing Addison covertly. In the week since he'd joined the crew, they'd chatted a few times, just small talk. He liked the way she gave him her undivided attention when he spoke. The way she laughed at his jokes. He liked everything about her.

She glanced his way as she went about tidying up the lower deck. She did that a lot, and each time Will's nervous system went on hyperalert. Was it possible she liked him too?

Yesterday he'd decided he would step up his game, but he hardly said two words to her during today's tours. Who was he kidding? He had no game.

"See ya, Will." Addison gave a wave and a smile.

It was the smile that did the trick. "Hey, Addison, wait up." Will stepped out from the snack bar, drying his hands on his khakis, a move he'd surely regret later. "I'll walk you to your car."

"Sure."

He followed her off the boat where they said good-bye to Josh and Big D, who were changing an exterior lightbulb.

Addison and Josh were parked a short distance from the marina so he had only a minute or two.

"How are you liking the job so far?" she asked.

"Love it. I wasn't sure how I'd feel about working on a boat. But I enjoy making conversation with people from all over, and Josh is a pretty cool boss."

She cut Will a glance. "And the rest of the crew?"

There were only her and Big D. Was she angling for a compliment? He slid her a smile. "They're not so bad either."

She ducked her head but not before he caught her shy grin. "So you haven't been around the water much? Aren't you from around here?"

"Oh, yeah, I was born and raised in Wilmington. I've been swimming since I was little and I fish a lot with my buddies. I just haven't had access to a boat."

"What kind of fishing?"

"Mostly from piers. I caught a six-pound mackerel last summer at Kure Pier."

"Wow, that's big."

He spotted her car just ahead. "People even catch sharks sometimes. I mean, I haven't, but it happens sometimes."

"I've never been fishing before."

"Seriously?"

"I grew up in Atlanta." Addison slowed as she came alongside her Honda. "The only fish I saw was on a plate at a restaurant."

"It's a lot of fun." Now or never. His mouth went suddenly dry but he forced out the words. "You should go with me to Kure Pier sometime."

"I've never been there." She turned at the driver's door. "I think I'd like that."

"Really?"

"Sure. How about tonight?"

136

Will blinked.

"We don't have a sunset tour and my mom's been on a cleaning rampage—my grandparents are coming this weekend. I could use the break."

"Oh, well, yeah, then. That'd be great. Can I pick you up at seven?"

"I'll text you my address if you give me your number." She handed him her phone.

His thumbs shook as he entered the digits. When he was finished, he handed the phone back to her.

"What should I bring? I don't have a fishing pole or anything."

"Don't worry about that. I have an extra I'll bring for you."

His phone buzzed and he checked the screen. It was from Addison. Her wide smile knocked him for a loop. "Now you have my number too."

AFTER ASSISTING ADDISON into the passenger seat, Will closed the door. He'd spent an hour at the car wash trying to transform his old Dodge from a heap of junk to a decent-looking vehicle. He scoured and vacuumed the interior and bought one of those fragrant pine trees. But any pride he'd felt in the results had evaporated as he pulled alongside Addison's newer Honda.

The sight of her parents' nice home only a block from Seabrook Beach did nothing to assuage his self-doubts.

Oh well. Nothing he could do about any of that. She might as well know from the start he was a poor college student. He slid into the driver's seat and started the car, a glimpse of his beautiful passenger stealing any words that might've formed on his tongue.

"You got me out of mopping floors tonight, so thanks for that."

"Happy to help. I'm pretty lucky. My mom does most of the cleaning. I do the dishes, which she hates, and my own laundry, of course."

"What does your dad do?"

"Oh, they're divorced. But before that he mostly just took care of the lawn and outdoor stuff, the cars."

She chuckled. "I meant for a living."

His face heated. "Oh, yeah. Sorry. He's an electrician. And yours?"

"He's a lawyer—but don't hold that against him. And my mom stayed home with us, but she sells baked goods on the side. She's a really good baker. I'll bring you one of her brownies sometime. They're so good they'll make you cry."

"Yeah? I love brownies. Any siblings?"

"Oh boy, do I. I'm the youngest of five, all boys except me."

"Wow, you must be scrappy to have survived that."

"I can hold my own. Any siblings for you?"

"Only child."

"So, spoiled then?"

He chuckled. "What gave it away, my mountain of student debt or my crappy car?"

Addison patted the dashboard. "Shhh. She'll hear you." She pulled back her hand, a pretty blush blooming on her cheeks.

She was so cute. "So your parents are still married?"

"Still married, still in love. It's a little sickening. Is it hard having divorced parents?"

"Not really. They fought a lot when they were together, and me and my dad don't get along very well. So when they told me they were getting a divorce, I wasn't too upset."

"How old were you?"

"Sophomore in high school."

"Do you see your dad much now?"

"Occasionally." The last time they'd spoken was last week when Will called on Dad's birthday. After the pleasantries his father asked after his grades, then went on to tell him how the trades were out-earning college graduates these days and Will was making a mistake with all that debt. As usual he walked away from the conversation feeling uncertain and irritated. But he wasn't admitting that to Addison.

The conversation turned to their jobs for the rest of the ride. When they arrived at the pier, he parked, unbuckled, and reached for his door handle.

Addison set her hand on his bare arm as her gaze locked on him. "I have a confession to make."

He tried to read her expression and came up empty. "Okay . . ."

"I don't actually want to go fishing."

"Oh. I see." But he didn't really. And the long pause that followed only confused him further. Did she want him to take her home?

"The thought of slimy fish kind of makes me ill." Uncertainty flickered in her eyes. "I only said I wanted to go fishing because I want to spend time with you." The admission tumbled quickly from her mouth.

And Will didn't even try to stop the smile from spreading across his face.

Chapter 23

*J*osh had changed outfits three times. Now, on his way to the restaurant where he was meeting Maggie, he wished he'd stopped at number two. The button-down and khakis were too dressy for the casual restaurant. Too dressy for *him*. She'd probably show up in a pair of shorts and a tee and he'd feel really dumb.

Too late now. He muttered a quick, desperate prayer that tonight would go his way. This had been so long in coming. How would Maggie react to the news that he wanted more from their relationship? With disbelief? Incredulity? Disgust?

Or would she be open to the idea?

The uncertainty made his palms sweat as he signaled to turn into the restaurant's lot. He'd selected a new place—one that held no old memories for either of them. A new place for a fresh start.

He hoped.

It had been three days since he'd requested this dinner and they'd exchanged only the briefest of texts since then. Did she suspect what was coming? Had she purposely distanced herself from him? He would know soon enough.

He'd arrived a few minutes early to make sure they got the private booth he'd requested and try to compose himself. But when the hostess led him to a booth in the far corner of the restaurant, Maggie was already seated there.

She offered a smile that seemed strained. "Hey."

His heart took a dive as he slid into the opposite side of the booth. "Hey yourself. Been here long?"

"Just arrived. I thought it might take Zoey a minute to acclimate to Sharon, but she practically dragged the woman off to play."

"Sharon—Mom and Dad's next-door neighbor?"

"Yeah." Maggie glanced down. "I wasn't sure how to, uh, explain to Erin . . ."

That they were having dinner alone. He should've considered that. "Right."

She glanced up at him, eyes full of questions and uncertainty.

But he wasn't ready to plunge into the conversation. If it ended badly, he didn't want either of them suffering through an awkward hour-long meal. Better to save it for later.

Like a gift from heaven a male server appeared tableside. "What can I get you two to drink?"

They ordered their drinks and then, when the server left, began perusing the extensive menu. They made small talk about the offerings, and a few minutes later when the server returned, he took their order. Maggie went for the fried flounder and Josh ordered barbecue.

But the very thought of food made his stomach churn. What happened in the next thirty minutes would determine the entire course of his future. But this uncertainty had to come to an end. He couldn't continue to live this way. She'd had such a hold on him for so long—and she didn't even realize it.

"So . . . how's it working out with Will so far? Learned anything helpful?"

He expelled his breath, glad to be on familiar footing. "He's doing great at the job. I haven't learned anything new about his homelife, though. I think he and Addison are infatuated with each other."

Maggie gave a wistful grin. "Ah, young love."

"They stare at each other when they think the other one's not looking. Addison blushes when they're talking and Will gets all flustered. It's kind of hilarious. I just hope it doesn't end with someone quitting."

"Is she a nice girl?"

"She is. She comes from an affluent family and hasn't been in the area long, but she seems to have her head on straight. She's reliable and organized. I'd take her over Penny any day." Penny had filled the job before Addison. "And you? Have you had time to do any more research?"

"I've done quite a bit but I haven't learned much. I can't find a connection between Robyn and your dad. If they worked together at some point, I haven't been able to figure out when or where."

Disappointment warred with relief. Even though Josh wanted answers, and even though it seemed likely his dad had done this, he didn't want to believe it. "I thought for sure we'd find something."

"Even if they didn't work together, they must've run in the same circles. It's possible they met at a conference or fundraiser or something."

"True."

They began discussing the many ways Brad might've met Robyn. As they chatted they eased into their comfortable patterns.

By the time the food arrived they were on familiar footing. Maggie raved over the flounder and hush puppies, but as the clock ticked away, Josh's mind returned to the matter at hand. It was all he could do to finish the pork. By the time the server collected their plates, the heavy meal sat like a cement block in his stomach.

Time to get down to business. What he said could give rise to an even closer relationship. Or it could drive a permanent wedge between them. If Maggie didn't feel the same way, their easy relationship might never be the same.

She was staring at him in the muted light, no doubt wondering why he'd invited her here. Her eyes held questions.

And he had the answers.

He drained the last of his drink, mustering courage. Then he took a deep breath and met her gaze. Now or never. "You're probably wondering why I wanted to speak with you alone. The thing is, Mags, I've been wondering about something lately." Like for about the last twenty years. He cleared his throat. "I've been wondering if . . ." He got caught in the pull of her pretty brown eyes and forgot the phrasing he'd planned to use.

She shifted in her seat. "Yes . . . ?"

Man up, buddy. Way past time to get this out on the table.

"I was wondering if you'd be open to the idea of a . . . a shift in our relationship."

The whole room seemed to shrink down to just Maggie and Josh. Time seemed to stand still as his words replayed in her mind. The reason for this meeting was just as she'd suspected. Just as she'd hoped.

Just as she'd feared.

And despite all the time she'd given to this possibility over the past few days, her emotions on the subject were still a tangled skein of yarn. "A—a shift?"

He glanced down to where his fingers mangled a cloth napkin. He set it aside and leaned onto his elbows as one side of his mouth lifted. "I think you know what I mean, Mags."

She swallowed hard. "Right."

"We already know each other very well."

It was true. She'd always felt so comfortable around Josh. It was so easy with him.

"And you can't deny we're compatible. We share the same values, the same religious and political views."

"It takes more than compatibility to make a relationship."

He slowly lifted a brow. "You're absolutely right."

She was referring to chemistry, of course, and he was practically daring her to refute the sparks between them. She couldn't. Especially now as the low rumble of his voice and intensity of his gaze lit a fire inside where a pile of cold ashes had lain for years. Since the night he'd kissed her. Since that amazing, sensual kiss she'd never been able to forget.

But she wasn't about to own up to it. The thought of changing everything between them might kindle a fire inside, but it also shook her to the core. Josh and Erin were her best friends. Brad and Becky were the parents she'd never had. If a romantic relationship with Josh ended badly, she risked losing her family. She had to quash this as delicately as she could.

"Don't you think—? You're my husband's brother, Josh."

"Late husband."

"What would Ethan have thought of this?" Before he could respond she rushed ahead. "People might find it a little odd. And what about your parents? Don't you think they might be upset by the very notion of—"

He set his hand on hers and waited until he had her full attention.

"Hold up. Slow down. One thing at a time. How about if we focus on us before we bring everyone else into it?"

The solid weight of his hand distracted her from the words coming out his mouth. It took considerable restraint to keep from weaving her fingers through his.

No. Stop thinking like that. You could end up losing virtually everyone who matters to you. This can't happen.

But what if it did? What if they followed this road and it didn't end badly? What if Josh was the answer to her heart's every question? A wave of longing hit her so hard, she struggled to draw a breath.

"Sometimes you look at me like that and I think maybe I'm not crazy. Maggie . . . remember that kiss a couple years ago?"

Remember? She'd only memorized every glance that had led up to it. Every touch they'd shared. Every sigh they'd emitted. Even now her lips tingled at the thought of it. She glanced at his mouth, then darted her attention back to his eyes.

"I didn't kiss you because I was sad and lonely. I kissed you because I wanted you. No one else, Maggie. Just you."

Her heart gave a slow roll as she fell into his smoldering gaze, where she could've happily drowned.

"I let you believe that because you weren't ready for the truth. I'd been feeling differently toward you for—for a while. I've thought about that kiss a million times. Best kiss of my life. Am I the only one who felt that way?"

When he looked at her like that, when he made her remember that night, she forgot all the reasons she'd been fighting this. And she *had* been fighting it. She hadn't allowed herself to admit it, but it was true. Sometimes their hugs extended a fraction too long. Sometimes their gazes connected in a meaningful way. For months she'd been engaged in a quiet battle to keep Josh in the friend zone.

"But we're—we're good friends, Josh." It was a last, half-hearted effort to keep things as they were. Safe. Unthreatening.

He squeezed her hand. "But is that all we can ever be, Maggie?"

The naked yearning in his eyes made her heart ache. How long had he felt this way? How long had he been pretending to be just her friend? Her brother?

And she was no better. Maybe that kiss had been the truest thing that had ever happened between them. Because if she was gut-level honest—she had not been thinking of her late husband that night.

"Maggie? Have I scared you to death?"

A laugh trembled out. "Yes."

He leaned forward, his eyes like a laser on her. "Tell me what you're afraid of. Let's talk this through."

"I don't want to lose you," she blurted.

He offered a compassionate smile. "You will never lose me."

"You can't know that. Relationships go sour all the time. Things happen and feelings get hurt and people get angry. How often do breakups end in friendship? Almost never."

"We haven't even had a first date and you already have us breaking up."

"I'm serious, Josh. Take you and Samantha. You guys were in love and now she can hardly stand the sight of you."

Something undecipherable flashed in his eyes. He shook his head. "That would never happen between us. We have a long history, you and me. We've already been through a lot together, and I care way too much about you not to want you in my life."

"You say that now."

"I promise you—Maggie, look at me—I promise you I will always

146

be part of your life—yours and Zoey's—no matter what happens."
His countenance fell and his eyes softened as pain flickered there.
"The way I feel about you won't change—even if you say no tonight."

It might just break his heart if she did, though. It was suddenly as
clear as air. And oh, she didn't want to hurt him. She squeezed her
eyes closed. She didn't want to hurt herself either, and that seemed
destined to happen if things didn't work out. If they broke up. If he
got bored with her.

Josh didn't exactly have a great track record. With the exception
of Samantha, his average relationship had lasted approximately three
seconds. He'd had so many women Maggie couldn't begin to remember their names. He'd told her once, after the breakup of yet
another brief relationship, that he'd gotten bored with her.

Just the thought that he might find her lacking opened a hollow
spot inside. Made her feel achy and vulnerable in a way that triggered
sheer terror.

"You're thinking awfully hard over there. Anything you wanna
share?"

"Just . . . walking through this." She couldn't tell him the truth.
He'd just deny that she could ever bore him. He'd say they knew each
other well already and he didn't find her boring in the least—and
he'd have a good point. Still, there was that terror.

"If I ask you a question, will you tell me the truth?"

Her pulse thrummed in her temples as their gazes mingled. "Of
course."

He glanced down at the table, then back up at her. "Do you think
you could—" His Adam's apple bobbed. "Could you ever feel more
for me than friendship?"

She already did. That kiss had proven it to her, even if she had denied it. Blocked it. Buried it. Because there was so much to lose here.

"Stop, Maggie. Stop weighing the pros and cons and just tell me the God's honest truth."

"Yes." The word left her tongue before she could stop it. She bit her lip.

His eyes lit and that quirky grin followed.

Oh yes, she could fall in love with that face. With this man. She was afraid she was already halfway there.

He took her other hand in his. "Then go out with me, Maggie. Let's see where this leads. We don't have to make an announcement or plan out the future. Just a date. Don't look now, but we're practically on one at this very moment."

Oh, man. She was really going to do this. Her nerves rattled until her hands trembled. "One step at a time?"

"We can go slow. Handle it however you want." His eyes pierced hers.

She felt it down to the soles of her feet. Tension crackled between them. She was losing that battle. And wasn't altogether torn up about it.

"I just want a chance with you, Maggie. Will you give me a chance?"

She would've given him the world right now, the way he was gazing at her, saying these things. All he wanted was a chance. And in her heart of hearts, she wanted that too. The problems that might possibly happen somewhere down the road faded at the longing in his eyes. At the yearning in her heart. There'd been something more between them for a long time. She couldn't quell it anymore. Not after he'd put his feelings out there so bravely, so sweetly.

"Okay," she said.

His hands tightened on hers as if by reflex. "Okay?"

At the hope on his face, joy bubbled up from deep within, from a well she hadn't known existed. Laughter followed. "Okay, Josh. Let's see where this goes."

"All right." His eyes warmed as he lifted her hand to his lips and placed a kiss in the center of her palm. "You won't regret this, Maggie. I promise."

As they lingered at the table, chatting quietly, Maggie hoped the magic spell that seemed to envelop them would never go away.

Chapter 24

"Nice lap, Keondre." Maggie squatted at the end of the pool where the fourteen-year-old boy waited, panting. "Good elbow position that time. Remember on your breaths to keep one goggle in the water. Do one more lap, focusing on that, then we're done for the day."

"Aww . . ."

"I have some killer drills planned for next week—you'll be begging me to leave. Now let's see what you've got."

He nodded, eagerness flaring in his eyes behind the goggles, and pushed off to a freestyle swim.

Better. He was still pulling to the right, though. She'd have him do some closed-eye laps next week. But she'd given enough instruction for one lesson.

The Johnsons' pool was regulation length—longer than the ranch house in front of it—but only three lanes wide due to the shallow yard.

Keondre's mom, Kyra, met Maggie at the side of the pool. Her son had inherited her lean height, almond-shaped eyes, and wide grin. "Only two lessons and he's already improved."

"He puts in the practice. That's half the battle."

Kyra laughed. "The battle is getting him out of the pool. The boy would live in there till he grew fins if I let him."

"He's got a lot of potential. That tall frame and those big hands and feet are real advantages. But his discipline and teachability will be what takes him a long way."

"Really? You think so? I know he's only just about to enter high school, but he's really hoping for a swimming scholarship to Duke."

"If he keeps up the hard work, I think that's a reasonable goal."

Keondre stopped at the pool wall and glanced Maggie's way.

"Much better on the sneaky breaths," Maggie called. "Work on that this week—and the elbows."

"Yes, ma'am!" He adjusted his goggles and pushed off for another lap. He'd have both mastered when she returned on Tuesday. It was exhilarating to teach an adept athlete who was also highly motivated.

"I'm so glad you agreed to coach him the rest of the summer," Kyra said. "He'd learned all he could from the instructor at the Y. I hope the high school coach is as good as you."

"I don't know him, but they seem to have a good program over there. They won state a couple years ago and made it to the finals last year."

"He's so excited to try out. He'll make the team?"

"I can't imagine why not."

Keondre dragged himself from the pool and headed toward the house. "See ya next week, Miss Maggie. Don't worry, I'll be practicing."

"I have no doubt."

Keondre turned at the sliding door. "Hey, Mom, when's supper? I'm starving."

"Supper's in the oven. Grab a towel—don't you drip all over my clean floor."

MAGGIE GOT IN her car and checked her phone for any texts that might've come in during the lesson. Nothing. Then, just because she couldn't help herself, she opened Josh's text from this morning.

Still like me?

She'd waited a full ten minutes before texting back. *I think I can tolerate you.*

After lunch he'd texted that one of his favorite local bands was playing at Beats on the Boardwalk. She hadn't answered yet.

Last night as he'd accompanied her to her car, they walked closely, their arms brushing. And even though they'd done that a million times, it felt awkward. Everything had changed. She was giving them a chance. Giving Josh a chance. The future was uncertain. And despite her agreement to see what happened, she couldn't help but fret about the damage a bitter breakup might cause. About Josh's short attention span in the romance department. About what his family might think. He was her brother-in-law. She winced as the silence lengthened between them. Was this too weird?

No weirder than you enjoying his kiss two and a half years ago.

The recollection provoked another thought that made the fried flounder in her stomach churn. What if he tried to kiss her now? Did she want him to? Her heart rate couldn't seem to keep pace with her lungs. Her palms grew sweaty, her mouth dry.

They reached her car and she unlocked the door with her fob. The sun had set, ushering in darkness, and the scent of honeysuckle carried on a breeze.

"I'll text you." Josh opened her door, putting it between them.

No kiss then. She dredged up a smile. "Okay. Good night."

"Night, Maggie."

As she drove away she wasn't sure if she was disappointed or relieved that he hadn't tried to kiss her.

Now she gave her head a hard shake and the Johnsons' house came into focus. Josh had promised to take it slow. Grabbing her for a kiss two minutes after agreeing to this *shift* was hardly slow. They needed to find their footing. Surely going out with him wouldn't be much different than what they'd been doing for years. And dancing might be the perfect activity, the perfect tension breaker. They'd always excelled at having fun together.

They'd just go out and have fun. What harm could come from that?

She lifted her phone and replied to his text about dancing tonight.

Bring it on.

Chapter 25

*B*eats on the Boardwalk sat just two blocks from Seabrook's carnival grounds. On this busy Saturday night, the rustic building teemed with locals and tourists alike. Sounds of chatter and laughter punctuated the space between the band's songs, and the smell of grilled burgers dominated.

Josh and Maggie had been fortunate to score a table far enough from the speakers to allow communicating. Though conversation had started out a little stilted.

Probably didn't help that he could hardly take his eyes off her. Her brown hair fell past her shoulders in soft waves. Her doe eyes seemed large and luminous under the pendant light, her sun-kissed skin flawless.

He could hardly believe he was here with her, on a date. He'd waited so long for this chance.

Since their conversation the night before, he'd been unable to keep the smile from his face. The wonder from his heart. It had been hard putting himself out there, risking her rejection. But her admission that she could feel more than friendship for him had turned his world upside down.

Across from him, Maggie shifted in the booth.

He was staring. And his daydreaming had ushered in a long, awkward pause.

Don't blow it now, idiot. He needed to get them back on familiar ground.

He dropped his napkin on his empty plate. "How did your lesson go today? This was the teenager who's hoping for a spot on the high school team?"

"Right. Keondre's a strong athlete, a good swimmer. He'll have no trouble making the team."

"Do you prefer teaching the advanced swimmers or the beginners?"

"Definitely the advanced. Having the swim team back home is what gets me through my day job."

She talked about teaching sometimes, but she'd never really admitted that. "Teaching isn't what you thought it would be?"

She propped her chin on her hand. "Oh, I don't know. I guess it's actually more than I thought it would be. I like the actual teaching part. But it's almost impossible to get parental support. A lot of high school students still need monitoring with their schoolwork, and some parents aren't able or simply won't give them the help they need to be successful. And then, of course, it falls to the teacher."

"That's a lot of students to monitor."

"Then there's discipline in the classroom, which has become complicated if not impossible. Also, pressure from administration to teach to the tests is frustrating. And don't even get me started on school politics." She took a sip of her tea. "Sorry you asked?"

"Not at all. I've heard other teachers say the same things."

"It's the students who keep us coming back. I see one of them grasp a new concept or discover a passion for writing or reading, and I forget all about the frustrations."

He tilted his lips. "I'll bet you're a great teacher."

"I try my best."

"I'll bet you have a dozen high school boys with massive crushes on you."

Her laughter rang out over the lively country tune. "They're more likely to be scheming up ways to get even with me. I'm a stickler for the rules. And what about you? Is captaining your own boat everything you dreamed it would be?"

"No regrets there. I get to spend my days on the water and be my own boss—not that that doesn't come with a few headaches. But overall I've been blessed with a healthy share of business and a good crew. I can't complain."

"You're lucky to have found your calling so young. You've wanted to be a captain like your uncle Clyde since I can remember."

"Good ol' Uncle Clyde." He'd passed away almost twenty years ago, but all those boat rides had made an impact on Josh. "I think my dad wanted to throttle him. But then Ethan decided to be a doctor and he eased up on me."

Maggie gave a wan smile and glanced down.

Maybe he shouldn't have mentioned his brother. Josh wished she didn't feel weird about dating him. "Should we talk about him? About Ethan?"

She took her elbows off the table and offered a real smile. "Not necessary."

A woman passed their table. Darcy Stuart. He started to avert his face but was too late.

She did a double take and backed up, beaming. "Well, hey, Josh. How you been?"

"Doing all right, Darcy. This is Maggie. Maggie, Darcy."

Maggie offered a polite smile. "Nice to meet you."

The woman barely spared Maggie a glance. "Haven't seen you in ages. We've missed you around here."

He'd met Darcy through a mutual friend and gone out with her once. She'd spent the whole night talking about herself. "Been busy, I guess."

Darcy glanced back at a table where someone was motioning for her. "Well, I'm being summoned. It was good to see you, Josh. Don't be a stranger. Nice meeting you, Maggie."

"Same." She regarded Josh with a lifted brow. "Old girlfriend?"

"Just a blind date gone awry."

Her lips twitched. "I see. Well, not to change the subject, but . . ."

"Please, feel free to change the subject."

She chuckled. "I wanted to ask about something that involves our investigation into Will, but I wasn't sure if you wanted to talk about that tonight."

He leaned forward. "It's just you and me, Mags, whether we're on a date or sleuthing around Seabrook. We can talk about anything you want."

"Oh good, because I had this idea the other day. We talked about DNA testing, but you didn't want to go there with Will's DNA. I get it. But what if you just did yours?"

"What good would that do?"

The music crescendoed and she leaned in. "This would be a long shot, but there are huge databases of people out there who've had their DNA tested to find family and complete their family trees and such. Once the database has your DNA, it automatically sends you matches. It can even differentiate between maternal and paternal matches. If Will has his DNA in the database and your dad is his biological father, Will would turn up as a sibling match for you."

"It seems unlikely that Will would've done a DNA test."

"You're probably right. But if he's had any questions about his paternity, it seems like it would've been the place for him to start."

"That's a big 'if.'"

"It is. Will might believe the man who raised him is his biological father. But we have to do something and there's really no downside to doing a test. It's relatively inexpensive and the results, if he's on there, would be proof positive. The only negative is that it takes five to eight weeks to get database results."

That seemed like forever. But Josh hadn't made any headway with Will. And he wasn't yet desperate enough to ask his dad point-blank. If they were wrong, it could cause irreparable damage to their relationship. "It's worth a try, I guess. There's really nothing to lose."

A playful gleam entered her eyes. "I thought you'd feel that way. I already have the test in my possession."

Of course she did. A laugh rumbled from his chest. "You're incorrigible. Now, will you dance with me already, or were you planning to drag me off somewhere and stick a swab in my mouth?"

Almost an hour later Maggie had forgotten all about the DNA test. Josh was a riot on the dance floor. What he didn't have in rhythm, he made up for with boldness and creativity.

The band's upbeat songs kept the dance floor full and energized. Her sleeveless sundress kept her adequately cool and she'd long ago stopped worrying about her fallen curls or melting makeup.

Josh had a way of making her feel comfortable in her own skin. She'd always been able to relax around him. Years ago it had been a point of contention between Ethan and her. He'd once accused her of liking Josh more than him. It wasn't true, of course. She'd loved Ethan. But with Josh she didn't worry about how she looked or sounded or what he thought of her. And the less she'd worried about it, the more he seemed to like her. He was safe somehow in a way that Ethan hadn't been. It was . . . refreshing.

The chorus of "Country Girl" kicked up and Josh did a slow turn, waggling his hips as he went.

Maggie laughed and imitated his move. As she turned she caught a pretty brunette eyeing Josh. It hadn't escaped her notice tonight that he'd caught the attention of other women—including the one who'd stopped by their table, Darcy. His confidence and muscular form offered plenty of appeal. His blue eyes were a thing of beauty, and that impish grin didn't hurt either.

And he was *her* date. A feeling of pride washed over her as the band segued to a country ballad, the first of the night. The lead guitarist picked out the stirring melody of "In Case You Didn't Know."

Smiling broadly, Josh sauntered up to her and swept her into his arms.

She placed a hand on his shoulder and took the one he offered. Any awkwardness from the beginning of the date had long since faded. She was almost giddy with pleasure now. "I'd forgotten what a clown you are on the dance floor."

"Dancing's supposed to be fun, and you've always been a great partner."

She'd only danced with him a handful of times and always the fast kind. Now as they shifted back and forth, turning in a slow circle, they were so close she could feel the heat rolling off his skin, smell the hint of his woodsy cologne.

He was five inches taller than her five-seven, and her heels added another two inches, putting her at the perfect level for slow dancing.

She fell into the music, into the poignant words as the first verse played out. Their thighs brushed as they moved smoothly together, her right foot tucked between his.

And that's when she realized—for all his wild flailing and exaggerated moves on the dance floor, he wasn't lacking rhythm at all. He was actually graceful!

She leaned back as she slapped him on the shoulder.

"What?"

"You're a good dancer! You goofball. All this time I thought you were rhythmically challenged. I almost felt sorry for you."

"Ouch."

"Why do you hide that you can dance?"

"I don't—I just like having fun, messing around, making people laugh."

"You like making people laugh *at* you?"

He chuckled. "Sure. Why not?"

"Oh boy. You really are the typical baby of the family."

He hiked a brow. "Shall we discuss all the ways you're like an only?"

"No, thank you." The chorus kicked in, the melody stirring and romantic. "Now hush, I like this song." She moved in closer and rested her head on his shoulder. His skin was warm beneath the soft material of his button-down, the curves of his shoulder solid beneath her fingertips.

He tightened his arm around her until their torsos pressed together. Until his hand settled at the small of her back.

She shivered. Tucked their clasped hands into the space between their shoulders. He felt so good pressed up against her. He didn't feel like a friend. Friends didn't make your heart wobble in your chest. They didn't make your knees go noodly or your skin vibrate with life.

He released her hand and slid his arm around her in a full embrace. His breath feathered the hair at her temples, stirring every hair follicle.

Maggie placed her palm on his chest as the sentimental lyrics rang out, taking root in her heart. It was almost as if Josh were singing the words to her. Telling her he was crazy about her. That she'd had his heart for a long time now.

Last night he said he'd kissed her all that time ago because he wanted her. But that was over two years ago. Exactly how long had he felt this way? How long had he been patiently waiting for her to notice him? Josh, who'd been there for her in her darkest days.

Her eyes stung at the thought. She blinked against the tears, her arms automatically tightening around him.

She'd asked him to help her find a man! She'd overlooked him because—

No, not overlooked exactly. She'd been in denial. Her feelings went deeper than friendship. She was just afraid to trust him with her heart. Afraid of the ramifications of caring about him in that way.

But she did care about him in that way.

She did.

As if sensing her internal struggle, he leaned back until their gazes mingled. His expression held questions she didn't want to answer. Did he notice her eyes were swimming with tears?

He set his hand tenderly on her cheek. "It'll be okay, Mags."

Her breath escaped. How did he do that? Read her mind like that?

"I'm not gonna let anything bad happen to you."

He was worried about *her* when she'd been so insensitive about his feelings. She'd only been worried about what she was going through and what she might lose. Guilt pricked hard. "Josh . . . I'm sorry if I hurt you."

His lips turned up as a gleam of humor lit his eyes. That quirky eyebrow bounced. "Worth it."

Chapter 26

Once Josh parked outside Maggie's place, she whipped the DNA test from her purse.

Talk about a mood buster. After that amazing slow dance and romantic stroll on the beach, this wasn't how he'd seen the night ending.

Moments later the swab tickled Josh's inner cheek as she swished it around. Apparently she'd already read the directions because the whole thing was over in twenty seconds flat. "Brings a whole new meaning to the phrase 'swapping spit.'"

"Funny." Maggie slipped the swab into a plastic bag and sealed it. "All done. I'll get it in the mail Monday."

"This has to be the weirdest first date on record."

She turned a wry glance his way. "It had its moments. But the sooner we send this, the sooner we get the results. Now walk me to the door and we'll say good night."

He reached for the handle. "Will I get a kiss?"

"You said we'd take it slow."

His attention drifted to her luscious mouth. "You're the boss."

Outside the car a welcome breeze greeted him. It was past eleven and a million stars twinkled in the black sky above the moonlit sea.

The constant roar of the surf carried over the distance, as familiar as the beat of his own heart.

By the time he reached the passenger side, Maggie had already exited. "Hey now. You should let me be a proper gentleman."

"You can carry me up the stairs. These heels are killing me."

He started to sweep her into his arms.

She skittered away, laughing. "I was kidding. I'm no lightweight, you know."

His gaze took a quick tour down the length of her and back up. "You're perfect."

She didn't reply but her lips twitched as she skirted him and took the steps to the porch. She'd told him once that in high school she'd wanted to be one of those petite girls who looked as if a strong wind might blow her over. But instead she was as tall as some of the boys, with swimmer's shoulders and muscular legs.

But to him Maggie was everything a woman ought to be: resilient, beautiful, feminine. If she could see herself through his eyes, she'd never wish herself any other way.

They reached the landing where the porch light dispersed an amber glow. Maggie dug in her purse for her keys. "I wonder if Sharon managed to get Zoey down."

"I wonder if Sharon is asleep and Zoey has free rein of the house."

"Now there's a scary thought." She withdrew her keys and looked up at him. As the moment lengthened, a wistful smile tipped the corners of her mouth. "Thank you for tonight, Josh. I had fun."

"Me too."

"I always have so much fun with you."

He arched a brow. "Even when we're solving mysteries that might have devastating consequences?"

"Even then."

It was true. Even in the midst of this strange journey they'd been on this summer, they'd found a way to laugh. He wouldn't want to go through this with anyone but her. "Maybe we can do it again next week."

A twinkle glinted in her eyes. "Dancing and swabbing?"

"Maybe we'll skip the swabbing next time."

"Spoilsport." She leaned in, wrapping her arms around him.

He reciprocated the hug, his hands finding the small of her back, the dip between her shoulder blades. She tightened the embrace and he followed her lead, letting her set the pace. Her body was flush against his. She was warm and soft in all the right places. Could she feel the heavy thump of his heart?

Her hand followed a path to the back of his neck and her fingers stirred the hair at his nape. She tucked her face in the cradle of his shoulder, and her breath teased the sensitive skin there. He relished every sensation. Tucked away the memory for later.

Having her in his arms was a piece of heaven on earth. Maggie didn't trust easily. Who would, with her mother, her childhood? Adulthood hadn't been much kinder. That she trusted Josh made him feel like a superhero somehow. She might not see it, but she was a strong woman. A fighter.

A squeal sounded from beyond the door.

Maggie drew back. "Uh-oh. Sounds like I have a wound-up little girl in there."

"Want me to come in and play tickle monster with her?"

"That would be a no. I probably won't get her down till midnight as it is." She placed a quick kiss on his cheek. "Good night, Josh. Thanks again for tonight."

"Night, Maggie."

With one last smile she slipped inside, careful to keep Zoey from spotting him. Then Josh descended the steps, his mind whirling with all that had happened tonight.

As he got into his car he couldn't stop smiling. At long last he and Maggie were dating. She was giving him a chance. He'd had his arms around her in a meaningful way on that dance floor—and again just now—and she'd been responsive. He could still feel the slight weight of her head against his shoulder, the press of her palm to his heart.

Maggie Reynolds felt something for him.

And it wasn't just pity.

Chapter 27

*H*ey, guys." Josh sat in his living room, smiling at his parents, who stared back from the screen of his laptop. It was good to see them. But the main purpose of the conversation made the frozen pizza he'd downed for lunch roil in his gut.

"Hey, honey. It's so good to see your face." Mom's brown pixie cut framed a petite face that sported a fresh tan. A bright shade of coral adorned her lips, and as usual, a pair of elaborate earrings dangled from her lobes.

Dad adjusted the angle of the phone. "The Wi-Fi's spotty, so if we get disconnected, I'll call back." Having lost most of his hair in his forties, Dad resembled the father on *Everybody Loves Raymond*—a fact that made Josh grateful he'd taken mostly after his mother in looks.

"No worries." Josh's gaze drifted to the wood-paneled background behind the sofa with a funky painting of . . . he wasn't sure what. "Where are you now? I can hardly keep up with you guys."

Mom squeezed into the frame. "We're in this adorable apartment in Athens."

"By 'adorable,' she means miniscule and expensive."

"Oh, stop it. It's not that small."

"It makes the cabin on the cruise ship seem like an estate. She rented it solely based on the picture of the balcony."

"You should see it, Josh! It's beautiful. I have my own little garden of Eden right outside the door." The image bobbled, cutting to the ceiling, then the floor as Mom swiped the phone and went outside to show off the space. She flipped on a porch light because it was evening there.

"Look at this bougainvillea!" she said over the noise of traffic. "Have you ever seen anything so lush and lovely? We sit out here every morning with our coffee."

"It's the only space besides the bed big enough for both of us."

"Oh, stop it. We should sit out here and talk to our son."

"He won't be able to hear over the noise."

"Well, that's true. We'll take you back inside, honey." The background noise lessened as they slipped back through the patio door. "Tell us what you've been up to."

"Yeah, how's business? Last time you mentioned you were looking for a new crew member."

The opening was too good to be true. He and Maggie had discussed how Josh might bring the conversation around to the subject. But now that the moment was upon him, his nerves quaked. Was he ready for the truth? "Um, yeah, I already hired a new guy. He's only nineteen but he's working out really well so far."

"I'm so glad to hear it," Mom said. "A good crew makes all the difference."

"He's a real go-getter and he's terrific with the passengers. Neat and tidy behind the bar. Couldn't ask for better." His smile felt plastic as he zeroed in on his dad's face and forced out the words. "His mom actually knows you, Dad."

"That so?"

"Yeah . . . her name's Robyn Jennings."

Furrows formed between Dad's brows. Otherwise his expression remained the same. "Doesn't sound familiar. Where am I supposed to know her from?"

"Not sure. She's a nurse, though, so I assumed you worked with her at some point."

"Doesn't ring a bell. Maybe if I saw her. Sound familiar to you, honey?"

Mom's earrings tinkled as she turned to Dad. "Didn't you work with a Robyn at Parkfield? The RN who always ate her lunch at the workstation?"

"That was Rowan."

"I thought Rowan was the one who always wore the rainbow scrubs."

"It is. That's the same woman."

"Oh." Mom shrugged. "Well, what do I know?"

Relief buzzed through Josh's veins as his parents carried on about the nurses Dad used to work with. There had been nothing suspicious in his expression or response—nor in Mom's.

That relief carried him through the thirty-minute conversation, then Mom yawned and they admitted they'd been up before sunrise for a tour.

Seconds after they ended the session, Josh called Maggie.

She answered on the first ring. "How'd it go? Did you find a way to bring up Robyn?"

"I did. Dad didn't recognize her name."

"Are you sure?"

"If he did, he's one heck of an actor. Mom didn't miss a beat either. They were both calm and casual as could be."

"Well, I guess he doesn't know Robyn then." Her voice held a note of confusion.

"Or he doesn't remember her name."

A beat of silence ensued. "Surely you're not suggesting your dad slept with a stranger."

"I don't want to believe it." During the conversation with his folks, Josh's mind had strayed a time or two. "He mentioned he might recognize her if he saw her. What if I produced a picture?"

"How are you going to do that without seeming like you're on some kind of mission?"

She was right. He sighed. "I don't know. I can't screw up my relationship with Dad unnecessarily. Maybe we should just wait for the DNA results."

"That won't be for weeks. Are you okay with waiting that long? Also, it's entirely possible we won't learn anything at all, and then what?"

"I don't know."

"I don't either. But I was wondering this morning . . . What if other family members are in that DNA database and you show up in their matches? Will they wonder why you had yours checked?"

"As far as I know, none of our immediate family has done anything like that. If there's a match, I'll just say I was curious about our ancestry. I am, in fact."

"Ethan always said you guys have Irish roots."

"That's the family scuttlebutt. Along with a little English on Mom's side. But I wouldn't mind finding out for sure."

Zoey's sleepy voice sounded on her end.

"Guess who just woke from her nap hungry as a hibernating bear?"

He wished he could be there to wrap Zoey in a big hug. "I'll let you go then. Tell Cupcake I said hi."

"Okay. See you tomorrow at seven. Wait. Can you at least give me a clue how to dress?"

He was picking her up for a surprise date. He'd been tempted to take her dancing again—just to be certain he got his arms around her at least once. But for the sake of variety, he decided on something different. "Definitely casual, comfortable shoes."

"Like T-shirt and shorts casual?"

"That's perfect. See you tomorrow."

"See you." He could tell she was smiling by the soft tone of her voice.

And by the time he disconnected the call, he was smiling too.

Chapter 28

*M*aggie loved surprises—the good kind anyway—and the Carolina Beach State Park was definitely a good one. Happiness bloomed inside as Josh turned into the park. "I love this place. Haven't been here in years." The kids from her graduating class, including Erin, used to hang out by the Cape Fear River, eating junk food, gossiping, and goofing off.

"Hope you're hungry. There's a picnic in the trunk."

"Well, aren't you resourceful." Not to mention romantic. She glanced at him from beneath her lashes. He was dressed as casual as she was in khaki shorts and a black T-shirt. He did very nice things for that tee. She cleared her throat. "I'm actually kind of starving. I took Zoey to McDonald's for lunch and only had a salad, then we got caught up playing at the beach and before I knew it, it was time to get ready."

"We'll eat first then. There's plenty of food. I thought we could take a short hike later if you want."

"Perfect weather for it." It was a balmy eighty degrees and partly cloudy.

The park's two-lane road wove through the lush forest. He drove all the way to the back, past the marina, and turned at the lot for the

Sugarloaf Trailhead. A picnic table squatted unoccupied beneath a canopy of towering pines.

Maggie carried the tablecloth while Josh grabbed a genuine picnic basket from his trunk. He'd definitely made some dating upgrades since the old days. She used to tease him about it. He had one or two cheap restaurants to which he brought his dates, and the night usually ended at Baron's Point, a quiet parking spot with ocean views.

"What's that little smile about?" he asked as they settled at the table.

"I was just remembering your affinity for Baron's Point."

He smirked. "I hope you can see my repertoire has improved with age."

"I'd have to agree."

"It's a little disconcerting dating someone who knows me so well."

She laughed. "You know me just as well."

"Yeah, but you didn't use to be such an idiot."

"Used to be?"

"Hey now . . ."

"And just in case you forgot, you got to see me being all dopey-eyed for your big brother."

His expression sobered as something flared in his eyes, possibly hurt. He covered it with a smile. "True enough."

She hadn't meant to bring up Ethan. Josh had gone to all this effort to please her and here she was, bringing up her late husband before they could take their first bites. But Ethan had been his brother. He was there between them whether they wanted him to be or not.

Maybe it was better to get it out in the open. "I can't change the past, you know."

His expression softened. "I wouldn't want you to, Mags. He was my brother and I loved him too. We'll always have that in common."

And yet, something else simmered under the surface of his expression. She wanted to set his mind at ease. "I don't compare you with him—if that's what you're thinking."

"Yeah?" He gave a wry laugh as he began unpacking the basket. "That's probably for the best. We were always very different, Ethan and me."

Where Ethan had been all intellect and straitlaced, Josh was athletic and carefree. They'd come from a long line of mostly doctors and teachers. Their parents valued intellect above all else, and while Josh was smart in his own way, it hadn't been in the way measured by academic tests. And his Bs and Cs didn't impress his folks.

Oh, they supported him, attended his games. But it was always clear to Maggie that it was just a game to them, especially his dad. The love and adoration he received from his peers never seemed to balance out the fact that, to his dad, his performance on the field didn't translate to real-life success.

Brad loved all his children. But when it came to his approval, Josh always seemed to come up a little short.

She leaned forward, put her hand on his, and waited until he looked at her. "You don't fall short, Josh. Not with me. I can be having the worst day ever and you show up and make me smile. Or you hold me and let me cry it out with no expectations whatsoever. You have a way of bringing out my best. You just let me be me. And, Josh . . . that's just the greatest gift ever."

His lips lifted in a smile. "That might be the nicest thing anyone's ever said to me."

"It happens to be true." She slid her hand away and they resumed unpacking the basket.

"Let's not make Ethan a taboo subject, okay?" he said. "He was a big part of both our lives and he'll always be a part of us."

"Agreed." There would be no better time to ask what had been on her mind since their first date. "So, while we're on the subject, I have to ask . . . What do you think he'd think of this? Of our going out like this?"

Josh chuckled. "He'd be wondering what in the world you could possibly be thinking."

She gave a mock scowl. "He would not. He always said I lit up around you."

Josh's brow jumped. "He did?"

"And he was right. You bring out a different side of me."

"Is that good or bad?"

She liked the way she felt with Josh. She liked who she was with him. And she really liked the way he made her feel these days. The way her stomach fluttered at his nearness. The way tension seemed to crackle between them sometimes. She loved the gentle way he touched her and the way his eyes softened when he gazed at her.

Like now. "It's a very good thing."

"So the other day Dad decided they should take the public bus across Athens to save money, and he and Mom squeezed onto this crowded bus. It's like a hundred degrees and no air-conditioning. The windows are down, blowing hot air around. It's standing room only, but Mom got an aisle seat. There's this guy in a tank top crushed right up against her. He's holding on to a ceiling strap, so she's got this sweaty, hairy armpit in her face. And she keeps leaning away, but the more she leans away, the more he leans into her space."

Maggie chuckled at the scene he painted. He'd always told a good tale.

"Dad was watching from down the aisle. You should've heard him telling the story. He was laughing so hard I could hardly make out his words. And Mom was just sitting there, her mouth all pinched, saying, "It was the foulest stench I've ever smelled! And he kept encroaching on my space!"

Maggie laughed, her eyes tearing up. "Your parents are a trip. They're having such a great time."

"Hairy armpit notwithstanding."

They were resting on a pier bench overlooking the Cape Fear River, Josh's arm draped over the back. The sun had dropped low behind a bank of clouds and now glowed golden, turning the clouds a vibrant shade of orange. A slight breeze drifted across the water, cool and refreshing.

After the picnic—her favorite foods from Dilly's Deli—they'd taken a short walk through the woods. The sandy path, strewn with pine needles and protruding roots, made her glad she'd worn tennis shoes. They chatted easily the whole way and returned in time to enjoy the stellar sunset.

She'd caught him up on the swim lessons. Word of her coaching had spread throughout Erin's circle, and she'd added two more summer clients to her schedule. She'd had breakfast at Erin's this morning, where Maggie was careful not to mention her upcoming date with Josh. "So how long do you think we should hide this from your family?"

"Hide? Is that what it feels like to you? I guess I was thinking we were being discreet."

"Okay, that's fair. It's just that I tell Erin pretty much everything, so it feels as if I'm holding something back."

He cupped her shoulder and gave it a squeeze. "You should do whatever you're comfortable with. Just remember my family has an opinion on everything and is quick to offer it."

How would Erin feel about Maggie dating Josh? She wasn't sure. Anyway, there was nothing to tell yet, really. They were only on their second date.

And what if their relationship was short-lived? Why cause needless tension or concern in the family? Better just to give the relationship time and space to see if it grew into anything. "You're right. We should use a little discretion for now."

He leaned in and whispered in her ear, "I've never sneaked around with anyone before."

"We are not sneaking around. We're using *discretion*—your word."

"Sneaking sounds more fun."

Their gazes met, locking together. It was that beautiful time of evening when everything took on a lovely rosy glow, and the sight of him stole her breath.

The hint of humor fell from his expression as his eyes grew more serious. "I had a wonderful time tonight."

"Is it over already?"

"I didn't want to forget to tell you." His focus dropped to her mouth.

Her lips tingled with want, even though a week ago she'd cautioned him to take it slow. Nevertheless, she could've cheered when he leaned closer and brushed her lips with his. So soft. So reverent. So delicious.

And already over. He withdrew a bit, his warm breath still a whisper on her lips. "Slow enough?"

Her body clamored for more. More kissing, more touching, more, more, more. But as seconds ticked away, her brain engaged cell by cell. Taking it slow was smarter. There was a lot on the line and they had all the time in the world.

"Perfect."

Chapter 29

*H*ey." Will greeted his father, who joined him in a corner booth at Applebee's. Dad wore work pants and a button-down with the Dane Electric logo. His mouse-brown hair seemed to have receded in recent days, making his forehead seem broader. He had ruddy skin and hooded hazel eyes that made him appear tired.

"Hey yourself." Dad grabbed the menu. "I only have forty minutes for lunch. Know what you want?"

"Yeah." Dad was ten minutes late so Will had had plenty of time with the menu. But at least his father had been the one to reach out for a change. Will hadn't heard from him since he'd called his dad on his birthday two and a half weeks ago and hadn't seen him in a couple months.

The server appeared and took their orders, promising to return shortly with drinks.

"So what you been up to lately?" Dad asked. "Your mom said you had a girl."

Their parents spoke on occasion, mostly about Will, and managed to keep it cordial. "Addison. But it's new—we've only been on two dates. She's part of the crew where I work."

"What's she like?"

"She's great." His lips curved of their own volition. "She and her parents recently moved to Wilmington from Atlanta and she finished her senior year here. She's saving up for college like me, so she's really understanding when it comes to being frugal."

"That's good."

Will warmed to the subject. He'd been bitten by the love bug, something he never expected at this point in his life. "She wants to be a psychologist. She's very smart."

"Like a therapist?"

"Yes, specifically she'd like to work with children." Will told him more about Addison—her favorite high school subjects, a little about her personality, and her dog, Mason, that she'd found abandoned at a park last summer.

When the server returned with their drinks, Will noticed his dad's eyes had practically glazed over, so he changed the topic. "What do you think of NC's chances this year? They've really beefed up their defensive line with their recruits."

His dad embraced the new topic and they talked about sports for a while. The conversation then turned to Dad's girlfriend, Jody, who had two young boys and worked as an administrator at a local community college. She was nice enough to Will, though he sometimes got the feeling she wished her boyfriend were unencumbered by a son.

Soon the server returned with their food—a whisky bacon burger for Will and a pasta dish for his dad.

"So how's it going with you?" Will asked after he finished his burger. "How's your job?"

Dad's eyes lit at the subject. "Going good. They keep me busy, which keeps the money coming in. There's a shortage of trade workers right now, so I'm putting in a lot of hours and making good money."

It was nothing Will hadn't heard before. "That's great."

Dad set his fork down and leaned into the table. "So you remember my buddy Steve, who owns Hardin Home Improvements? He helped me install our windows way back when."

Will sensed where this was going. "Sure."

"Last week he was telling me about this program he started. They hire apprentices for their trade workers and it serves as a training program. They have a similar setup for plumbers, carpenters, and electricians. You can make money while learning a trade that'll pay off big-time down the road. You should think about it."

So that's what this lunch was all about. Why should Will be surprised? And yet a hollow spot opened in his gut. "I already have, Dad. I respect what you do, but I want to go to college."

"You'll waste all your good years in school and graduate with a mountain of debt. Then what are you gonna do?"

"It'll be worth the time and money to follow my dreams. And the debt won't be that bad. I've got grants and academic scholarships to help subsidize the cost."

Dad's lips twisted. "Well, ain't you smart. You shouldn't turn your nose up at the trades—we make good money."

"That's not what I'm doing. I realize the trades are a valid choice. It's just not for me."

Dad tossed his napkin on his empty plate. "But good enough for your old man, huh?" He pulled a credit card from his wallet and swiped it in the tabletop kiosk. "I told your mother she was spoiling you. Coddling you. Told her it was a mistake. *Following your dream.*" He rolled his eyes. "While you were screwing around on the basketball court after school, you shoulda been working a job."

"I worked all through—"

"If you'd played your cards right, you'd be making a good living by now, but instead you're planning to spend half your life in school racking up a bunch of debt."

Will gritted his teeth. "Why can't you understand that I want to study science? Maybe be a neurosurgeon? I could make a difference in people's lives."

His brows furrowed. "Unlike me, you mean?"

"No, Dad, that's not what I mean. It's my life, isn't it? Shouldn't I get to choose what I do with it?"

Dad grabbed his card from the machine, then slid from the booth. "Sure, you're nineteen years old and know it all. I'm only forty-eight—what do I know?"

Will's heart sank as his father strode from the table. He'd never approved of Will. He was always undercutting him, making him feel like he should be ashamed for getting good grades or playing on the basketball team. Was it any wonder Will wanted to find his biological father?

If Will could flip a switch and be like his dad, he would. The man could fix anything. He was the handiest guy around. And he did make good money.

But Will wasn't like him. He wasn't like him at all, and he was tired of feeling like a failure for it.

Chapter 30

The sound of rushing water greeted Josh, Maggie, and Zoey as they entered the aquarium at Fort Fisher.

"Look at the otters, Mommy!" Zoey rushed over to the window to watch the animals frolic in the water.

"Aren't they cute?" Brad and Becky had brought her daughter here a few years ago, but Zoey didn't remember.

"Do you hear them chirping?" Josh asked.

The sounds echoed through the cavernous building.

Zoey cocked her head, listening. "Otters *chirp?*" Her voice rose on the last word as she crinkled her nose.

He chuckled at her expression. "They sure do."

Josh strolled along the pavers with Maggie while Zoey rushed from one lookout to the next. When they stopped he brushed Maggie's hand with the back of his in a way that could've only been deliberate.

Her skin tingled at the touch, and a sidelong glance revealed Josh gazing longingly at her.

Awareness flickered between them, reminding Maggie of last night's amazing sunset kiss. What it had lacked in length, it more than made up for in warmth and fervor.

"I do love that little girl of yours," Josh whispered. "But I sure wish we were alone right now."

"What would you do?"

His gaze dropped to her lips, lingering there for a beat. "Exactly what you want me to do."

His lips were inviting, the lower one slightly plump and pink. She could almost feel the bristle of his five-o'clock shadow against her cheek.

"Look, Mommy! Look at the funny fish."

They joined Zoey at the tank and pointed out the different kinds of fish, then followed along as she wandered from one display to the next. Josh took her picture by a fake alligator, then they moved on to the next section where Zoey dropped to her knees to play in the man-made tide pool with several other children.

Josh and Maggie had been careful to keep their interactions platonic around Zoey. She was verbal enough to tell anyone who might listen that Uncle Josh and Mommy had been holding hands.

And it was becoming increasingly difficult to keep those boundaries in place. It seemed that ever since she'd given herself permission to care for Josh, her heart had been in a free fall. When he wasn't there, she missed him and made mental notes of the things she'd share with him.

And when they were together, she wanted to touch him. She wanted to bask in his obvious affection. She was starting to wonder why she'd been so insistent they take it slow. She knew him better than practically anyone. Admired him. Respected him. He'd always been so good to her and Zoey, offering support and comfort. The romantic feelings were a natural extension of the foundation they'd built over many years.

But it was already the end of July and she was due back at school August 18. Just over three weeks away. Somehow summer was almost over. How would their relationship evolve in the long term?

She couldn't believe she was even thinking long-term—they'd only been dating one week!

He caught her staring and the corner of his lips tipped upward.

That familiar buzz of chemistry washed through her like a drug. To heck with all the fretting. She just couldn't resist that face. "After the aquarium why don't you stay for supper?" No idea what she'd fix. She hadn't been to the grocery store in a week. But she wanted more time with him. Time alone with him after Zoey went down.

"Why don't we pick up pizza on the way home?"

She smiled. "Perfect."

"JELLYFISH ARE MY favorite," Zoey proclaimed as they headed toward the exit.

"What do you like about them?" Maggie asked.

"They're weird and swooshy."

"Couldn't have said it better myself, kid." Josh pushed open the door, and they exited to a huge deck that offered a play pad with climbing equipment. Picnic tables surrounded the playground.

"Come play with me, Uncle Josh. Please."

"Very nice manners. I'll come play but you have to go through the tunnel with me."

"You're too big for the tunnel."

"Wanna bet?"

"I'm gonna grab some water," Maggie called as Zoey dragged him toward the playground.

Maggie got two bottles from the vending machine and settled at an empty table where she could watch them. A while ago, near the fish tank, they'd run into a pretty young thing, Amanda, whom Josh had gone out with "a time or two." It seemed they couldn't go anywhere without running into one of his former girlfriends.

But Maggie had put the encounter from her mind as Josh seemed singularly focused on her and Zoey. They gawked at the sea creatures in the two-story aquarium, took the requisite photos with the giant megalodon jaw, and stood hypnotized by the graceful movements in the towering jellyfish tank. She was sorry she hadn't brought Zoey here earlier this summer.

But she'd been busier than she'd expected with four swim students, meeting with each of them twice a week. She'd also been squeezing in some lesson plans, though her heart wasn't in it.

She got out her phone and returned a text from Erin and a teacher friend from back home, asking about a lunch date before the school year started.

She was halfway done with her water when Josh sat on the other side of the table. "She found a few friends."

"She usually does." Maggie lowered her phone and watched Zoey lead three younger children through the rope maze, giving instructions as they went. "Do you think she's too bossy?"

"She's a born leader. It's a good quality." He smiled as Zoey helped a little boy across the rope bridge. "She's a good kid, Mags. You're doing a great job."

"I hope so. It's not been easy."

"Ethan would be so proud of you. I hate that he's not around to see how sweet and spunky she is—that's all you. But sometimes she has this expression that reminds me so much of him."

"When she discovers something new? I've noticed that too. Also that pouty look when she sulks."

Josh gave a wistful smile. "He did sulk on occasion."

It used to drive her crazy. But she'd give anything to see that pouty face again.

Neither of them had to mention that the five-year anniversary of his death was just twelve days away. It was no doubt heavy on all their minds. His parents would return in about a week, and they would release Ethan's ashes on the seventh as planned. "Are your parents looking forward to coming home?"

"I think Dad's ready. Mom's having a blast, though. But she's missing the grandkids pretty bad."

"We FaceTimed a few days ago. And they'll get to spend some quality time with Zoey before we head back home." They'd invited Zoey and her to stay until Maggie had to return to work.

"I'm glad you're staying a bit longer. After that I guess we'll be doing some long-distance dating." His gaze locked on her. "Is that too presumptuous of me?"

"I was wondering the same thing. I haven't dated long-distance since Ethan was in college—and that didn't go so well if you'll recall." They'd argued a lot during his freshman year. Maggie felt so insecure about his being away at college. So afraid of losing him. What if he found another girl? What if he forgot about her? She was so sure he'd break up with her.

She didn't relish the thought of going through that again.

"You guys were kids. I'd like to think we've both matured enough to handle any issues that might crop up. We just have to be honest with each other about what we're feeling."

"You're right."

"It's only two hours and we're both off on Sundays."

"And Zoey and I could come here some weekends."

"I'd love that—and so would the rest of the family."

But would they love the idea of Josh and her together? That remained to be seen. She hated the thought of causing turmoil in the family. They should probably talk about when they'd tell his family. But Maggie was loath to spoil the beautiful day with worries about that.

"Do you think you could ever live in Seabrook again?"

Her attention darted his way even as surprise stole the words from her mouth. Somewhere in the recesses of her mind, she'd thought about it this summer. But she hadn't expected him to address the subject so soon in their relationship.

He gave her a sheepish look. "Sorry. I'm getting ahead of myself."

She laughed. "Well, we have only been dating one week."

"Right. No, you're right." He glanced back to the playground, a mottled flush climbing his neck. "I didn't mean to rush you."

She'd never seen him blush and it was so darn cute. She put a hand over his and waited until she had his attention. "For what it's worth, I'm enjoying every minute of it. And I realize your business roots you here. I'm dating you with a full understanding of that fact."

"Fair enough."

On the table her phone buzzed with an incoming call. She glanced down as Derrick's name flashed on the screen. And now it was her turn to blush. She rejected the call, but not before Josh noticed the caller's name. And she could see by his downturned lips that he recognized the name.

"He's only called a couple times."

"I didn't say anything."

"You didn't have to."

He offered her a thin smile. "Like you said, we've only been dating a week. We haven't even talked about exclusivity."

They hadn't. But the truth was, Maggie wasn't warming to Derrick, and the thought of Josh going out with another woman—like that pretty Amanda—pricked her with jealousy. She didn't want to date anyone else, and she didn't want Josh to either.

She folded her arms on the table, holding his gaze as silence rolled out between them. "Maybe we should."

He searched her face for a long moment. "Talk about being exclusive or . . . ?"

The radical thumping of her heart created a tsunami of thoughts. Had she spoken out of turn? Maybe she was the one rushing things now. But her feelings for him had grown more quickly than she'd ever expected. "How would you feel about that?"

His eyes lit and his brow did that quirky jump just before he broke into a smile. He took her hand. "I'd feel pretty dang good about it."

Relief swamped her. "We're on the same page then."

"Same paragraph, same sentence."

"Same word even."

Her phone buzzed, drawing their attention. Derrick had left a voice mail.

She squeezed Josh's hand. "I'll take care of it this week."

Chapter 31

*M*uch to Josh's dismay, the pizza night at Maggie's never happened. On the way out of the aquarium, Erin called. It was her and Patrick's anniversary and their sitter canceled last minute. Owen had plans with his friends and could Josh please, please come watch Mia for a couple hours so they could make their reservation?

He never minded spending time with his nieces and nephew, but he'd been anticipating some alone time with Maggie. That didn't happen, however, and now, after a long week at work, complete with an engine problem and bad weather, Josh was eager to collect on that rain check.

The delicious tangy scent of the pie rose from the box on his passenger seat. They'd have supper and he'd play with Zoey for a bit. And then, at long last, he'd take Maggie into his arms as he'd been dying to do all week.

He'd replayed their recent conversations in his head a dozen times. Recalled the way she'd gazed at him. He couldn't believe she had broached the topic of exclusivity. Couldn't believe that, after all these years, she was officially his girl.

Glancing in the mirror, he caught a glimpse of his dopey grin. Couldn't even blame himself for it. He was the luckiest man in the world. Hopefully she'd dealt with Derrick this week. Josh didn't care to see the man's name appear on her screen again. After watching her with Ethan all those years, he'd experienced enough jealousy to last him a lifetime.

In fact, he was feeling so optimistic that on Monday morning he'd called Jonathan Wells at the Charleston Yacht Club and graciously turned down his job offer. Thank God Josh wouldn't have to sell his business and move away. He would've done so if Maggie hadn't given him a chance, but he was grateful things hadn't worked out that way.

He caught himself whistling as he took the steps to his parents' place. He was a goner. If he didn't know it before, he knew it now.

Seconds after he knocked, Zoey flung open the door and her eyes lit on the box. "Pizza!"

"Hey, what about me?" Josh said.

"Hi, Uncle Josh. Can I carry the pizza?"

Maggie appeared in the foyer, the spiral curls she'd placed in her hair not yet brushed out. "Zoey, I told you not to answer the door without me."

"It's just Uncle Josh."

"But you didn't *know* it was Uncle Josh." Maggie sent him a chagrined smile.

"Sorry!" Zoey scooted off with the pizza.

"That girl." She lowered her voice. "She called me *Maggie* earlier."

Since Zoey was now conveniently around the bend, Josh leaned forward and took advantage of Maggie's sweet lips. She returned his kiss and when her fingers skated up his chest, he reached around and pulled her closer. Aah, this was more like it.

The intended quick peck turned into a long, searching kiss that made Josh go warm with want. When he deepened the kiss, her eager response had his hands roaming over the planes of her back.

"I can't reach the plates!"

They sprang apart at the sound of Zoey's voice, so close by.

Maggie sent him an apologetic look and turned for the kitchen. "Don't climb on the counter."

Sure enough, when they entered the kitchen, Zoey had already pulled up a barstool and was climbing onto it.

Josh lifted her down. "I'll get them, Cupcake. You grab the silverware." He glanced at Maggie's hair. "While Mommy finishes getting ready."

Her hand flew to her head. "I totally forgot. Be right back."

He helped Zoey set the table while she prattled on about their day and finally about the movie they'd watch after pizza. Zoey expounded on the plot as they sat at the table to wait for Maggie.

"She's locked in a tower and her hair is magical." She lifted the pizza box's lid and peeked inside. "Maggie said we can watch it after pizza."

"You mean *Mommy*."

"But you call her Maggie."

"That's true, I do. Everyone else calls her by her first name. But there's only one person in the whole wide world who gets to call her Mommy."

"That's me!"

"Exactly right. It's a special thing to have a wonderful mommy. You're a very lucky little girl."

Maggie entered the kitchen, bestowing a grateful smile on Josh. "The table looks so nice."

"You're late, Mommy. The pizza's getting cold."

"Well then, I guess we'd better get started."

192

The lights were dim and the movie was only halfway over, but already her daughter's eyes were drifting shut. Zoey snuggled between Maggie and Josh on the sofa in her unicorn pajamas, clutching Bunny to her chest.

"She's almost out," Josh whispered.

"I'm not surprised. She woke up early and didn't take a nap."

"You seemed a little frazzled when I got here. Everything okay?"

"It's been a busy day. I had two swimming lessons, then I stopped to get a new water filter for the fridge. The warning light's been on for a few days and I didn't want your parents to come home to a problem. But we went to three different stores to find the right one so I was running late on the way home, and then I got pulled over for speeding."

"Uh-oh. Get a ticket?"

"Just a warning. He was really nice about it. But then I was running even later, which is why I wasn't finished getting ready when you got here."

"You don't have to sweat that stuff. Next time just text me and I'll come later. Or I can entertain Zoey while you get ready."

He was right. Why hadn't she thought to do that one simple thing rather than get all stressed out over being ten or fifteen minutes late? "I should've. But I was distracted all day because apparently my mom found out that I put an end to things with Derrick. She's been calling since yesterday and every time the phone rings, I tense up."

"You haven't called her back?"

"I'm waiting for her to calm down. There's no talking to her when she's frantic." Putting her off might also be a bad idea, but Maggie just couldn't deal with her today. She wanted to anticipate her quiet evening with Josh.

She glanced down at Zoey, whose eyes were closed, her lips parted loosely in sleep. "I think she's out."

Josh's lips curved as he gazed down at Zoey.

She loved the way Josh adored her little girl. He would've made such a good father. Way back he'd mentioned that he and Samantha were considering adoption, but only months after mentioning it, he told Maggie they were separating.

"I'll carry her to bed." Josh carefully eased Zoey into his arms and carried her down the hall. Maggie followed so she could pull back the covers. In a matter of seconds Zoey was sprawled in her bed sound asleep.

The night-light lit the way as Maggie turned on the sound machine. Then they slipped from the room, pulling the door partly closed behind them. Josh took her hand and they settled again on the couch.

"I've been waiting all week for this," he whispered.

"Me too." They'd been dating two weeks now. That was still slow, wasn't it?

She was only vaguely aware of the movie playing in the background, the TV light flickering, as he drew her into his arms. His lips, soft and warm, invited hers to move with his in a dance as old as time.

And she gladly acquiesced. Her hands slid up to his face, where the soft scrape of his whiskers tickled her palms. He smelled so good, tasted so good. He was simply delicious. A little mewl escaped her throat.

Josh eased back a fraction of an inch, his breath falling hot and ragged on her lips. "You're killing me."

"But what a great way to go."

His chuckle was caught when his lips met hers again.

What a way to go, indeed. She'd wondered if their first kiss had been exaggerated by time and imagination. But no. He was as skilled as she remembered. His gentle caresses, the soft sweep of his lips . . . She was intoxicated with it. With him.

She fell backward into the nest of the couch and his weight came down on her.

"We always seem to end up this way," he said against her lips.

She brushed her mouth against his. "Mmm."

"Tell me to slow down."

"Slow down."

"That wasn't very convincing."

"We're just kissing."

"You wanted to go slow."

"Stop talking." She reached up and took his mouth, her fingers sliding into the hair at the nape of his neck. She didn't want to rush things. But his kisses were like a drug. He swept her away, filled her with sensations she'd never had. Or maybe she just couldn't remember. A thought for another time and place.

Right now she just wanted to relish the reverent way he touched her face. Savor the soft exploration of his mouth. Wallow in the way he made her feel so wanted and adored.

"So this is how it is!"

They sprang apart at the shrill voice.

It took Maggie's drugged mind a moment to clear.

Then the light snapped on.

And like a bad dream, there, at the threshold of the entryway, stood her mother.

Chapter 32

*O*f all the times to leave the door unlocked. Maggie blinked against the sudden brightness. *"Mom?"*

Her mother's eyes swung to Josh and flew open wide. Her hand shot to her mouth. "Oh!"

Maggie sprang to her feet. "What are you doing here?"

"You're—you and *him?"*

"Lower your voice, Mom. Zoey's sleeping in the—"

"Maggie!" Mom grimaced. "Dear God in heaven, what can you possibly be thinking?"

Josh rose, his face like stone. "She asked you to lower your voice, Mrs. Hughes."

Mom narrowed her eyes at Maggie. "How *could* you? He's your *brother.* It's immoral what you're doing. What would Ethan say about this?"

Maggie's face went nuclear. Not only because of her words but because Josh was hearing them too. "What are you doing here, Mom? You can't just barge in and—"

"What am *I* doing here? What is *he* doing here, alone with you, making out on the couch with you like you're a couple of teenagers?" Her gaze drifted pointedly over Maggie's hair.

Face burning, she smoothed it down. "Mom, this isn't a good time."

"I can see that! If you'd simply returned my calls, this could've been avoided. I came to talk some sense into you regarding Derrick. But now I see the truth. I can't believe this has been going on behind my back all summer." She clutched her heart and muttered something to herself—possibly the Hail Mary prayer, though she hadn't set foot inside a Catholic church for forty years.

Josh stepped between mother and daughter. "Maybe it would be best if you got a hotel room tonight. You and Maggie can talk in the morning after you've settled down."

Mom's spine stiffened. She tossed her short black hair. "Don't you tell me when I can speak with my own daughter. She clearly hasn't the sense God gave her."

Maggie closed her eyes. If only the floor would open up and swallow her. "Please don't, Mom."

"This is not the way I raised you! Have all my efforts gone to waste that you'd shame me this way? Ethan must be rolling over in his grave, and who could blame him! Messing around with his brother of all people. *Your* brother."

"We don't see it that way," Josh said firmly.

"Oh, I'm sure." Mom gave a harsh laugh. "But I'll bet your parents do!"

Maggie glanced at Josh, but he hadn't taken his eyes off her mom. A shadow flickered on his jaw as his muscles twitched.

Mom's gaze toggled between them. "You haven't told them. You've been hiding this from them. They're gallivanting all over Europe, clueless that their daughter-in-law is betraying their dead son!"

"Stop it, Mom!" She had to get her out of there. Maggie sidled around her and snatched the door open. "You need to leave now. Please. We'll talk tomorrow."

Mom didn't budge. "I'm only telling you the truth. If you're embarrassed, it's because what you're doing is shameful. I go out of my way to set you up with a nice young eligible man and you betray me this way—and after all I've done for you. You're ungrateful and you only think of yourself."

"That's it." Josh took Mom's elbow and ushered her toward the door, his expression lethal. "Your daughter asked you to leave."

At the door Mom shook off his hand, glaring at Maggie. "We are not finished talking about this, Maggie. I have to drive back tonight, but I'll be calling you tomorrow."

She wouldn't be staying. Maggie almost sagged in relief.

"And you'd better answer! Hopefully you'll have come to your senses by then." Mom slammed the door behind her.

Maggie didn't realize she was shaking until Josh pulled her into his arms. It felt as if all her energy had drained through her feet, leaving her as weak as an overcooked noodle. She buried her heated face in the cradle of Josh's shoulder. She couldn't even look at him! The things her mother said repeated in her mind on an endless loop. Shame washed over her.

His hands moved over her back, soothing. "You okay?"

The knot in her throat choked off her words. She nodded.

"I wanted to throttle her. I've never seen her like that. I mean, I knew from the things you've said she could be a real piece of work. But wow. I'm so sorry, honey."

"I'm fine." This wasn't even anything new, though her mother usually saved her worst behavior for when they were alone. Mom preferred that everyone else adore and respect her, then they'd believe that Maggie was crazy when she complained about her.

"She's wrong about all of it, Mags. You know that, right?"

Maggie wasn't so sure. She was too busy trying to forget all the times her mother had flung many of the same words at her. She'd realized sometime during high school that her mother was a narcissist. When Maggie was older she'd researched the topic, read a dozen books on the subject. But that knowledge gleaned never seemed to stop the damaging effects of her mother's harsh words.

"I'm not your brother. Your mother's only mad because you dumped the man she wanted you with."

"I know."

"What's so special about this guy anyway? Why does she even care who you're dating?"

"He's the son of one of her board members."

Josh sighed. "Of course. It's all about her. Having him as a son-in-law would give her some kind of advantage at work, I take it."

"I guess so."

"You can make your own decisions. You're a perfectly capable woman. A wonderful person. It was all I could do to stand there and listen to her say those things about you."

"Thank you for making her leave."

"I wanted to clap a hand over her mouth. She's wrong about you, Maggie." He took her face in his hands and stared intently at her. "You know that, don't you?"

"I know." In her head anyway. When Mom was slinging words like darts, however, it was sometimes hard to convince her heart.

But what if Mom had a point about Josh? Deep down Maggie had been worried his parents might view things the same way as Mom. Might see her relationship with Josh as a betrayal to Ethan. "Do you think your parents will be okay with this?"

He didn't answer for a moment. "I don't know. It'll probably come as a surprise. They might need some time to adjust. I was thinking we should wait till after the anniversary to tell them."

She'd hoped he would allay her fears. But he'd given her honesty at least. Brad and Becky definitely shouldn't come home to this startling news on top of the anniversary they were all facing. Waiting a couple weeks made sense. They'd tell them before Maggie went back home.

"Maggie . . ." His gaze sharpened on her. "You're not having second thoughts, are you? About us? Please don't let what your mom said scare you off."

"I'm not." She gave a wan smile. "She knows just how to get to me, though."

His thumbs swept her cheeks as he stared at her adoringly. "Don't let her ruin this. We're just getting started and I'm loving every minute. I think you are too."

Her heart buckled. Until ten minutes ago Maggie couldn't remember the last time she'd been so happy. He swept her away. "I am."

His expression softened. "I don't want to lose this. I don't want to lose you." He pressed a kiss to her forehead, then glanced toward the door. "Does she always bust right into your house like that?"

"Pretty much." Though at home Maggie was more deliberate about locking the door for that very reason. She had no reason to do that here.

He drew away and took her hand. "Come sit down with me. Let me hold you awhile."

"If you don't mind, I think I just want to go to bed. I'm so exhausted all of a sudden."

He squeezed her hand. "Of course."

She walked him to the door, where he turned and gave her a soft, soothing kiss. "If you need to talk, call me, no matter the time."

"Okay."

Then he pressed one last kiss to her lips and slipped out the door, leaving Maggie alone with her thoughts.

Chapter 33

*M*aggie watched with pride as Keondre took another lap across the pool. His hands sliced rhythmically through the water as his legs propelled him forward in a long, lean line. He was already faster than he'd been at their first lesson. He was swimming as straight as an arrow and his sneaky breaths were nice and smooth.

Kyra came up beside her, offering a glass of lemonade.

"Thank you." After standing in the August heat for almost an hour, she found the cold liquid welcome and refreshing. "Mmm. Very nice."

"The key to good lemonade is simple syrup."

"I'll take your word for it."

They watched Keondre turn at the far wall and begin another lap.

"I can't believe how far he's come with you in just a matter of weeks. We're ecstatic with his progress."

"He's eager to learn. It's a joy teaching such a coachable athlete."

"His confidence has soared. He's so sad you only have one more lesson together. We both are."

"I am too." Maggie also hated the thought of leaving—not only Keondre, but Erin and Josh and Seabrook. In all her efforts to avoid the island since Ethan's death, she'd forgotten this was her home too. There were good memories here. Memories worth hanging on to.

"He'll be fine. I'll give him some things to work on. He'll make the team and he'll learn a lot more from his coach."

"Are you sure we can't hide you away in our attic? We'll take real good care of you."

Maggie laughed. "Tempting. But I can't afford to quit my day job." Though the lessons had ended up being more lucrative than she'd imagined. She hadn't planned on making any money this summer.

Kyra sipped her lemonade. "Pity."

Ten minutes later, Maggie started her car and put the windows down to release the stuffy air. It was after one now. Keondre's lesson was her third today—she'd grouped them together to make childcare more feasible.

Today she'd left Zoey with Sharon. Her neighbor's granddaughter was visiting for the day, and the woman thought the girls might enjoy each other's company.

Maggie had just been glad for something to do. Ever since she'd awakened this morning, she dreaded her mother's phone call. Speaking of which . . .

Maggie checked her phone—and her stomach dropped at all the notifications from her mother. When Mom hadn't reached out first thing this morning, Maggie assumed she was planning to let her stew awhile. It was one of Mom's favorite games: Guilt Maggie, Then Ghost Her for Punishment.

But Maggie had made a tactical error. She should've checked her phone between lessons because Mom had called seven times and left three—no doubt scathing—voice mails.

Crap.

From the pier Josh waved good-bye to Big D. They had a one-hour lunch break between their morning and afternoon tours, which they often took together. But Josh had some bills to pay, and he often used a table on the main deck to work on them during his lunch break.

Will disembarked the *Carolina Dream*. "I'm off to lunch. See you at one."

"Hey, thanks for helping out with the sick passenger." A woman had gotten physically ill and didn't quite make it to the railing. According to Big D, Will cleaned up the mess and directed her to the middle of the boat once her misery subsided.

"No worries, man. All in a day's work." With a wave Will took off.

Josh went to the upper deck and grabbed the stack of bills from the pilothouse. When he came back downstairs, his sister was boarding. With her short blonde hair up in a stubby ponytail, she looked about eighteen. The summer sun had bronzed her skin and a pair of white shorts and a pale pink top set off her tan.

"Well, hey there," he said. "What are you doing here? Everything okay? The kids?"

Her smile didn't quite reach her green eyes. "The kids are fine."

"Well, what is it? You haven't been down here since I took the family on *Carolina*'s maiden voyage on the river."

"You got a minute?"

Something had upset her—hopefully she hadn't spotted Will on his way out and thought she'd seen Ethan's ghost. "Sure, my next tour isn't for another hour." He ushered her to one of the booths that overlooked the river and sat across from her.

Erin pinched her shirt and fanned herself. "Feels good in here. It's been miserable outside this week."

"Gotta be close to a hundred."

"It's the humidity. Even that storm the other day didn't help matters. You can't walk outside without melting."

He observed her as she glanced around the vessel. She'd always been one to settle into a conversation, and even though his curiosity was killing him, he let her.

"You've made some upgrades in here."

"Some paint, new upholstery on the booths, new flooring." He'd done a lot more than that, but he wouldn't bore her with mechanics—electric and plumbing updates. His sister only noticed the aesthetic stuff anyway.

"It's nice. Warm and welcoming."

"The old girl needed some love for sure. I wouldn't have gotten such a great deal on her if she'd looked like this when I bought her, though."

"Business still good? Mom said you hired someone recently."

"Uh, yeah. He's working out real well."

"That's great." Her attention drifted back to him and her expression turned serious. "A while ago I got a phone call from Nora."

He swallowed back a curse. "Maggie's mom?"

"None other. I would've gone straight to Maggie with this, but she tolerates enough from that woman. I wanted to spare her the drama if it just turned out to be a bunch of her mom's narcissistic bull."

He pressed his lips together. Leave it to Nora. She'd spilled the beans about their relationship. "Let's have it."

Erin aimed her eyes at him like a heat-seeking missile. "She was fuming because she's under the impression you and Maggie are seeing each other."

He maintained eye contact, resisting the urge to squirm in his seat. Their gazes tangled the way only a brother and a sister's could.

Erin could always see right through him. But Maggie was her best friend. Should he prevaricate? He put up a mental shield while he decided how to handle this.

Erin huffed. "It's true. You're dating Maggie."

So much for that shield. He couldn't lie to her or even distract her—she was like a dog with a bone at times like this. "It's brand-new, Erin. We've only had two dates." Three if you counted the aquarium and four if you counted last night's pizza—which he wasn't.

"My best friend is dating my other brother and neither of you bothered to mention it? This is a huge shift—and it affects the whole family." She gave her head a hard shake. "She was Ethan's wife, Josh. I feel like the whole world just turned upside down."

"Don't buy into Nora's irrational thinking. We're not exactly committing incest here, you know. Nora's only upset because she wanted Maggie to pair up with the son of a board member to further her own career. That's what this is really all about."

"Dr. Derrick?"

Josh blinked. "He's a doctor?"

"Listen, I know how Nora can be and I don't necessarily share her outrage. But at the same time, I'm having trouble wrapping my mind around this." Her eyes narrowed on him. "And a little heads-up would've been nice. She blindsided me."

He couldn't believe Derrick was a doctor. He was surprised Nora hadn't thrown that in his face last night. He shook the thought away. "Well, that's what she does."

"And yet Maggie confided in *Nora* about your relationship?"

Josh gave a harsh laugh. "Of course not. Her mom walked in on us at the beach house last night and had a hissy fit."

"Walked in on you . . . what?" Erin scowled. "Just two dates, huh?"

"It was just two dates."

"And already there was something to walk in on?"

He glared at his sister. He couldn't believe Nora had gone behind their backs like this. Stirred things up. It shouldn't have surprised him, though.

"All right, fine." Erin crossed her arms. "It's none of my business."

"Finally."

"But this does affect the whole family, whether you like it or not. And it would've been nice if my brother or best friend had at least mentioned it in passing."

"We wanted to let it play out without pressure from the family. We wanted to see how it went."

"And? How's it going?"

"It's going well, Erin, that's how it's going."

"Excuse me for being a little caught off guard here. Maggie and I tell each other everything—or so I thought. I've spoken with her almost every day this summer."

"Don't you dare give her a hard time about this. We were just waiting till the fifth anniversary passed. We didn't want to spring it on the family when we're all about to face that day. Nora's already scolded and shamed her over this—it was painful to witness and all I could do to stop myself from throttling the woman. Maggie was shaking by the time she finally left." Josh pinned Erin with an unwavering stare. "The last thing she needs is her best friend heaping guilt on her too."

Erin held his eye contact. Then she slowly leaned back in the booth, her gaze sharpening on him with a knowing look. "You're in love with her."

He gritted his teeth. He hadn't meant to give himself away like that. "If I am, you're sure not the first person I'd tell."

Erin's expression softened. Then she looked to the window where a model bow tug made its way upstream.

"Don't you dare tell her."

Erin glanced his way, all innocence. "Tell her what?" Then her lips tipped in a warm smile. "Does she feel the same way?"

"I don't know," he grumbled. Shifted in the booth. He knew he should've added some padding to the seat backs.

"I've never seen you quite like this."

"Testy?"

She chuckled, the smile lingering on her mouth. "In love."

He huffed. "Yeah? I was married for four years, remember?"

"Oh, I remember . . ."

He was not going there. Not with Erin, not with anyone.

"You're right about Nora," Erin said. "Maggie's been through a lot. It's a wonder she turned out to be such a wonderful person. Don't worry. I won't give her a hard time."

As Erin's approach softened, his shoulders relaxed. "Well. Thanks for that." He hated to even tell Maggie what her mom had done. Or maybe Nora had already called to gloat about it. She was a master manipulator. And Josh didn't relish the thought of opposing her in this battle.

"There's one more thing," Erin said.

At her serious tone, his gaze swung to hers.

"Nora asked me for Mom's number."

He stiffened. "You didn't give it to her."

"So she could blindside Mom too? Of course not. But she's clearly on a rampage, out to manipulate everyone to get what she wants."

His sister was no dummy. But now, thanks to Nora, they might have a real mess on their hands.

"You should talk to Maggie before this escalates any further."

"I will."

A moment later she leaned forward, eyes twinkling. "You know, I think I could get used to seeing you all dopey-eyed over my best friend."

"Shut up," he muttered. But his lips twitched as he said it.

Chapter 34

$\mathcal{M}$aggie's ears were still ringing with her mother's accusations. Sitting in the Food Lion parking lot, she'd listened to the tirade, steeling herself against the harsh words.

And as she pulled from the lot, she battled the familiar sense of shame and insecurity. She was so tired of feeling this way. Of letting her mother make her feel this way. For years Erin had advised her to seek therapy for the emotional abuse she had endured—was still enduring. Maybe Erin was right.

Maggie's recent therapy had been focused on her grief and loss, but now that those feelings had somewhat abated, maybe it was time to focus on her relationship with her mother. Figure out some way to manage her mother's behavior and maintain her sanity.

When she returned to the beach house, rather than go next door and pick up Zoey, she flittered through the house, dispensing with clutter. She cleared her mind as she did the breakfast dishes and started a load of laundry. By the time she finished she felt calmer.

She was about to run next door when her cell phone rang. At the sight of Josh's face on her screen, her lips turned upward. Remembering the way he'd come to her defense last night, she went all warm inside. Ethan had been supportive about her mother, but Mom only ever showed him her good side. She was quite charming when she wanted to be. He didn't fully understand why Maggie found her so exasperating. As painful as last night had been, at least Mom exposed her true self to Josh.

Maggie accepted the call. "Hi there. On lunch break?"

"Yeah, for a few more minutes anyway. Have you heard from your mom?"

"Oh yeah. She gave me an earful a little while ago. It was basically last night's scene, take two. I'm still trying to shake it off."

"I'm sorry. And I'm really sorry to add to your worries. But Erin tracked me down at the marina. Your mom called her this morning and told her about our relationship."

Maggie palmed her forehead "*What?* Why would she do that?"

"I think we both know the answer to that."

This was not how Maggie had wanted her best friend to find out. "How upset is she? I have to call and explain."

"It's okay. I talked to her. She's fine, honey. She's not upset with you."

"Are you sure?"

"She felt a little blindsided at first, but once I told her we hadn't wanted this to overshadow the anniversary, she understood. In fact, I think we can count on her support—if needed—when we tell my parents."

Maggie could hardly believe it. She wasn't sure she would've been so understanding in Erin's place. "Really?"

"Really. So try to relax a little. Your mom might be adept at getting her way, but she's not a magician. And she's apt to find that the Reynoldses aren't quite so easy to manipulate."

"I'm sorry she's causing all this drama. I hate that she does this stuff." Maggie had worked so hard to keep her mom away from the family. When they'd been planning Maggie's wedding, it was practically an Olympic event.

"This is not your fault. You don't have to apologize for your mother. This isn't exactly the way I hoped our relationship would start out, but we'll get through it. However, we're gonna have to tell Mom and Dad sooner rather than later."

"You're probably right. If Mom reached out to Erin, what's to stop her from calling them too?"

"She, ah, actually asked Erin for their number—but of course she didn't give it."

Why did her mother have to be so manipulative? "Grrr! I can't believe she's behaving this way. Well, yes, I can, but it's still infuriating."

"It'll be okay." Josh's voice was soothing. "Mom and Dad'll be home tomorrow, and we'll just head Nora off at the pass."

If her mother reached them first, she'd try to convince them that Josh and Maggie's relationship was inappropriate at best and incestuous at worst. "Are you sure we shouldn't call them? I'd hate to tell them over the phone, but it would be even worse if my mom ambushed them with this."

"If I thought Nora could get their number, I'd be in favor of calling them. But they're so private with their information—their phone number isn't available online. I checked."

His parents refused to even use a credit card on the internet. "That's a relief. And they don't have any friends in common since they live so far apart."

"Would your mom have any other way of getting their number? Is it written down in your house anywhere?"

"You think I'd actually give my mother a key to my house? I have a trusted friend who's watering my plants. She knows all about my mom. I can't believe she's doing this—and all over some guy she wants me to date."

"You mean . . . the *doctor*?" His tone held a note of humor.

"Erin mentioned that little detail, huh?"

"Are you sure you wanna pass that up for a lowly tour-boat captain?"

"Hey, I happen to be very proud of my tour-boat captain." She bit her lip. She'd felt so defensive of Josh that she'd just given away her feelings. But she had begun thinking of him that way. How quickly that had happened.

"You just called me *yours*," he said softly.

"Guess I did."

A beat of silence ensued. "I like it."

She wished he were here with her right now and not clear across the island. She was eager to build on their already-solid foundation. But they just might have to survive an earthquake first.

"Hold that thought," she said.

Chapter 35

*B*rad and Becky were due into the Wilmington International Airport at eight thirty tonight. Then Josh would pick them up and the rest of the family would meet them at the beach house. Maggie had tried to tell them they'd be jet-lagged, but Becky wouldn't hear of putting off the gathering till the next day. She'd missed her kids and grandkids.

All Saturday night and Sunday morning Maggie fretted about her mother finding a way to reach Brad and Becky. She'd been astonished in the past by her mom's craftiness. She had a wicked way of getting what she wanted.

But Josh was right—she didn't have superpowers. Maybe she'd decided she'd already caused enough turmoil just by revealing their secret to Erin. Maggie could only hope.

After her phone call with Josh yesterday, Maggie had called Erin and cleared the air, going so far as to apologize for hiding their relationship.

"You don't owe me an apology," Erin said. "I admit my feelings were a little hurt at first, but once Josh explained about the anniversary . . . I get it. I really do. And it's still a little weird thinking of you and Josh, you know, *together*. But I'm getting used to the idea. If you make each other happy, I'll be rooting for you guys."

Maggie was enjoying the sunny Sunday afternoon on the beach with Josh and Zoey when he got a text. She glanced his way as an ocean breeze, carrying the scent of coconut sunscreen, cooled her skin.

Josh lifted his sunglasses and squinted at the screen. "Oh boy. That was Mom. They're at LaGuardia and their flight to Wilmington was canceled."

Maggie deflated. Every minute ticking by made her nervous. "Oh no."

"What's wrong, Mommy?" Zoey dug a shovelful of sand from the hole nearby.

"Mamaw and Papaw will be a little late getting home."

"They've got another flight," Josh said. "But it's not till tomorrow morning." He gave Maggie a knowing look. They both wanted to get this big reveal over with.

"They won't be home tonight for the party?" Frowning, Zoey lowered her pail.

"I'm afraid not, honey. We'll have the party tomorrow when they get home." She glanced at Josh. "Did they say what time?"

"Their flight lands at one thirty. Erin will pick them up now since I have a tour." He glanced down when another text came in. "They'd still like everyone to come for supper. We'll have the party then, Cupcake."

"Okay . . ."

Zoey's sulk reminded her so much of Ethan's, Maggie couldn't help but grin. "We'll keep all the decorations up. And maybe you can draw some pictures for the front door."

"Yay! I'm gonna draw one of me with Mamaw and Papaw on the beach."

"I'm sure they'd love that," Maggie said.

Seemingly satisfied, Zoey went back to digging her hole.

"They're gonna be exhausted," Maggie said.

"They're getting a hotel for tonight." He lowered his voice. "They'll get some good rest. Maybe this will work out for the best."

"I'd agree with you if I could just believe my mom won't try to reach out to them."

"If she'd wanted to get hold of them and had a way, she'd have done it by now."

"That's true." Maggie tried to believe it, but she had been tricked by her mother one too many times to underestimate her.

The next evening Josh drove toward the beach house. The party was no doubt in full swing by now. He was eager to see his parents after spending the summer apart. But he was also nervous. He planned to stick around until after Erin's family left. That's when he and Maggie would break the news that they were dating.

He'd spent a lot of time weighing how that information might be received. Maggie was more optimistic than he was. When you grew up with a "golden child" for a brother, you came to accept that you would never quite measure up.

It would've been easy to resent his brother, but Ethan had always been so easy to love. He had been down to earth, humble, and well aware of his own shortcomings. He rooted for his little brother and tutored him when his grades fell—mostly because Josh was too busy with girls and sports to bother studying. But remaining eligible was important and Ethan always stepped in to help when Josh got desperate.

Ethan had always been Dad's mini-me, not only in looks but in interests and intelligence. He'd relished the position—who could blame him? He'd thrived under Dad's mentorship and taken his advice. Their mom was less biased. She'd attended Josh's every game and cheered him on. She was proud of him, though often frustrated by his lack of effort in his classes.

But once the siblings had left the house, Ethan and Erin off to college and Josh into the maritime academy, things seemed to balance out. By the time Josh earned his pilot's license, his parents seemed proud of him. And when he'd started his business and eventually bought the *Carolina Dream*, they'd cheered him on.

But then Ethan had died.

And then, as often happens when someone passes away, his brother became larger than life. The golden child was now immortalized as a hero.

And Josh was okay with that. His brother had been special. He *was* a hero and deserved to be remembered and celebrated. Josh would be the first in line to sing his praises.

All these thoughts haunted him as he turned onto Bayview Drive. A heavy feeling in his gut weighted him. Tonight he had to tell his parents that he was dating the hero's widow.

And he was almost certain that, once again, he would fall short.

"Welcome home," Josh called as he spotted his mom chatting with Erin in the living room, Mia perched on her lap.

Mom's brown eyes twinkled and a smile bloomed at the sight of her son. She set Mia aside, jumped up, and enveloped him in a hug. "Oh, it's so good to get my arms around you! You seem taller."

He chuckled as he let her hang on as long as she wanted. "Pretty sure I haven't started growing again, Mom."

She cupped the back of his head. "And your hair is longer. Are you growing it out? Because that didn't work out so well for you in high school."

He had a cowlick at the crown of his head. "I've just been busy."

She leaned back and took his face in her hands, her gaze sharpening on him. "You look tired. Have you been sleeping?"

"I should be asking you that. You guys have gotta be jet-lagged."

Mom tucked her short brown hair behind her ears. What looked like chandeliers jangled under her lobes as she spoke. "We got a good night's sleep at a Fairfield Inn last night. The staff was so nice. They hunted down a foam pillow for your dad—you know how he hates the feather ones. We went to bed at five and slept till eight this morning. I feel like a new woman."

Maggie entered from the kitchen and leaned against the wall.

It was all he could do not to sweep her up in his arms and kiss her right on her sweet mouth. "Hey, Mags."

"Hey."

"There's my hardworking son." Dad stepped through the French doors. He seemed a few pounds heavier, but a summer in Europe would have that effect.

Zoey slid from his arms, joining Mia on the sofa as Dad pulled him in for a quick hug. "Good to see you."

"You too. Seemed like a great trip."

"It was. But it sure is good to be home in the US of A. Business good?"

"Terrific. I don't think I've ever seen you so tan."

Dad patted his gut. "Or so f—"

"Dad!" Erin said. "Not in front of the kiddos, please." She'd lectured them about complaining of weight issues in front of the children.

"Oh, right, right." Dad's grin widened. "On that note, let's eat!"

By THE TIME they finished the grilled burgers, corn on the cob, and Maggie's deviled eggs, the sun was setting and the temps had fallen to a comfortable eighty degrees. The beach was deserted and the seagulls soared overhead, drifting on the breeze. The ever-present roar of the waves comforted Josh.

He'd been too anxious about the upcoming conversation to eat more than one plateful. But his family had been too busy talking, laughing, and catching up to notice. His parents were full of humorous anecdotes from their trip. And they wanted to know everything that had happened while they'd been away.

Maggie caught them up on the swim lessons she'd been teaching. Mia got a high five for her progress in the pool. Owen had been playing baseball and helping his dad with the landscaping around the church. Erin was preparing to return to her position at the high school in two weeks, same as Maggie.

"And what have you been up to this summer, Zoey?" Mom asked.

"I been building sandcastles on the beach!"

"I hope your mom took pictures," Dad said.

"Of course I did. She's the best little castle builder on the island."

"Only when Uncle Josh helps me. And then we eat supper and he always lets me help put the dishes in the dishwasher 'cause I'm good at that."

She'd made it sound like Josh was there all the time. Which, of course, he was. Josh glanced at Maggie, who began biting her nails.

Dad leaned back in his chair. "Been coming over a lot, have you?"

"Every night," Zoey said. "And he sings to Mommy and me sometimes, especially when he tucks me in. But not when Miss Sharon stays with me 'cause then she tucks me in, but she sings bad."

"Sharon from next door?" Mom addressed Maggie with a strained smile.

"Uh, yeah. She watches Zoey sometimes."

It grew quiet around the table.

Erin shifted.

A frown crouched between Dad's brows.

Mom wore a speculative expression as she glanced around the table, trying to read them like a detective reads a perp.

Josh studiously avoided looking at Maggie. But he didn't want to make eye contact with his parents either. Which left him fiddling with the saltshaker.

Finally Zoey's giggle burst the bubble of suspicion. "Sometimes Uncle Josh kisses Mommy."

Chapter 36

𝒥osh sucked in his breath. Had Zoey really just announced that in front of his entire family?

Everyone at the table froze in place.

A seagull cried out.

A breeze stirred the wind chimes.

He studied the seashell design on the tablecloth as if it held a secret code that would reveal the date and time of the rapture. Speaking of raptures, now would be good.

Erin leaned forward. "Um, Owen, honey, why don't you take your sister and cousin inside to play."

"Aww . . . it was just getting good."

Erin shot him a *Do it right now* look.

The boy stood, reluctance in his sluggish movements. "Come on, guys, let's go inside. I'm just dying to see Zoey's new Barbie doll."

Once the three of them disappeared through the French doors, silence prevailed for a solid century. So much for breaking the news to his parents. And when had Zoey seen them kissing anyway? They'd been so careful. Josh dared to look up.

Dad's frown spread. He glanced from Maggie to Josh. "What's going on here?"

"A lot's happened this summer," Josh said. "We were going to talk to you about it after everyone left."

Mom covered her mouth. "It's true then?"

"You know," Patrick said, "in biblical days it was customary when a man died for his brother—" A thump sounded beneath the table and Patrick winced. "Uh, never mind."

Dad threw his napkin on his plate. His jaw muscles twitched. His eyes bored a hole straight through Josh. "How long has this been going on?"

Josh frowned at the implication. "What are you trying to say, Dad?"

"I'm not saying anything. I'm just asking a question."

Mom set her hand on Dad's shoulder. "Honey . . ."

"It's a reasonable question." Dad shot Maggie an accusing look. "Is that what this summer has really been about? Being close to our son. Our *other* son?"

"Leave her alone, Dad." Every muscle in Josh's body strained against patience. "We've been seeing each other for all of two weeks, but thanks for the vote of confidence."

Mom's expression softened. "He didn't mean—"

"I know what he meant."

Maggie leaned forward. A mottled flush climbed her neck. "Brad, Becky . . . I know this must come as a surprise. It caught me by surprise too. Josh and I have been the best of friends for so long. He's always been there for me—you all have."

"What would Ethan think?" Dad asked Josh. "She's your sister-in-law."

"She *was* my sister-in-law."

"That's right, because your brother's *dead* now."

"Bradley!"

"And somehow, when he asked you to take care of Maggie, I don't think this is what he had in mind."

Maggie's gaze flew to Josh.

Because yes, when Ethan had enlisted he had made that request. "He asked all of us to look out for her. And we have. We would've done that even if he hadn't asked."

Maggie took his mom's hand, her eyes shining with tears. "You guys have been the best. I couldn't have gotten through these past five years without you. Without *all* of you. You're my family. I never expected my feelings for Josh to shift . . . but somehow that's exactly what happened." She squeezed Mom's hand. "I will always love Ethan. He was my high school sweetheart, my husband, the father of my child. But it's been five years and I'm . . . I'm lonely. It's time for me to move on. And I know that must be so hard for you."

"That's not the problem, Maggie." Josh pinned his dad with an unswerving look. "The problem is that I'm not good enough to step into Ethan's shoes."

"Josh!" Mom said. "That's not true."

"Maybe not for you, Mom."

"Oh, honey!"

Dad returned his glare.

His silence was crushing. Maybe Josh had thrown that out there hoping for a denial. Apparently he wasn't getting one. He had to get out of here. He didn't even want to breathe the same air as his dad. Not for another second. "I should go."

Dad leaned forward. "You just had to drop this on us the second we got home? Days before the fifth anniversary of your brother's death?"

Josh's chair gave a loud squawk as he bolted to his feet. "That's my cue."

Mom popped to her feet. "Oh, Josh, stay, and let's talk this out. Don't leave like this. We just need some time to get used to the idea. This is a shock. We never—"

"I think we all need time to cool down, Mom." He worked hard to level his voice. "I'm sorry to have ruined your homecoming party. We didn't want it to happen like this, but—" His gaze flicked to Maggie.

She swiped her cheek as she stood. "I'll explain later after I walk you out."

Josh beat a hasty path to the door. He needed air. He needed space to breathe. He needed to feel like he was good enough in his father's eyes.

But it didn't appear that would ever happen.

Maggie didn't catch up with Josh until she reached the stoop. She closed the door behind her. When he turned to face her, she threw her arms around him and pulled him close. He stood stiff and unresponsive. His muscles were taut, his body was overly warm, and he was shaking.

The scene had been awful on multiple levels. But worst of all was the hurtful blow his dad delivered with his silence. Why hadn't Brad refuted the statement? She tightened her arms around Josh, wanting to shield him from his father's response—or lack thereof. But it was too late. All she could do now was offer comfort.

Finally Josh's arms came around her. He set his cheek against hers. His breaths were slowing. "I'm sorry to leave you with them like this. I'll go back inside if you want me to."

He was thinking of *her*. She stroked his back in long, gentle sweeps. "No. I'll be fine. Josh, I wish you could just step inside my mind and know how much I respect and adore you. You're the best man I know. You're kind and selfless and sweet and strong and funny." She drew back so she could look him in the eyes. The defeat on his face started a dull ache in the center of her chest. "Your parents love you. You must know that."

"Of course they do."

Her husband might have been the golden child—the siblings had often joked about it—but Josh was the unsung hero. He had been by her side every time she needed him. He picked her up when she was a puddle on the kitchen floor. He held her as she wept. Walked the floor with a colicky Zoey when Maggie was exhausted. He was always just a phone call away.

And this summer had only drawn them closer. It only took an open confession from Josh. A shift in her thinking. Permission to open her heart. Once those pieces were in place, the inevitable had happened.

She'd fallen totally and irrevocably in love with Josh Reynolds.

She hadn't even realized until she'd watched him shrink under his father's silent glare. Maggie had always loved Josh. But now she was *in* love with him. How could such a tiny word make such an enormous difference?

"I just don't measure up to Ethan." His flat acceptance of the statement made her want to weep. "I never have."

Her heart cracked. She pinned him with a stare. "If you don't measure up, then why have I fallen head over heels for you? Huh, Josh? Answer me that."

He blinked. His gaze drifted over her face as if measuring her sincerity.

"Yeah, that's right. I said it." And maybe she'd live to regret it. But God help her, it was the truth and he needed to know it.

The muscles in his face seemed to loosen one at a time. Finally he exhaled, the tension leaving his body. "Say it again."

She cupped his face and fell into his hope-filled eyes. "I'm in love with you, Josh Reynolds."

"Oh, Maggie." He closed the distance between them. Brushed her mouth with his in the sweetest, softest touch imaginable. He touched her, kissed her like she was precious.

She wanted to melt right into him. Wanted to absorb his pain and heal his wounds and assure him that he was everything she knew him to be. She told him with her kiss.

A long moment later he drew away until his breath was just a whisper on her lips. "I love you too, Maggie."

A SHORT WHILE later Maggie said good-bye to Josh and slipped back into the house. She stopped in the foyer to catch her breath. Gather her thoughts. She needed a second to process that she and Josh had just professed their feelings.

He loves me.

She palmed her chest. The hope and happiness in Josh's expression heartened her. She clung to the image even as she steeled herself for an uncomfortable evening. She was a houseguest in enemy territory— or so it felt. Time to face the foe.

Erin and Becky fell silent as she entered the living room. Her mother-in-law's eyes were bloodshot, her mascara smudged.

Guilt gave a good hard pinch. "Where's Brad?"

"He and the others went for a walk on the beach." Becky gave her a pained look. "Is Josh okay?"

"He'll be fine."

"Sit down, Maggie. Please."

"I'm gonna go relax on the deck." Erin squeezed Maggie's arm as she passed.

Maggie took a seat catty-corner to the sofa and met Becky's gaze. "I'm truly sorry you and Brad were ambushed like that. That's not the way we wanted you to find out."

"Erin already let us know about your mom calling her and the, uh, implications of that."

Maggie's face tingled with heat. Sometimes it seemed as if her mother ruined everything. "As you know, she can be . . . unreasonable."

"You don't have to say another word. I apologize for my reaction, sweetheart. Maybe I shouldn't have been so caught off guard. You and Josh have always been so close. But in my mind . . . you're still Ethan's wife." Her voice trembled on the last two words.

"You don't have to apologize for being surprised. Honestly, if you'd told me at the beginning of the summer I'd be feeling the way I do—I think I would've been just as shocked."

"I'm sorry about Brad. He overreacted. He—he does that sometimes. You know that. The anniversary has been heavy on our minds these past few weeks. The sense of grief and loss—it just seems never-ending. Those things that came out of his mouth were just a reflection of his pain. I know that's no excuse."

No, it wasn't. "Josh is really hurt."

Becky's eyes teared up. Her lips trembled. "He does love that boy. They might not have much in common, but he's always loved both his sons equally."

Maggie gave a strained smile. "That's a conversation for the two of them."

"Yes, of course. And when Brad calms down he'll certainly have it."

That was good. They needed to clear the air. Josh needed to feel his dad's love and approval. Hopefully Brad could verbalize his feelings in a way that would set Josh's mind at ease.

Until then, maybe Maggie should clear out of Seabrook. She didn't relish the idea of going back home. Hated the thought of being separated from Josh sooner than necessary. But her presence would be a constant reminder of the problem, and she didn't feel like walking on eggshells for the next week and a half. Or subjecting Zoey to that kind of tension.

She turned to Becky. "Maybe Zoey and I should head home a little early. I don't want to make you and Brad uncomfortable in your own home."

Becky grabbed Maggie's hand. "Oh, honey, please don't do that. You are always welcome here and we've so looked forward to time with Zoey. Brad will apologize to Josh. He's already regretting his behavior—take it from a woman who's known him forty years. He'll make this right." Becky tilted her head, eyes glazing over again. "Can I just ask—can you give us a little time to catch up here? You've been 'Ethan's wife' to us for a long time. We didn't see this coming and—just a little time. Please, honey."

It was a reasonable request. It even sounded as if Becky might eventually come to terms with their new relationship. But what about Brad? "Of course."

"Thank you. And you'll stay?"

It might be a bit uncomfortable, but Maggie wouldn't deprive them or Zoey of their time together. "We'll stay."

Chapter 37

*J*osh was in dire need of caffeine. He planted his palms in front of his home coffee machine as the brew trickled into the carafe. The morning news faded into the background as he inhaled the robust aroma of his favorite java.

He'd hardly slept last night. His emotions wavered between crushing disappointment over Dad's reaction and rapturous joy at Maggie's profession of love. Despite the argument with his parents, he'd gone to sleep with a smile on his face.

He couldn't believe after all these years of unrequited love, she finally, *finally*, returned his feelings. It was a day he'd feared would never come. Too good to be true. If he'd known it would only take a heartfelt confession and two weeks of blissful dating, he'd have done it years ago.

But years ago she hadn't been ready. Not even when they'd kissed that first time. Waiting had been hard, but it was the right thing to do. She was ready to move on now. Ready to move on with him.

And that brought him to his parents. He'd called Maggie late last night, wanting to check on her. He hated leaving her there in the middle of so much tension. But she said she was fine. Relayed her conversation with his mom. Dad had apparently been quiet the rest of the night, but Maggie was optimistic they would come around.

He hoped she was right. At this point he couldn't even envision a future without her and Zoey. Now that their feelings were mutual, his thoughts fast-forwarded. She'd hinted that she was open to moving to Seabrook. Was it too soon to go there?

Yes. Too soon. He needed to give her a chance to settle into the relationship. Into her feelings. He needed to give his parents time to accept it. Once they did, they would love the idea of Maggie and Zoey moving back to town. That was just the beginning.

Josh wanted to marry her.

But it was definitely too soon for that. He was getting ahead of himself—not to mention Maggie. But he glanced around his house anyway, planting the seed of thought a little deeper. Would she like living here or would she prefer to buy something together? He enjoyed his little ranch with its open floor plan and cozy backyard, but he wasn't that attached to it. If she wanted to look around, he could be flexible. Who was he kidding? He'd live in a tent in Squire Park if that was what she wanted.

The coffee had stopped brewing and he'd been so busy mooning over his woman he hadn't noticed. He poured himself a mug and took that first glorious sip of the morning.

As he swallowed, the doorbell rang. It was too early for visitors—the sun was barely up. Maggie would've texted him, which left only one possibility.

Barely presentable in a pair of knit shorts and a tee, he set down his coffee and headed for the door. His dad stood on the porch, wearing a sheepish expression, a basketball hooked under his arm.

Josh really needed that coffee. "Good morning."

"Morning. Thought we might shoot some hoops."

This was new. "It's seven o'clock, Dad. And isn't it the middle of the night in Europe?"

"You said you had a court and no one to shoot with. Here I am."

He'd mentioned that in passing last night. "Ooo-kay . . ." Josh opened the door wider. "Guess I'll get my shoes on. Want some coffee?"

"No, thanks."

That made one of them. Josh put on his shoes while Dad wandered around the living room, peering at his photos, browsing his bookshelves.

When Josh was ready he stopped by the kitchen, grabbed his mug, and started chugging. *Ow, ow, ow.* He managed to swallow half, then set down the mug and headed toward the back door. "We can go out this way."

Dad followed him across the patio and toward the unattached garage, complete with basketball court. Once there, Dad bounced the ball to Josh and he made an easy layup.

He'd used the court only a few times since he installed the backboard in the spring. Big D had come over to play once. Maggie and Zoey had played HORSE with him. A fun afternoon. He lifted Zoey to the hoop for her shots. And it turned out that as athletic as Maggie was, she was a terrible shot.

Dad wasn't much better. When he shot from the free throw line, the ball hit the rim and bounced off.

Josh rebounded and passed it back to him.

Dad dribbled the ball awkwardly. "Hey, um, I'm sorry about last night. I was caught off guard. I know I handled it badly." He shot the ball, which hit high on the backboard.

Josh rebounded. "I'm sure the news was a shock."

"Honestly, I just never . . . I need a little time to adjust to that one. But I want to clear that other up first."

Josh jumped and released the ball. It swished through the net.

"You and I have never really talked about . . . when you got sick." Dad caught the ball and turned it over in his hands. "It really scared me, Josh. I dealt with medical emergencies all the time, but when it's your son . . . I didn't cope with it well. I didn't realize it at the time, but I think I pulled away from you. I was so scared of losing you."

Josh thought back. He'd thought his dad had just been busy working all those months. "Are you trying to say you were running from it? From me?"

His dad swallowed hard. Took a shot that missed the board entirely. "I know. What a coward, right? At first I focused on finding you the best doctors around. But after that I guess I left your mom to handle the day-to-day care, using the excuse that she was off in the summer. I practically deserted you in the name of 'providing for the family.' But really . . . I was just scared to death. I kept long hours because when I was working, I didn't have to think about the fact that my son could die." He blinked back tears.

Josh stood motionless. He'd been a boy trying to cope with the effects of chemo, becoming the "sick kid" in his class, trying not to be afraid for his life.

"By the time you were well, I'd put a wall up. To protect myself, is what your mother says. She's probably right about that. She's right about most things. And your brother . . . it was always so easy to find things to talk about. Even Erin, with her interest in psychology and science—we had so much in common. Whereas you and me, we're so different. I know I should've tried harder."

Josh's thoughts were stuck on the first part—the part where he'd been sick. Dad had buried himself in work to run away from it. Josh hadn't had the luxury.

"I know I let you down when you needed me most. I let my wife and the whole family down. You'll never know how sorry I am for that. The regret eats me alive."

Wait a minute. While Dad had been running so hard—had he run straight into the arms of Robyn Jennings? He stared at the man standing before him, looking tired and defeated. Josh tried to dredge up some sympathy. But all he could think about were the times he'd spent bent over the toilet bowl, his mom always nearby taking care of him, comforting him. While his dad was out doing his own thing, succumbing to his fears.

Josh had to know the truth. He had to ask the question. "Is work the only thing you lost yourself in, Dad?"

Dad blinked. Tilted his head. "When you were sick? What do you mean?"

"Yes, when I was sick." He could hardly stand the thought of it. He pinned his father with a look. "Was there another woman? Did you cheat on Mom?"

Dad's head jerked back. *"What?"*

"I want the truth. I need to know."

"What—? Why—?" Lines furrowed Dad's forehead. He broke eye contact and then, seemingly in a daze, wandered over to where the ball lay in the grass and picked it up. When he faced Josh again, his eyes were like ice. He advanced on Josh, stopping an arm's length away. "I'm guilty of a lot of things, son. But I have *never* cheated on your mother. I don't know where you get off suggesting such a thing. I know I said some things yesterday I shouldn't have. I'm sorry for that. And I'm even sorrier for withdrawing when you were sick— sorrier than I can ever say." His voice trembled, his eyes flickering with hurt. "But I don't know where you'd get the idea— Your mother is the love of my life. I haven't so much as touched another woman since the day we met."

He was telling the truth. Dad wasn't capable of lying to his face like that. And now Josh felt like a dog for making the accusation. Wished he could take it back. "I'm sorry, Dad. I was out of line."

He opened his mouth to explain about Will. But unless this whole look-alike thing was just some crazy fluke, he could think of only one other person who could've fathered him. And Josh wasn't opening that can of worms right now.

Dad closed his eyes. Exhaled a breath. Then gave him a questioning look. "Where did that come from?"

"I was angry and I spoke out of turn. I'm sorry." He couldn't take back those words. But at least he knew the truth.

After a moment Dad clapped a hand over his shoulder. Gave him a mirthless grin. "Like father, like son, huh?"

They shot the ball in silence awhile.

Dad finally had a shot that nearly went in. "You know, Josh, I don't say it nearly enough, but I'm proud of you. You're a good man and I love you."

Josh swallowed against the lump in his throat. He'd needed that. "Thanks, Dad."

"How 'bout we just put all this behind us, okay? Can we just move on from this?"

Josh expelled a breath. A lot had been said by both of them. Things he'd have to process later. But he could forgive now. "Gladly."

Dad handed him the ball and Josh dribbled it, then faced the basket. "I hate to bring it up, but there's still the issue of Maggie and me—it's not going away." He shot the ball. It hit the backboard and sank through the net.

Dad retrieved the ball and went to the free throw line. "I can hardly wrap my mind around that right now. But give me a little time, okay? You know I'm not good with change."

A reasonable request. "You got it. I'm sorry to have dumped all this on you guys. I know the timing's bad with the five-year anniversary coming up. We're all a little out of sorts."

"Erin explained all that." Dad shot the ball, releasing it like an arrow from a quiver. It hit the front of the rim and pinged off. Dad grimaced. "Maybe you could give your old man a few pointers. If I'm going to be shooting hoops with my son, I should at least challenge him a little."

Josh grinned at him. "That could be arranged."

"Mom and I thought we'd come along on one of your tours next week. Would that be all right with you?"

"That'd be great, Dad. I'll set you up with some tickets." It hadn't been easy, but they'd somehow managed to clear the air.

Even though Josh now had a new problem to process.

Chapter 38

*T*he gilded sky brightened in increments on Thursday morning. The wind tugged at Maggie's hair as Brad guided the Reynoldses' offshore fishing boat across the water. Maggie hugged the urn on her lap. The entire family had come out for the somber occasion.

Becky sat with Brad in the pilot's cabin. The rest of them sat quietly in the front of the boat. Maggie and Josh were on the starboard side, Zoey on Josh's lap. Across from them Patrick held Erin's hand and Mia sat between them and Owen.

Tensions in the family had faded over the past two days. She and Josh were respectful of Brad and Becky's feelings. It was only fair to allow a period of adjustment, especially in light of today's date.

The casting ceremony had been heavy on Maggie's mind. She'd been talking to Zoey about it for days, making sure her daughter understood, in the simplest of terms, what would be happening.

It had been five long years for all of them. Today they were symbolically releasing Ethan. Giving themselves closure. It was another step in the grieving process—and one she felt ready for. She hoped the whole family was.

The sea was devoid of pleasure crafts this morning, only a few fishing boats bobbing on the waves a distance away. Seagulls cried overhead, hoping for breakfast.

Maggie drew in the scent of briny air as she remembered all the evenings she and Ethan had spent boating as teenagers, fishing, talking, in a simpler version of the boat they now rode on. Together their skin had browned under the summer sun as they'd laughed until they cried and fallen madly in love.

She would store up those memories and pass them on to Zoey as she grew older. She would keep Ethan's memory alive for her, as would Ethan's family. They would continue making sure Zoey knew who her daddy was. Maggie peered at the point where the golden sun melted into the shimmering sea.

I promise.

Brad slowed the boat and it soon came to a stop, bobbing in the water some three miles out to sea. When Brad and Becky emerged from the pilothouse, the group came to their feet.

"All right then." Brad took Becky's hand and the others continued the spontaneous chain of connection around the circle.

Then Brad bowed his head and the morning seemed to hush all around them. Maggie closed her eyes, letting the stillness of the moment wash over her.

"God in heaven," Brad said, "we know our boy's already with You, and we're so grateful for the peace that knowledge brings. We want to thank You for giving Ethan to us for thirty-two years. While we wish it had been longer, we're grateful for every day he was with us and we'll treasure the memories the rest of our lives." His voice broke off at the last words.

After a brief silence Becky picked up the prayer. "Be with us, Lord, as we continue on without Ethan. Comfort us, guide us. Help us remember that though we're releasing his ashes, we're not letting go of him. We'll just hold him in our hearts from now on. Amen."

"Amen." Maggie swiped a tear from her cheek and offered a re-assuring smile to Zoey.

Brad and Becky stepped quietly to the railing and the others followed. Maggie stood beside Becky, and Josh came along on her other side. He lifted Zoey into his arms so she could see over the railing.

Together Becky and Maggie tipped the urns, releasing the ashes into the air. The wind caught the remains and carried the gray cloud until it dispersed like a vapor over the sea.

"Look, Mommy," Zoey said in wonder. "Daddy's flying."

Maggie swallowed against the lump in her throat as she grabbed her daughter's hand. "He sure is, honey. He sure is."

Chapter 39

*T*he next week passed uneventfully for the Reynolds family. They seemed to emerge from the scattering of Ethan's ashes in a more peaceful place. Josh was relieved at the passing of the anniversary. All the momentous occasions surrounding Ethan's death had been marked with both sadness and closure. A feeling that he'd overcome yet another hurdle in this long journey called *grief*. This one seemed more significant than the others.

This week his parents had joined him on the *Carolina Dream* for his two-hour tour. It felt good to have their support, their approval. Josh had been processing all his father had told him. In the end, parents were only human. They did the best they could. At least his dad told him the truth and was trying to improve their relationship. Josh would do his part.

He'd also enjoyed time alone with Maggie this week. His parents had even offered to watch Zoey. Everything seemed to be heading the right direction.

But inside Josh a storm was brewing.

His dad's denial of the affair was never far from Josh's mind. Because if Dad hadn't fathered Will, as far as Josh could see, that left only Ethan. But he'd been dating Maggie back then, and Josh couldn't believe his brother would've cheated on her.

239

Was it possible Will's dad was his biological father and the boy's uncanny resemblance to Ethan really was just some random fluke?

In an effort to learn more, Josh decided to do a little fishing. So a few days ago when he'd been eating with the crew, he asked Big D about his adoptive father. Josh was just trying to figure out how to finagle the information from Will when, like a gift from heaven, the boy offered up that his dad hadn't come into his life until he was five.

A gift, and yet a punch in the heart. Every moment since then, Josh had been torn up inside. There was too much evidence for this to be a coincidence. He had to tell Maggie about his dad's denial. About Will's dad. He couldn't keep that knowledge a secret from her. He just wasn't built that way.

Not to mention all the other people involved. If all was as he suspected, his parents had a grandchild they didn't know—from the son they'd lost. Zoey had a brother. Owen and Mia, another cousin. Erin and Patrick, a nephew.

And Josh couldn't forget about Will—especially not when they worked together daily. He'd gotten to know the guy pretty well the past month. He was a good kid. Thoughtful, hardworking, helpful. They shared a love of sports, even if they rooted for different teams. And it seemed Will had a biological father he didn't know about—would never have a chance to meet. But he also had an extended family. A family who would embrace him and love him unconditionally.

Josh ruminated on the situation as he drove to pick up Maggie for what was sure to be a difficult date. The more he weighed the facts, the more convinced he became. Dread simmered in his stomach. The rain picked up and he put the wipers on. Had Ethan known about the boy? Josh couldn't imagine he had. Josh had enough trouble conceiving that he'd ever cheated on Maggie—and left the mess for his brother to clean up.

"Did you really do this, Ethan? She did not deserve that. Doesn't deserve this. And now I have to be the one to tell her. Thanks a lot."

Maggie was gonna take this hard. Who could blame her? She would learn her dead husband had likely cheated on her—albeit when they'd been dating. But loyalty was everything to Maggie. When Ethan had gone off to college, she'd been so worried he'd fall for another girl. Josh and Erin had done everything they could to allay her fears.

But she'd been right after all.

She would be so hurt, confused, and angry. This would turn her world upside down—and so soon after she'd finally found her footing again. Josh felt like a heel for doing this to her. He just didn't see any other option. She would return home in two days and he'd put it off as long as he could.

He tried to focus on the positive. They had made some wonderful memories this week. His thoughts drifted back to Friday night, when they'd gone to Erin and Patrick's for a barbecue and a swim. After supper he and Maggie had a few moments alone in the deep end. He'd caught her around the middle and tugged her to the side where he'd kissed her the way he'd been wanting to all week. He lost himself in the coconutty smell of her hair, the sweet taste of her mouth, the gentle curves of her waist. Her skin was warm and silky smooth. Her lips pliant beneath his own. He wanted to stay right there all night, wrapped up with her like—

Suddenly, she was gone, fluttering away, as peals of laughter carried from the patio. His nieces had invaded their private party. Maggie tossed a coy glance over her slender shoulder. His mind and body slowly shifted gears as she sliced across the pool. He'd forgotten how effortlessly she glided through the water. Moments later when she emerged from the pool, he half expected her to have sprouted fins or a mermaid's tail.

On Saturday Maggie had finished the last of her swim lessons. She was feeling a bit melancholy about leaving her students, so Josh distracted her with a trip to the aquarium with Zoey. On Sunday Josh had taken Maggie to The Wharf, arguably the nicest restaurant in town. They danced afterward—only slow songs for that swanky establishment. Josh wasn't complaining. Ever since she'd professed her feelings, he'd felt free to hold her and kiss her and show her how much he adored her. When she did the same in return, he felt like a new man.

They hadn't seen each other for three long days, but they'd spent hours on the phone each night and exchanged frequent texts during the day.

Josh turned into his parents' drive and shut off the ignition, a heaviness weighing him down. He would take Maggie out for supper and then he'd break the news.

Josh was in an odd mood. Maggie couldn't put her finger on it. His exchange with his parents and Zoey seemed normal enough. He swept Zoey into his arms, then chased her around the house with tickle fingers. And the second they stepped outside he swept Maggie into his arms. "You look beautiful. I missed you."

"I missed you too."

He brushed his lips slowly across hers. "Three days is too long."

But now as he drove to the restaurant, she couldn't banish the suspicion that something was wrong. Maybe it was the way his hands gripped the steering wheel. Or the tension of his thigh beneath her palm. Whatever it was, it nipped at her like an icy wind.

The wipers arced across the windshield, momentarily clearing the glass. A bank of gray clouds obscured the evening sunlight as a storm front closed in.

She glanced at Josh. "Everything okay over there?"

He tossed her an unconvincing smile. "Yeah. You hungry?"

"For seafood gumbo? Always. I've been meaning to get over to the Seafood Shack all summer. I can't believe how fast it's gone by. That I'm going back to school in four days. That Zoey's about to start her second year of preschool. She's growing up so fast. Also, I'm not quite ready to face my mother. She called today. She's still angry about Derrick and when I wouldn't give in to her demands, she hung up on me. She won't make it easy, and living in the same town again, it'll be difficult to avoid her."

She glanced at Josh as he turned into the restaurant's lot. His brows bunched together and his eyes were focused straight ahead.

He rarely missed an opportunity to tease her about Dr. Derrick. Had he heard a word she'd said? "Josh?"

"What?" He glanced her way before swinging his truck into an empty space. "Sorry. My mind's someplace else."

"I can see that. Why don't you tell me what's going on."

Josh turned off the ignition and the wipers stopped their incessant swishing. They unbuckled their belts. "Why don't we eat first? I have an umbrella in the back." He reached between the seats.

She set a hand on his arm. "Did I do something to upset you?"

"No, of course not. These past few weeks have been . . . They've been the best, Maggie."

At the tender look in his eyes, a warm, happy bubble rose to the surface and gave a soft *pop*. "For me too. And your parents have been great this week. Offering to watch Zoey, asking about our dates after you leave. They're coming around to the idea."

He nodded. "That's great."

"It is . . . which is why I'm wondering what's bothering you. I'd rather just talk it over now. Maybe you'll feel better once you get it off your chest."

He closed his eyes for a long blink.

Thunder rumbled in the distance. "Is it something at work?"

He opened them again. The intensity in his expression sent a trickle of dread through her veins. "I found out a few days ago that Will's dad isn't his biological father. He mentioned it during a conversation at lunch."

"You didn't tell me." No wonder Josh seemed so distracted tonight. He must be torn up about his father, his parents. "Oh, Josh . . ."

"Maggie . . . remember when my dad came over last week? When we shot hoops and squared things away?"

"Of course."

"Right. Well, there was a point when I got angry with something he said. Doesn't matter what—the point is that I lost my mind a little and accused him of having an affair years ago."

"Oh, wow. You didn't mention it till now? What happened? Did he own up to it?" Everything had seemed so normal around the house this week. But maybe Becky already knew about the affair.

Josh took her hand as his gaze sharpened on her. "Maggie . . . he didn't do it. Will isn't his child."

"What?" She frowned. "He denied it?"

"I know my dad—so do you. He looked me right in the eyes. He was adamant about it. He was hurt that I would accuse him of cheating on Mom. I felt like a heel."

But that didn't make sense. Maggie shook her head.

"I'm telling you, Maggie . . ." His words were gentle. "He didn't do it."

"Okay . . . if you say so." But cold fingers of dread inched up her spine. Because . . . "If he's not Will's father, then who—?"

She stiffened. *"No."*

Josh tightened his grip on her hand. The pity in his eyes turned her stomach. She wrenched her hand away. *"Ethan?* He would've been, what, nineteen? We were together then. He never would have cheated on me."

Rain pattered on the roof. Ethan was as loyal as they came, and surely Josh knew that. But clearly he believed Ethan had been unfaithful to her. Josh's silence made heat flush through her body. Made sweat prickle the back of her neck.

She fought through the fuzz in her brain and forced herself to be objective and analytical. She needed proof, not emotions, to convince Josh. "Not only were we together back then, but Robyn was in her midtwenties, and Ethan was away at college. It doesn't make logistical sense."

Except . . .

Something flashed in her mind. Something from her research earlier that summer. Robyn Jennings had also attended NC State.

But lots of people attended that university. It was the largest in the state.

Maggie stared out the windshield where rivulets of rain spilled like tears down the glass. Ethan's first year of college they'd gone through that rough spot. Being separated was harder than she expected. She saw him on social media at this party or that event, girls everywhere. Prettier girls, smarter girls, more interesting girls. She never knew how insecure she was until he left, and her mother's insults buzzed like bees inside her head.

"You're so jealous and insecure, Maggie. No wonder no one likes you."

"Don't be so boring."

"You'll never keep a man if you're not interesting."

Every time Ethan came home that first year, Maggie feared he'd break up with her. She hadn't relaxed until the next year when she moved with her mother to Fayetteville, cutting the distance between them to a one-hour drive. Then the following year she joined him at college.

He welcomed her into his world, showed her around campus, introduced her to all his friends. She made a name for herself on the swim team and did well in her classes. Everything seemed good between them. They had a wonderful college experience. With the unsupervised hours studying and hanging out together, their relationship bloomed.

If Ethan had cheated on her during that first year apart, she would've known. His guilt would've exposed the truth.

"Talk to me, honey," Josh said. "Tell me what you're thinking."

"It can't be true, Josh. He wouldn't have done that to me and he couldn't have kept a secret like that for all those years."

Josh took her hand in both of his. "No matter what, he loved you very much."

"He wouldn't have cheated on me." There had to be some other explanation. "Maybe it really is all just a fluke. Maybe Will's resemblance to Ethan is just one of those one-in-a-million things. Maybe we've been tearing our hair out all summer over some stupid genetic fluke."

But the odds were so greatly against that happening right here. Even she couldn't dismiss it as a coincidence. She studied Josh's somber expression, his sympathy-filled eyes. "You believe he did it." Her words came out as an accusation.

He was quiet for a long beat. "I don't want to believe it, honey. But I can't find any other plausible explanation."

If it were true, if Ethan really had cheated on her, he would've lied to her for *years*. And if he could hide something like that, what else could he have lied about? Their relationship would've been a lie.

Their whole marriage would've been a lie.

"No, he didn't do it. *He didn't do it.*" But a sob built inside like a cresting wave. She tried to push it down, but there was no holding back the swell of emotion. It crashed into her with the force of a tidal wave.

Josh pulled her into his arms as sobs wracked her body. "He didn't do it," she repeated.

If Ethan could do this, then everything she believed about him was a lie. If someone loved you, they didn't betray you. They didn't lie to you about something so significant. They didn't look you in the eyes and deceive you. Ethan was innocent.

But she cried anyway. Sobbed.

Josh tightened his embrace. His hands swept over her back, soothing. "I'm sorry. The last thing I wanted to do is hurt you."

The rain pounded the roof. Her head throbbed. A golf ball lodged in her throat. By the time she pulled away from Josh, she felt like a gutted fish—raw, exposed, and rotting.

"Do you"—her breaths stuttered—"have a tissue? I'm sorry about your shirt."

He reached into the glove compartment and came out with a napkin.

She blew her nose even while more tears trickled down her cheeks. It was getting dark now. Past the wet windshield the restaurant's lights gleamed. She was a wreck. She was deflated and her appetite was long gone. "I'm not hungry anymore."

"What do you want to do? Anything. Just name it."

She wanted to go home, pull the covers over her head, and forget the doubts swirling in her mind. But that wasn't an option. Her in-laws and daughter were there. "Does your dad know about Will?"

"No, I didn't tell him anything. It's up to you what happens from here, Maggie. And you don't have to do anything right now. Nothing at all."

"I don't wanna go home. I'm a mess and I don't think I could possibly act normal."

"Okay."

"Can we go to your place? I just want to hide until they're all in bed. I can't face them tonight." Not with so many unanswered questions. Not with this boulder sitting on her heart.

"Of course, honey. Whatever you want."

Chapter 40

*J*osh sipped coffee as he stared into his backyard, which seemed much the same as it did every morning. The sun had risen a couple hours ago, casting his yard in shade. Last night's rain had darkened the flower beds' soil and dampened the cushions he'd forgotten to bring inside. Weeds seemed to have sprung up overnight. Twigs littered his lawn.

The storm had passed but evidence of its visit remained.

Josh drained his coffee, then glanced at the time. He had to leave in twenty minutes for his first tour. He set the empty mug in the sink, grabbed a fresh mug, and filled it, adding a generous splash of cream. Then he headed down the hall and turned into his bedroom.

Maggie slept on her back in the center of the bed, the sheet pulled to her chin. The sun filtered through the curtains, giving her skin a translucent glow. Her lashes were spiky from crying, the remnants of makeup smudged like shadows beneath her eyes.

He hated to wake her. As long as she slept she was blissfully unaware of last night's revelation. It had been late when she'd fallen asleep on the sofa, exhausted. But his family would know something was up if she didn't return home to her daughter soon.

He sank onto the bed and caressed the soft skin of her inner wrist. "Maggie? It's morning, sweetheart."

She stirred. Her eyelids fluttered, then opened. Her gaze fixed on him, flickering with confusion. Then reality settled over her features, the hazy memory of last night as palpable as a spring fog.

"I slept here?" she croaked.

"It's okay. I texted Mom last night and told her about your migraine."

Her hand found her forehead.

He'd given her ibuprofen when they'd gotten home. "Feeling any better?"

"Um, yeah." She was speaking only of the headache, of course. The rest of her pain was less treatable and no doubt more debilitating. She sat up in bed. "Time is it?"

"After nine." He handed her the coffee.

"Thank you." She sipped the brew. "I can't believe I slept so late. You have to leave soon, don't you?"

"I have about twenty minutes. Unless you want me to go with you over to Mom and Dad's. I can call Big D and—"

"No, don't do that. My mind is clearer this morning. I can handle it. Besides, your parents would wonder why you weren't working."

That was true.

"I don't know how to handle all this. I still can't believe it."

"You don't have to do anything. Just take one minute at a time. One hour at a time. Give yourself a chance to breathe."

Sounded familiar. After Ethan's death she'd spent months just getting from one moment to the next. They all had. She sent him a wry look. "We're back to that, huh?"

"And we'll get through this together. Just like last time."

The minute Maggie walked through the door, Zoey ran over and embraced her. "You weren't here when I woke up this morning, Mommy."

"I'm sorry, sweetheart. But I'm here now and we'll have a fun day with Mamaw and Papaw."

"Papaw made Mickey Mouse pancakes, but they were burnt."

"Only on the bottom," Brad called from the living room.

Zoey scurried to where he waited on the floor with a copy of *How to Catch a Mermaid* and squirmed onto his lap. "It's okay, Papaw. Sometimes mistakes happen."

Becky stepped from the kitchen, drying her hands on a towel. Her brow furrowed as she homed in on Maggie's face. "Feeling better, honey?"

"Much better, thank you. Last night was pretty rough." That was putting it mildly.

"Josh was worried about you. Must've been the storm front. Barometric pressure and all that."

"A good night's sleep helped. Thank you for taking care of Zoey."

She smiled. "Oh, it's a pleasure, believe me. I hate that you have to leave tomorrow. It seems like we just got home from Europe."

To Maggie yesterday seemed like a year ago. "Don't worry, I'm sure we'll be back to visit soon."

ALL DAY MAGGIE felt as if she were walking around inside someone else's body. The sort of sensation you experienced when you stayed up all night. But lack of sleep was not her issue.

Her problem was that she was considering a new reality, and no one around her was aware of it—or could be made aware of it. It was as if her body had somehow split into two halves. One was aware of the new possible reality—but this side she pushed into the background. The other half sleepwalked through the day, saying and doing all the normal things.

They took Zoey to the park where she scuttled between the equipment. Maggie pushed her on the swing and posed for Brad and Becky's photos. They went to Burgers on the Beach for lunch. Maggie made conversation, laughed in all the right places, made sure her daughter went to the potty and was buckled into her car seat. They went shopping for new sandals for Zoey, who was outgrowing her favorite pair. Two stores later Zoey emerged, skipping between Brad and Becky, in a pair she declared her new favorites.

Then there were errands: the post office, the pharmacy, and a trip to the gas station. Back home they made supper, then sat on the deck while Zoey played with her Magna-Tiles. And then it was time to put her daughter to bed.

Josh had checked on her a few times via text. She was glad he hadn't called. She couldn't deal with the emotions with her in-laws so close by. He offered to come over tonight, but it was Big D's birthday and Josh had promised to take him out to celebrate weeks ago.

Still, as she tucked Zoey into bed and listened as she "read" books aloud, Maggie allowed yesterday's bombshell to surface. She envisioned telling Brad and Becky what Ethan might have done all those years ago. They'd be as adamant as she, insisting he couldn't have been unfaithful to her. Not their golden child.

But they hadn't yet seen Will's incredible likeness to Ethan. Once they did, they'd waver too. And if it was true—*please, God, don't let it be true*—they'd have the unexpected joy of another grandchild from their beloved son. That would sweeten the bitter pill.

Maggie would have no such comfort. Even the prospect of a

brother for Zoey wouldn't soothe her spirits. Will would be a constant reminder that nothing was as Maggie had once thought. Would she ever get over that feeling?

She had no idea how many books Zoey read, but when she reached the end of *The Cat in the Hat*, Maggie placed it on the bedside table. "All right. It's time to go to sleep, sweetheart."

"Just one more, Mommy?"

Always *just one more*. "Pick one out for Mamaw to read in the morning. You know how she loves to read to you."

"*Giraffes Can't Dance*! That's her favorite."

"Good choice." Maggie grabbed it from the pile. She bent down and kissed her daughter's forehead. "Sleep tight."

"Do we have to go home tomorrow?"

"I'm afraid so, sweetie. I know you'll miss Mamaw and Papaw—"

"And Uncle Josh and Mia and Owen and Aunt Erin and Uncle Patrick."

"I know. But we'll be back to visit soon, and when we get home you'll get to play with Pokey. And soon you'll start preschool again and get to play with your friends."

"I like school."

Her daughter was growing up so fast. Soon she would be reading words for real. "That's because you're so smart." Maggie pressed another kiss to her forehead. "Good night, Chickadee."

"Night, Mommy."

Maggie turned off the light, then slipped through the door and pulled it almost closed. Once in the hallway she found her thoughts shifting gears.

Normally she would join Brad and Becky in the living room and watch a comedy. They would laugh at the funny parts and Brad's commentary would make them laugh even harder. Becky would tell him to shush when he talked over the dialogue and Maggie's lips would twitch at their comical bickering.

But not tonight.

Their routine would be disrupted. Because even though she'd put the situation from her thoughts, her unconscious mind had been chewing on it all day. And as she walked down the hall toward the living room, she knew what she had to do.

Chapter 41

*R*obyn Jennings lived in a small ranch on the southwest side of Wilmington. Maggie used the address from Will's application that Josh had texted her weeks ago. She pulled along the curb, studying the property.

Darkness obscured the unattached garage, and the home itself boasted a tiny stoop centered between two large lit windows. Someone was home—hopefully not Will. But it was a Friday night and he was young. Probably out with friends.

Maggie's heart thudded at the thought of coming face-to-face with the woman who might've had Ethan's other child.

Ethan's other child.

No, it wasn't true. She was about to prove that to herself.

She squeezed her eyes closed, welcoming the black void. If only she could make all of this disappear so easily. But she couldn't. She opened her eyes again. She was here for answers.

Gathering courage, she opened the door and slipped into the night. Gravel crunched beneath her sandals as she walked up the short driveway. An old white Dodge hunkered just outside the garage. Her legs wobbled as she followed the pavers to the steps leading to the stoop.

The night air smelled of lilacs and earth. Cars whipped past on the main road just outside the subdivision. Somewhere in the distance a siren pealed. As she climbed the steps a warm breeze lifted her hair.

On the darkened stoop she drew a steadying breath and then knocked. Her respirations were quick and shallow as if she'd just finished a run on the beach. Questions buzzed inside her head like a dozen angry bees.

She was biting her nails. She lowered her hand.

God, help me. She winged the ancient plea heavenward. She hoped He would forgive the ambiguous request. She couldn't seem to formulate anything more meaningful.

The door swept open and a woman appeared, silhouetted by the light behind her and shielded by the patio door between them. Was it the woman they'd found online?

"Can I help you?"

"Are you—are you Robyn Jennings?"

The woman tilted her head. "Who's asking?"

"My name's Maggie. Um, I wondered if I could have a minute of your time."

"What's this regarding?"

Maggie gathered her courage. "Your son."

The woman glanced over her shoulder, then thrust open the patio door. But rather than inviting Maggie inside, she scurried onto the porch.

Maggie made room for Robyn, who closed the entry door behind her and remained inside the enclave of the open patio door. Maggie's stomach sank like an anchor at her suspicious behavior.

"What do you want?"

"I've recently become aware that"—she swallowed hard—"that you may have known my husband, Ethan Reynolds. Is that true?"

Maggie whipped out her phone and pulled up the photo of

young Ethan. She turned it around, hands trembling. "This is my husband—my late husband—when he was twenty. Did you know him?"

Robyn gasped. A solid five seconds passed before she tore her eyes from the photo. "I—I never knew that man. Never knew anyone by that name." She reached for the doorknob. "You should go. I'm in the middle of something."

She was lying. "Please. I need to know—"

"You have to go." The patio door was falling shut.

"Did he love you? Did he know he had a son? Please, you have to tell me."

Robyn whipped around. "I already told you I never knew him. I'm sorry but I can't help you."

"Wait." Maggie shoved a piece of paper at her bearing her phone number. "Could we talk another time? I'm leaving town tomorrow. I don't live here."

Robyn stuffed the paper into her jeans pocket and closed the door firmly behind her. A second later the pneumatic closure released the patio door and it, too, clicked shut.

The encounter had been so quick. Mere seconds. But as she turned and took the steps, Maggie's knees wobbled precariously. She steadied herself with the railing.

Robyn couldn't get away from her fast enough. Her denial had contradicted her response. Maggie hadn't had to see the woman's expression to know she was evading, lying.

It wasn't DNA but it was awfully close. She fled to her car and closed herself in, wishing the darkness would swallow her up. She wanted to get as far away from this place as possible. She started her car and pulled from the curb.

Vision blurry, she dashed tears from her face. Could he really have done this terrible thing? She pressed a hand to the ache in her chest, her mind whirling with questions. If her suspicions were true, had Ethan known about Robyn's pregnancy? About his son? Had he kept in contact with her? With Will?

This was just too much to bear. *Isn't it enough that You took him from me? Couldn't You have just left it at that? Now he's gone and I can't even get answers. And now my memory of him, of what we had, is forever sullied.*

"Mom?"

Will's mother jumped at his sudden appearance. Then she dashed into the connecting kitchen and grabbed a dishrag. "Will. I thought you were in your room."

His gaze sharpened on her even as dread roiled in his stomach. "Who was that at the door?"

"It—it was just someone selling . . . cookies."

Mom was a terrible liar. Even if her ridiculous response didn't give her away, the tremble in her voice and the frenetic cleaning would've. He was shaking a little himself. The knock on the door had pulled him from his room. Only one of his friends would come over this time of night. But it hadn't been Levi or Braden. It was a woman.

"I heard what she said, Mom."

His mother's widened eyes locked on him for a moment. Then she glanced at the closed door.

"The window's open. *I heard what she said.*" His own voice trembled. When you were the product of a sperm donor, you didn't hold out much hope of ever knowing your biological father. But that hadn't stopped Will from wondering and searching.

And now the answer seemed to have washed up like a seashell on the shore. He'd been too shocked to move. And by the time he'd gathered his wits, the woman was gone. "Her husband must be my biological father."

Mom scrubbed a spot on the counter. "We don't know that."

It was one thing not to know the answers to his questions, another to simply withhold them from him. "I can tell you're lying, Mom. Were you lying about the IUI too? She talked like you knew him. Like you had a relationship with him."

"No! I swear that's the truth. She was mistaken about that."

Her expression and tone seemed sincere enough. "What's his name?" He'd stepped into the hallway too late for introductions, if there'd been any.

The rag stopped its frantic motions. His mom slumped her shoulders, her whole body heaving with her breaths. "I couldn't say, but—she showed me his picture." Mom met his gaze, her expression softening. "Did you hear the part about him . . . ?"

"Being dead? Yeah, I heard that part. So you think it was him? That her husband is my biological father?"

Mom set down the rag and came over to him. Her eyes teared as she regarded him warily. "I don't know."

Will's throat swelled closed. "But now he's gone and I can never know him. Never have a conversation with him."

"I'm sorry, honey." Mom touched his shoulder.

He flinched away. "Why did you lie to her? Why did you chase her away? I could've talked to her and learned about him at least."

"I'm sorry. Her husband died a-and she seemed so distraught."

"What about me? Did you think for a minute about what I might've wanted?" She knew he'd always wanted to find his biological father.

Something about the woman snagged in his memory. She'd said something about leaving tomorrow. Something about not living here. "What's her name? Where's she from? I have to find her."

Mom's face crumpled. "I wish I could tell you, honey. I'm so sorry."

Chapter 42

I went to see Robyn."

Josh had barely registered that Maggie was on his doorstep before she spilled the words. He pulled her inside. "What did she say? Was Will home?"

"I think so. She didn't say much. Couldn't get me out of there fast enough."

"So you didn't learn anything?"

Maggie let out a humorless laugh. "She denied knowing Ethan, but she was obviously lying. She seemed . . . guilty." Her lower lip wobbled.

"Oh, honey." He pulled Maggie into an embrace. She was trembling, stiff in his arms. He held her tight as she wept. He closed his eyes, wished he could spare her this pain. He could hardly believe Ethan could've done this to her.

God, hasn't she suffered enough?

"I didn't want it to be true. Didn't think it could possibly be true. But her behavior was so suspicious. As soon as I said I was there about her son, she rushed out onto the porch and closed the door behind her like she didn't want whoever was inside to hear what I had to say. Once she found out what I wanted, she wouldn't answer anything else and insisted I leave. The whole encounter took less than a minute."

He rubbed her back, murmuring words of comfort until her tears stopped. Then he eased away, taking in her pain-ravaged face and feeling it like a kick in the gut. "Can you take me through it from start to finish?"

Maggie did as he asked while he listened intently.

"She was definitely evading the truth," he said when she finished. He wished he'd known Maggie was going over there so he could've gone with her. Maybe it wouldn't have changed the outcome, but he would've been there to support her. "I'm so sorry this is happening."

"Part of me still can't believe he'd do this, Josh. But the evidence is sure stacking up."

He used his thumbs to brush away the remnants of tears. "What do you want to do now? How can I help?"

"I just want to go home and forget about all this."

He could only imagine. But life wasn't that simple. And there was an innocent young man involved.

She peered up at him with tear-filled eyes. "Do you think Will should be told?"

"This might be an unwelcome revelation since Ethan is—"

"Gone." Maggie stepped from his embrace. "I think I should step back from this point on. I'll leave the rest to you. That's not really my place."

She sounded numb, disconnected. Not at all herself—and who could blame her? But her demeanor sent a tremor of unease through him. "Let's sit and talk awhile. I have some leftovers in the fridge if you're hungry."

She glanced around the room, seeming a little lost. "Thanks . . . but I think I'll just head back to the house. Go to bed early. It's been a long day."

"Sure, honey." As they headed toward the door, he took her hand. It was cold and lifeless. She'd had a shock. He wished he could take her in his arms and make the rest of the world disappear for a few hours. If only he had such magical powers.

When she paused at the door, he took her chin and searched her eyes. "Hey. I'm worried about you."

She offered a wan smile. "I'll be fine. I just have a lot to process. It'll be easier to do that back home where I can be alone."

Having his parents underfoot and unaware of the weight she carried left her no space to work through this. But the last thing he wanted was to be so far from Maggie right now. She needed support more than ever—and she sure wouldn't get it from her mother.

He gave her chin a soft pinch. "I'll be over in the morning to help you load up."

"Okay."

"And if you need to talk, just call me. Anytime, day or night."

Her smile didn't reach her eyes. "Thanks, Josh."

"We're gonna get through this." He brushed her lips and found them as cold as her hand. "Love you, honey."

"Love you too." And then she was leaving.

Moments later he stared after her as she pulled from his drive, and that sense of unease traveled through him in waves of energy like an impending earthquake.

That night Maggie tossed and turned, replaying the scene with Robyn a hundred times, hoping for a different read. Trying to find something she might've missed. But she was convinced Robyn had been lying.

Could Ethan really have done this? Abandoned her, not once but twice now? It triggered her deepest fear. Her most painful wound—that of her father's abandonment. She couldn't believe she was dealing with this all over again. It was the gift that kept on giving.

She reexamined her courtship with Ethan, their marriage, one memory at a time. And then came this thought: If Ethan had cheated on her once, he could've cheated again. He could've cheated many times. After all, if he'd gotten away with it the first time . . . He hadn't seemed guilty or suspicious, but maybe her radar was broken. Maybe she couldn't trust her own feelings, her own judgment—and where did that leave her?

Tears flowed in the dark. As the hours inched by, she craved the blissful escape of sleep, but it was as elusive as a rolling wave.

In the middle of the night another thought barged in like an unwelcome guest. If Ethan could cheat on her—Ethan, whom she'd believed was loyal and trustworthy and honest—couldn't anyone?

Couldn't Josh?

She'd fallen for him so quickly and completely. She was in love with him, there was no denying it. But his past relationships were as brief as a sneeze. He had lost interest, gotten bored, met someone new. Someone shinier. Even his marriage to Samantha hadn't lasted that long, and it had ended in ruins.

She thought of all the women, old flames, however short-lived, that they'd run into this summer. If all those women—most of whom Maggie considered beautiful and interesting—couldn't hold his attention, why would Maggie think she could?

"You're so boring, Maggie. Even your friends think so."

"Why don't you do something with your hair? It's so frizzy."

"Get your head out of that book and do something fun. What are you, eighty?"

"You'll never keep a man's interest like that."

She tried to shut down the voice but it kept coming, filling her with insecurity.

If Ethan cheated on you, how long will it take Josh to do the same? He's the fickle one, after all.

She turned over for the dozenth time. Feeling suffocated, she flung off the covers. How could she go back home and trust that Josh would be faithful to her? How could she believe he wouldn't tire of her the way he had all the other women?

Sure, he loved her now. He'd loved Samantha, too, and now she was his bitter ex. Maggie didn't want to be Josh's bitter ex. He'd been her rock for so long. And how would an acrimonious breakup affect her relationship with the rest of the family? The family she'd come to depend on as her own?

Much later when she finally fell asleep, she dreamed of Ethan's first year at college. Only in the dream she was there. She walked across a darkened parking lot toward a lone car. She peered through the rain-dappled windshield. Ethan and Robyn were tangled together in the back seat.

Maggie jerked awake. Her eyes burned. Her throat thickened. Back then she'd blamed her mother's mental abuse for her insecurity. She reassured herself that Ethan wasn't cheating. That it was just her imagination.

He'd tried to convince her of the same thing!

How could he have been so cruel as to gaslight her? It wasn't at all like the Ethan she knew and loved. *Thought* she'd known and loved. She would have to reexamine their past in light of this awful possibility. She dreaded the thought of traipsing through the ashes of her marriage once again.

Maggie slept only a few hours. And when her alarm blared she silenced it with a jab. As the memory of the dream surfaced, heat simmered through her. It built inside until it produced a full boil. She gripped her pillow in her fist, squeezing. Gritted her teeth.

Hello, anger stage.

That had been quick. Shortly after Zoey's birth she'd flown into a rage. Run outside and kicked the garage door until it was pockmarked with dents. Another time, frustrated with a fitted sheet, she'd screamed into a pillow until her throat felt raw.

Maggie slowed her breaths. Released her fist, her jaw. She had a long day ahead. She and Zoey were going home—and until then she had to pretend everything was fine. She dragged herself out of bed.

LATER THAT MORNING Maggie wished she had a pillow handy as she shoved a suitcase into her trunk, making room for the box of toys Josh carried down the steps. They were nearly finished loading her things.

Brad and Becky had taken Zoey for one last walk on the beach. She'd taken her pail to collect seashells. It was all too convenient. Because last night Maggie had come to a difficult decision and she was running out of time.

Josh set the box in the trunk. "Last one."

Maggie pulled out a few of Zoey's favorites to keep her occupied on the drive, then he closed the trunk and shelved his hands on his slim hips, peering at her. His gaze cut into her like a laser.

"What?"

He tilted his head, regarding her quietly. "Can I do anything to help?"

The sweetness of his offer brought the sting of guilt. She didn't want to hurt Josh. It was the last thing she wanted. "Sorry. I'm a little on edge this morning."

He pulled her into his arms. "It's okay. I understand. You're dealing with a lot." He wrapped her up tightly and pressed a kiss to her temple.

In a few minutes Josh would probably be just as upset. But she'd worked it all around in the night and she had to do this. With his track record, a breakup was inevitable, and she'd rather end things now before her feelings grew any stronger. Before he broke her heart. If he cheated on her, she didn't know if she could come back from that. But if they parted ways now, maybe they could remain friends.

She told herself to step back. But she needed just a moment more in his arms. She needed to soak in the sense of safety and acceptance he'd always given so freely. Needed to memorize the feel of his strong arms around her. The familiar scent of his cologne. The wide slope of his shoulders. She memorized it all. Every little detail so she could reflect on it later, close her eyes and remember what being loved by Josh had felt like.

She swallowed past the tightness in her throat and pulled away. "We need to talk, Josh."

Chapter 43

*N*othing good had ever followed those ominous words. A sense of doom spread through Josh like venom. Maggie had hardly fooled him this morning with her fake smiles and can-do spirit. The minute his parents took off with Zoey, she dropped the act. But since then she'd been edgy and quiet.

Until that hug. She'd gripped him so tightly it made him ache. But it also made him heady, how easily she'd fallen into his embrace. Like she trusted him to keep her safe. Like he was her shelter in the storm.

He'd thought it was a good sign.

Not a good-bye. And now, staring into her guarded eyes, he realized that's exactly what it had been. A fist tightened in his gut. "Don't do this, Maggie."

"I love you, Josh, I really do."

"Then don't do this!" He couldn't lose her. He couldn't. Not when they were finally together. Not when she finally loved him the same way he loved her.

Dial it back, Reynolds. He sucked in a breath.

She was hurting, she was reeling. He had to remember that. "Listen, honey . . . You've been through a lot. I get it. You're overwhelmed and questioning everything you knew to be true. But you'll process it and come out the other side and realize Ethan really did love you like crazy. Maybe he did make a terrible mistake years ago, but that doesn't negate everything that happened between the two of you. And it doesn't change *anything* between us."

She looked away. Blinked back tears. "I'm sorry, Josh. I really am. But I just can't do this. It—it's too much."

He reached out and took her shoulders, waited until he had her full attention. "Don't push me away, Maggie. Let me be there for you. I want to help you through this. We can talk on the phone and I'll come up every weekend." He'd cancel tours if he had to. Nothing was more important than Maggie.

Compassion flickered in her eyes. Her lips trembled. "It's not that. I don't even think I— I don't know if I believe in love anymore. And even if I did, I don't want to. Love ends. Love hurts. And I'm so tired of hurting, Josh." Her voice wobbled.

He tried to pull her into his arms.

She shrugged away.

"Let me hold you."

"No. It won't help. The only thing that'll help is going home and forgetting this summer ever happened."

He flinched. This summer had been the highlight of his life. Having Maggie had been a dream come true.

Her face softened. "Not you, Josh. Not us. I didn't mean it that way."

Her words would've soothed his crumbling spirits, but they didn't change the fact that she was ending things. Anxiety bit at him like a thousand fire ants.

"I just want to forget about Will and what Ethan did or didn't do—I wish I'd never seen him at that stupid carnival. I just want to—I want to stop hurting."

"I don't blame you. Let's just forget about Will for now. Let's give it some time. I'll come up next weekend and we can talk it through."

Frustration flared in her eyes. "You're not listening to me. I can't do this, you and me. I just can't."

"So, what, we're just . . . friends again? You're in my life. In my *family*. It's not that simple."

She raked her fingers into her hair. "I just need everything to go back the way it was."

He gaped. *The way it was?* Before she was his? Back to when he'd quietly suffered with unrequited love? Back to when he pretended she was just his friend, his sister-in-law? No. He couldn't go back to that. He just couldn't.

He turned and paced to the end of the drive. Stared unseeing into the neighbor's yard, breaths heaving. *God, no, please. I can't go back there.* It had been hard enough, harboring those secret feelings before. But now he knew what it was like, having her in his arms, in his life, in his heart. How could he ever go back to the way it had been before? She was asking too much. His eyes burned.

Some deeper, unselfish part of him whispered in his ear. What had happened wasn't her fault. She'd suffered so much. If he loved her, shouldn't he give her the space she needed to heal? He pressed his fingertips in his eyes.

She touched his arm. He hadn't even heard her approach. "Josh? Please don't be mad at me. I can't stand the thought of losing you on top of everything else." The last words quivered.

He dug deep, through his own pain and misery. He didn't want to heap more hurt on her. It wasn't her fault he'd fallen so deeply in love with her years ago. Wasn't her fault he couldn't even look at another woman without comparing her to Maggie. "You haven't lost me, honey. You just . . . do what you have to do, okay? It'll be fine."

He'd be fine. If Maggie could get through this, somehow he'd find a way to survive it too.

A squeal carried from the direction of the beach. Zoey dashed toward them on the walkway, his parents trailing her. "Stay off the street!"

"Mommy, come see my shells! We found a big scallop and Papaw found a whelk. But it's a little broken on the tip. I'm gonna make a project and mail it to Mamaw and Papaw. Will you help me make it, Mommy?"

Maggie offered Josh a sad smile, gave his arm a brief squeeze before she headed toward her daughter. "Of course I will."

Josh watched her go. And just like that he'd lost her.

Chapter 44

The next morning Maggie took Zoey to church, but only because she'd begged. Maggie was in no condition to greet people she hadn't seen all summer. But her daughter had missed her church friends and it wouldn't hurt to stay busy.

So Maggie sat in the pew and tried to focus on the sermon. But her mind kept wandering back to Seabrook. Back to Josh. Back to that gutted look on his face when she'd ended things yesterday.

At the memory her stomach clenched. Hurting him had been painful. A stew of emotions simmered inside: guilt, regret, heartbreak. She was exhausted from two nights of little sleep. Tomorrow she'd return to school and begin preparing for the students who would come the following week. The thought of it only made her more exhausted.

She closed her eyes and envisioned herself diving into a still pool, slipping through the water, all her worries sinking to the bottom, leaving her weightless, buoyant.

But there would be no time for swimming today. She had lesson plans to prepare—work she'd put off in favor of spending time with Josh.

She pushed away all thoughts of him and his tragic eyes. He would be fine. He would soon find another woman to keep him company.

As her mother had reminded her many times, she was hardly irreplaceable.

When the service ended Maggie made a beeline for Zoey's classroom. After she'd collected her daughter, a number of friends and acquaintances stopped them, wanting to catch up. Maggie pasted on a smile and made small talk. Then, using her busy afternoon as an excuse, she bustled out the door. Zoey talked the whole way home and Maggie was glad to see Pokey in the yard next door, waiting for Zoey.

Because she had a phone call to make.

Inside the house Maggie glanced at the time. Erin would be home from church by now and Patrick would likely have a new members class or something that detained him. It was a good time to call. She'd planned to do it yesterday but didn't have it in her.

Erin answered on the second ring. "Hey, girl! How's Fayetteville?"

"Exactly the same as when I left."

"You have great timing. I just walked in the door. Mia went home with a friend and Owen is helping Patrick at church. He's leading a GriefShare group."

Maggie had attended those meetings locally following Ethan's death. That seemed so long ago. "That's great."

"You sound a little down. Aren't you excited about the new school year?"

Maggie peeked out the back door where Zoey threw a stick for Pokey, who retrieved it and carried it off. She chased after him. "Not really. I should've spent more time on lesson plans and less time on swimming classes."

"Don't act like you didn't enjoy every minute."

"I really did. But now I've got the school year right up on me and I'm unprepared." And emotionally drained.

"That's not like you. What's going on?"

She wished she could tell her best friend about Will, about what Ethan had possibly done all those years ago. But she'd left all that to Josh. It would be hard explaining her reasons for breaking it off with Josh when she couldn't divulge why she'd had a sudden change of heart.

"There is something I need to tell you. Yesterday before we left town . . . I broke up with Josh."

"*What?* But you guys just got together."

"I know." And it had been so good. Maggie squeezed her eyes shut, trying to block out the memory of his infectious laughter, the twinkle in his eyes, that quirky twitch of his eyebrow.

"You seemed pretty great together—I mean, once I got used to the idea. He must be so upset. He's over the moon for you, Maggie."

Maggie gave a mirthless laugh. "Oh, you know Josh."

Silence stretched out like a taut wire. "What do you mean by that exactly?" Erin's voice was strained.

"Come on, Erin. You know I love Josh, but he isn't exactly known for longevity when it comes to romantic entanglements."

"That didn't seem to bother you a week ago."

Maggie winced. "Please don't be angry with me. I just . . . I'm overwhelmed with—with school starting and my mom and a bunch of unresolved stuff with Ethan. I just can't deal with a new relationship right now."

"This is exactly what I was afraid of, Maggie. Now things are strained between you and Josh, and it affects the whole family."

"It doesn't have to."

"You can't be that naive. Any fool can see he's in love with you."

"I'll always love Josh. Nothing will ever change that." Her voice wobbled on the last words. She was afraid of exactly that. That she'd live the rest of her life loving someone who was sure to abandon her when something better came along.

Just like Ethan.

Just like her dad.

"I know you must have your reasons. I don't mean to be defensive of Josh. I'm just—"

"He's your brother. You should be defensive of him."

"But you're my best friend and I want the best for both of you."

"I appreciate that." A beat of silence passed while Maggie paced the floor, wishing she could find something to say that would smooth things over.

"Can I put on my counselor's hat for a second?"

Maggie gave a wan smile. Erin always prefaced her advice that way. "Of course."

"I feel like there's more going on here. After Ethan died we discussed your abandonment issues and how his dying triggered them. Is that what this is? Are you afraid Josh will leave you because of his dating history?"

Erin's words slammed into her heart. Tremors quaked through her body. She pressed her fingers to her temples. Her friend knew how to cut right to the matter.

"It's just you and me here," Erin said. "This won't go anywhere else."

"I just can't do it, Erin. I don't have the emotional bandwidth to deal with a relationship right now."

"I realize Josh must seem like a poor risk, but I do believe he's capable of settling down. I wouldn't have gotten on board with your relationship otherwise. You've had a lot of loss and I want the very best for you."

"I know that."

"Losing Ethan was bound to make you leery of falling in love again. But, honey, at some point you'll have to take that risk if you want love in your life. If you want Zoey to have a father—and I know that's a priority for you."

Maggie couldn't even think about all that right now. "You're about to suggest I return to therapy."

A pause played out over the distance. "It wouldn't be the worst thing."

True words. Because what else could she do when what she wanted most was also what she feared most?

"Have you seen your mother yet?"

Maggie was grateful for the shift in topic. "She called yesterday but I didn't pick up."

"I'm surprised she wasn't on your doorstep the minute you got home."

"She's giving me the silent treatment. She's still angry because I wouldn't date Dr. Derrick." Pokey barked as he led Zoey on a merry chase.

"Is that back on the table now that you and Josh aren't an item anymore?"

"I meant what I said. I can't do a relationship right now—and somebody slap me if I ever agree to get involved with anyone my mom recommends." Of course, her mom was bound to do just that, and Maggie's refusal would cause more friction in their relationship. Not to mention manipulation, guilt trips, and passive aggression. She could hardly wait. The thought of it was like an anchor around her neck.

As much as she dreaded stirring up the pain with counseling, it was probably time—past time—to figure all this out.

Chapter 45

Almost two weeks passed without word from Maggie. Then on the Thursday before Labor Day weekend, after his morning tour, Josh checked his phone.

How are you? she'd texted.

He gave a wry laugh. Well, funny she should ask. He was pretty miserable in fact. He thought about her all the time. His arms ached for her. His heart was broken. He'd written her a dozen texts only to delete them.

Also, the Charleston Yacht Club had already given that job to someone else. Yes, he'd checked. Because the thought of sticking around here, seeing Maggie every time she brought Zoey to see the family, was something he'd sworn he was finished with.

He waved good-bye to the last guest, reboarded the vessel, and joined the crew in cleanup. He'd search for another job. Or maybe move the *Carolina Dream* to another port and start over somewhere else. But he sure hated the thought of letting down Big D and his crew.

Will.

He felt a ping of guilt every time he saw the guy. Like now. His nephew was elbow deep in the greasy popcorn machine. Josh would have to address that soon. But first he had to tell his family. And before that he needed to check in with Maggie, owner of his heart.

He rolled his eyes at his melodrama, put down the broom, and whipped out his phone again.

Just friends. Just good ol' Josh checking in on his sister-in-law. *Doing okay. How's school going?*

After he sent the text, three dots appeared immediately. Josh waited, his heart skittering in his chest.

Her reply came seconds later. *It's going well.*

When more dots appeared, Josh delayed his response.

Have you told your family yet?

I told you I'd wait awhile.

Go ahead. You shouldn't put it off any longer.

He was feeling exactly the same. It was hard being around Will, being around his family when he held this bombshell. He'd been avoiding his family because of his discomfort, but he could hardly dodge Will. Though he was only part-time now that his classes were underway again. But the guy deserved to know the truth.

He reread Maggie's text. Had she thought about how this might change things going forward? *Sure you're ready for that? We can put it off a bit longer.*

Her reply was immediate: *I'm sure.*

Josh paused, thumbs hovering over the keyboard. *How are you doing?* Would she be more forthcoming than he would? Three dots appeared. But there was such a long pause that he almost grabbed the broom again.

Then her reply appeared. *I've been better. I've starting seeing Miss Allison again. Hoping to sort some things out.*

Good. That was good. Between her mother and everything with Ethan, Maggie had had a lot to deal with. *You're stronger than you know.*

Hope you're right.

He was about to reply when she added, *Gotta run. Time for my next class.*

Chat later, he replied.

But would they? Once he told his family and Will, the boy would likely become a part of family gatherings. Would Maggie want to be around him? Wouldn't he be a constant reminder of Ethan's infidelity?

Josh stuck his phone in his pocket and grabbed the broom. Will was still cleaning the popcorn machine, blissfully unaware his life was about to change.

Josh had considered approaching Will's mother first, but Will was nineteen and a legal adult. Plus she hadn't exactly been receptive to Maggie, which made it pretty clear she didn't want her son to know the truth. She wouldn't welcome their intrusion into Will's life. But he had a right to know who his biological father was.

But first . . . Josh's family. How would they react to the news that their golden child had apparently cheated on Maggie? They would undoubtedly find it hard to believe at first, just as he and Maggie had. But once presented with the evidence, how could they deny it?

The weekend was full up with tours, being the last weekend of high season. But there were no tours on Labor Day, when Mom and Dad were having the family over for their annual picnic.

He would tell them then.

Chapter 46

Saturday nights had taken on a whole different flavor since Will had begun dating Addison six weeks ago. She liked strolling Seabrook Beach and walking Wilmington's historic downtown and boardwalk. There they enjoyed sampling coffee from local vendors and window-shopping.

She was beautiful and kind, smart and compassionate. He'd discovered the latter when he opened up about his dad's unrealistic expectations. And two weeks ago, after the woman had visited his mom, he'd admitted to Addison he didn't know who his biological father was. Lounging in a cozy coffee shop near the Cape Fear River, she listened intently as he relayed the story of the woman who'd recently appeared on their doorstep and his frustration with his mother over the situation.

Addison did little more than hold his hand and validate his feelings, but it made him feel lighter than air. She came from such a solid family. Such an uncomplicated family. Yet she somehow seemed to understand his feelings. She'd even gotten teary at one point, which made Will want to wrap her up in his arms and hang on forever.

She would make a wonderful psychologist someday.

Tonight he'd splurged on supper at the Sea Grille near her house. The food was delicious and conversation pinged easily back and forth throughout dinner. The car ride had been comfortably quiet. He had to make it an early evening since his biology paper was due by midnight. All too soon he pulled into her drive, put the car in Park, and shut off the engine.

He offered Addison a regretful smile. "Sorry we couldn't stay out longer."

"Your grades are important. And you work so many hours. I don't know how you fit it all in." She cocked a coy glance his way. "Are you sure you have time for dating in your busy schedule?"

He fell into her sparkling green eyes. "Only for you." He leaned over and brushed her lips with his. He'd only meant it to be a quick kiss. But Addison was addictive. Once he started it was hard to stop. They'd become exclusive a week ago, and he was still pinching himself at the thought that she was his.

A long moment later she put a hand on his chest and leaned back until their breaths mingled between them. "I'd better go inside."

"Things were just getting good."

"Agreed. But my dad's peering out the window."

Will jerked back.

Addison chuckled. "It's fine. He knows you're my boyfriend. But it's hard to enjoy making out when . . ." She nodded toward the house.

No kidding. His own blood now ran ice-cold. "I'll get your door."

An hour later Will was shut away in his room, laser focused on his paper about Gregor Mendel and his groundbreaking work on pea plants. He'd loved high school but was enjoying college even more now that he'd gotten most of his gen-eds out of the way. Now he could focus mostly on the sciences.

A text pinged in. He'd forgotten to silence his phone and did so now. He did his best work when he was focused—and that deadline was quickly approaching.

It was almost ten when Mom brought him a Coke. "How's the paper going?" She'd been extra nice ever since that woman had come to their door.

"I'm almost finished with the first draft."

"How many drafts will you do?"

He flashed a grin. "However many it takes."

"My brilliant son. Well, don't stay up too late. I thought I might make pancakes in the morning since we both have the day off."

"That'd be great, Mom. Thanks." She made the best pancakes. And ever since she'd taken a part-time caretaker job a couple years ago, she didn't have many Sundays off.

When she slipped from the room, he went back to work, chugging the Coke as he went. Finally the first draft was done. He set it aside to clear his mind before he tackled revisions.

He grabbed his phone. It was too late to text Addison. She had the kids' class for early service in the morning. But the notification from earlier appeared on the screen. My Legacy had a match for him. He tempered his excitement—all the matches so far had been maternal.

He never mentioned the matches to Mom because she'd gotten upset three years ago when he admitted he'd sent in his DNA. He assured her his search for his biological father didn't mean he loved her any less. That she'd been a great mom and no one could ever replace her. But he'd obviously hurt her feelings. Or maybe it was because he'd done the test without telling her first. He must've known deep down that she wouldn't approve. And that recent visit from his bio dad's widow proved him right.

He logged in to the website and opened the screen that revealed the matches. His eyes fixed on the most recently added name.

He froze. Stared at the name until his vision blurred.

He blinked away the fog. But the name remained. As did the relationship descriptor beside it: *parent/child*.

His thoughts ricocheted through his mind. He struggled to make sense of it.

"Mom?" The word was nothing but a croak.

It was . . . a mistake of some kind. It couldn't be right. Could it?

He bolted from his bed. "Mom!"

Chapter 47

*J*osh was sitting on his patio listening to Patrick's sermon when a call came in, quieting his brother-in-law's voice. Since the number was unknown, Josh refused the call, and the sermon resumed. He had to hand it to Patrick—the guy was pretty insightful.

Josh had meant to attend the service this morning but he'd slept late—an aberration. What did you expect when you lay awake half the night thinking about the woman you couldn't have and wondering when it would be acceptable to text her again?

Maybe today. It had been three days since she'd texted last. "You're pretty lame, my friend."

While Patrick was preaching on "Five Ways to Let Go"—a sermon Josh needed like water—he opened Facebook and went directly to Maggie's page. He didn't glean any new information as she hadn't updated it in weeks.

"And that's what you get for surfing the internet instead of listening to the sermon."

His phone dinged, a voice mail. Promising himself he'd continue the sermon later, he stopped the live recording and tapped on the message.

"Um, hello. We've never met, but my name is Robyn Jennings. I'm Will's mother."

284

Josh bolted upright in his seat.

"Could you return my call as soon as you can, please?" A click sounded and the voice mail ended.

Adrenaline flooded his system. He shot to his feet and tapped Robyn's number. Had something happened to Will?

Or had the woman somehow made the connection between Maggie and Josh? Maybe Will had mentioned his last name and she'd pieced it together. And if she knew Josh was Will's uncle, did that mean Will knew also?

"Hello?"

The voice coming from his phone startled him from his thoughts. "Uh, hello. This is Josh." He omitted his surname in case she hadn't put it together yet. "You just left a message for me. Is Will all right?"

"Yes. I'm sorry. I didn't— No, he's fine. I hope I didn't call too early."

"Not at all. I was just sitting on my patio enjoying the weather before it turns sweltering. It's already pretty humid but it's supposed to get up to a hundred today." *The weather?* He palmed his face.

"Yes, I heard." Silence dragged out.

Josh sought to fill the gap and came up empty. He didn't know what she wanted and didn't want to give anything away.

"I was actually wondering if you might be able to stop over later today. There's something I'd like to talk to you about."

Josh squeezed the back of his neck. *Like why my girlfriend was on your doorstep two weeks ago? Or just exactly how your son came to work for the uncle he didn't know he had?*

"Hello?"

"Uh, yeah. I'm still here. Can I ask what this is regarding?"

"I—I really prefer that we talk in person, if you don't mind. Would one o'clock work? I know it's short notice. I can give you my address. We live on the southwest side of Wilmington."

"I know." *That's not creepy at all.* "I mean, Will's address is on his application. One o'clock is fine."

"Okay. Good. I'll . . . I'll see you later, then."

"See you later." The call ended.

What had just happened?

Josh paced to the other side of the patio and back. She hadn't seemed angry, but then again, he didn't know her. If she'd connected Ethan and Josh, she must believe he'd hired Will knowing he was Josh's nephew. And while that wasn't entirely accurate, it was true enough.

If Robyn was as skittish as Maggie had portrayed, she couldn't be happy about the turn of events. About the way Josh had invited Will into his life without divulging his identity. From her perspective his actions would seem underhanded. Sneaky.

Josh could only imagine the kind of protective feelings a mother might have over such sensitive information. Maybe Robyn had put it all together and would beg Josh not to tell Will about Ethan. That would put Josh in a terrible position. He couldn't keep this discovery from his family. And once he told them, there was no way they wouldn't insist on meeting Will, on being in his life—if that's what the young man wanted.

Josh's thoughts, still whirling, spun in an entirely different direction.

Maybe Maggie's visit had scared Robyn into telling her son the truth. That might be how she'd come to mention Ethan's surname—and then Will would've connected the dots. Reynolds was a common name, but Will was a bright kid. He would've gotten on the internet. He would've had to look no further than social media to find Ethan's Facebook page—and Josh listed as his brother.

That was probably it. Josh's duplicitous motives for hiring Will would've been revealed, which could've upset them both. But this scenario was much preferred over being asked to sweep the whole thing under the rug.

He glanced at his watch. Only five minutes had passed since he listened to the voice mail. Now he had three and a half interminable hours of waiting and wondering ahead of him.

By THE TIME Josh knocked on the Jenningses' door, it seemed as if three and a half decades had passed since his call with Robyn. He'd twisted himself into all kinds of knots, and now his empty stomach churned because he'd forgotten to eat.

The door opened and a woman appeared. Robyn Jennings couldn't have been much over five feet tall. She looked much like the photo they'd found online—an attractive woman with blue eyes and dark blonde hair flowing to her shoulders.

Her lips tilted in a strained smile that didn't quite reach her eyes. "Hi. You must be Josh." She opened the storm door, allowing him entrance.

"You're Robyn. Pleasure to meet you." He stepped into the small foyer, taking in the space. Original wood flooring, tasteful rugs, and throw pillows gave the home a warm, lived-in vibe. The savory scent of bacon, mingling with something sweeter—maple syrup?—reinforced the feeling.

Robyn twisted her hands. "Won't you come in?"

He followed her into the living room, where a recap played of last night's season opener between Notre Dame and Boston College. "Is Will home?" The answer to that question would reveal a lot.

"He's in his room, but I'd like to—" Her gaze darted back toward the door. "Excuse me, please. Would you like something to drink? I have sweet tea and, well, water. Unless you'd like a glass of milk." A flush swept up her neck.

"No, thank you. I'm fine."

"Please have a seat." She dashed away before Josh could tell her what a good worker Will was. He'd intended to open with that. He lowered himself onto the puffy beige couch.

The sound of a car engine reached his ears, growing louder. Then it shut off.

They had company. This was getting more intriguing. He'd know soon enough what was going on. He tried to focus on the game, which had been a blowout in favor of the Irish. But even his favorite team couldn't distract him from what was about to happen—whatever that was.

Voices drew his attention toward the entry hall. He blinked at the woman who appeared.

Maggie jerked to a stop. *"Josh."*

He popped to his feet. "Maggie." He tore his attention from her only long enough to get a read on Robyn—a pointless endeavor.

"Maggie, would you like something to drink?"

"Uh, no. Thank you."

"Okay then. Please have a seat." Robyn reached for the remote.

As Josh and Maggie sank onto opposite ends of the sofa, she sent him a questioning look.

He lifted a shoulder, but all he could think was *Man, she's so beautiful.* He'd missed her so much. Maybe she'd hang around afterward to talk. Maggie seemed to be as confused as he was about this little gathering—her shoulders were stiff, her expression guarded. But then, they were at the home of the woman with whom Ethan had apparently cheated. Josh wanted to give her hand a comforting squeeze, but she was too far away.

The TV went silent.

Get your head in the game, idiot. Robyn had obviously made the connection between Ethan and Josh, which meant she'd either called them here to beg them to keep her secret or—

No. Will was here. If he didn't already know the truth, she would've met them elsewhere. His nerves settled at the thought. Robyn had told Will the truth. And she didn't seem angry. She hadn't stopped twisting her hands since he'd arrived.

Robyn perched on the armchair across from them. "As I told Josh, Will's in his bedroom. I asked him to give me a chance to speak with both of you in private. But he does know everything I'm about to tell you. I told him last night." She offered Maggie a sheepish look. "First off, Maggie, I want to apologize for my behavior when you were here before. I—I was caught off guard and I responded poorly. I'm very sorry."

"I understand. Did my husband know about Will?"

Robyn shook her head. "I know you must have a lot of questions, but I'd like to tell you what happened. And I'll be happy to answer any questions you might have when I've finished, if that's okay?"

Maggie gave her a stiff nod.

"Of course." He hoped Robyn wasn't about to cause Maggie more pain. He wanted to shield her from this somehow. But Maggie had never been the type to bury her head in the sand. Her presence today was evidence of that.

Robyn drew a deep breath. "Please bear with me as I start at the beginning." She cleared the nerves from her throat. "I never wanted a marriage—or even a romantic relationship. My parents soured me on the idea. By the time I was sixteen, my mom had been married three times, my dad four. They had tumultuous relationships, the kind that made my childhood chaotic and stressful. They both put their romantic relationships in the position of priority. There wasn't much room left over for a shy little girl.

"By the time I was twenty, I knew I didn't want or need a man in my life. I got through nursing school—I'm an RN now—and once I got my first nursing job, my plan was to have a child. I didn't really have a family—certainly not my parents—and no siblings, and I wanted a child more than anything."

Maggie's spine stiffened and her expression hardened. "You used Ethan to get pregnant."

Robyn's eyes widened. "What? *No.* No, that's not what I did. Please just bear with me."

Josh peered at Maggie. Her hands were knotted in fists, her expression still guarded. "You okay to go on?"

"Yes."

Robyn shifted. "I didn't want the complications that might come with the usual manner of conception—a father pressing for rights or hoping for a relationship with the child or marriage with me. I decided to have an IUI—intrauterine insemination. Long story short, I chose a sperm donor and got pregnant with Will with the first procedure."

"Are you saying . . . ?" Maggie gave her head a sharp shake. "No. Ethan never put back sperm. Why would he? Are you suggesting he donated it in exchange for money? He never needed money that badly." She looked to Josh for confirmation.

He wanted to agree with Maggie—but then, they'd never dreamed

Ethan would've cheated either. "It's okay, Maggie. Let's just hear her out."

Robyn swallowed hard and wet her lips. Then her gaze fixed on Maggie. "Shortly after Will was born, the cryobank informed me there had been some kind of mix-up with the samples, and the gist of it is . . . Maggie, Ethan is not Will's biological father."

Chapter 48

*E*ver since Robyn had begun her story, Maggie had tried to reserve her judgment. Was she telling the truth? And as the story continued—insemination, switched sperm—it seemed a little outlandish. But now her assertion that Ethan wasn't the father of her child had hope surging to the surface like a sunken buoy. Maggie's upper body shot forward. "What?"

"Wait, Maggie," Josh said, then addressed Robyn. "If that's true, why didn't you tell Maggie when she was here before?"

"The cryobank couldn't tell me who the switched sperm came from. All I had was a donor number. And when she showed Ethan's photo—Will is a replica of him. I just knew he had to be Will's biological father." Robyn pressed a hand to her chest. "She blindsided me. I was scared! I was suddenly faced with having to share Will with some family I didn't even know. I was afraid to lose him. It was selfish. I know that."

She turned pleading eyes on Maggie. "I'm sorry I responded the way I did. When the shock of your visit faded, I felt terrible about my part in tarnishing his memory."

Maggie's head was spinning. Whirling. But she pressed ahead. "So you didn't even know Ethan."

"*No.* I swear."

Maggie pressed her palm to her chest. Her husband was innocent. He hadn't cheated on her. Hadn't even known this woman at all. The relief of the revelation made her dizzy.

Josh planted his elbows on his knees, his attention laser focused on Robyn, who was wringing her hands. "You're not telling us everything."

Maggie's gaze shot to him. "This is good news, Josh. Why would she make this up?"

"But it doesn't explain why Will's the spitting image of Ethan," he said softly before pinning Robyn with an unswerving look. "You said Will wasn't his."

"He's not."

"We're supposed to believe that some random sperm sample produced a child who's practically a replica of Ethan?"

Something flashed in Robyn's eyes.

Something that sent a bolt of fear through him.

"The sperm sample wasn't random," Robyn said. "It was yours, Josh."

"Mine?" Josh went still. Everything inside him froze. Except his mind. Thoughts reverberated through his head. *The cryobank in Wilmington. The sperm sample.* He struggled to process the information through the fog that swept into his brain.

He'd been fourteen, facing chemotherapy, when his doctor advised him to put back "samples" for future fertility. He'd been so embarrassed that day, walking into the clinic. Slipping into that room, the pretty nurse knowing what he was about to do. The mortification on top of the disease seemed cruel. When he left the clinic, he was angry and embarrassed as his mom drove him home. He vowed he wouldn't go back.

"I was sick and facing chemo." He gave his head a shake. "They told us they lost the sample."

"I didn't know any of that. Only that there'd been a mix-up at the lab." Understanding dawned in Robyn's eyes. "That's why they couldn't provide me with a donor file. You were never a donor."

He sat back slowly, mind spinning. A shiver passed through him as reality sank in. The room and everyone in it faded until it was only Josh and his thoughts.

Will was his *son.*

The boy resembled Ethan because Ethan was his uncle.

A tear slipped down Robyn's cheek. She silently handed him a sheet of paper.

It had the My Legacy logo at the top and just below it: *Will's DNA.* Under Matches—*Joshua Reynolds: parent/child.*

"He's *mine.*" Josh looked at Maggie, his vision blurring with tears.

"Oh, Josh." Maggie breathed the words.

He had a son. And the proof was right here in his hands. He was overwhelmed with emotion.

"When I called this morning, I wasn't 100 percent sure you didn't already know the truth. You couldn't have hired Will randomly."

"Back in June I spotted him at the carnival," Maggie said. "It was like seeing my husband's ghost. We had to find out who he was."

Josh barely heard them through the chaos in his head. All these years of infertility. He'd resolved himself to never having a biological child. The sudden shift of fortune was disorienting. "Does he know? Does Will know about this?"

Robyn nodded. "He's been searching for his biological father in one way or another all his life. Maggie, when you came to the door before, Will overheard some of that. He thought, like me, that your late husband must've been the sperm donor. A couple years ago he submitted his DNA to that database, and just last night, Josh, your name popped up as a match."

That DNA test Josh had taken actually came through—but not in a way he'd ever expected. He must have an email with the match sitting in his own inbox.

"From there, he got online and pieced it all together."

Josh glanced down the hall. Was Will upset Josh had hired him under false pretenses? Was he disappointed to discover his biological father was just some riverboat captain? Not a military hero who'd died in the line of duty? Maybe Josh couldn't live up to years of hopes and expectations.

"He's dying to talk to you," Robyn said. "I left him in his room, chewing up his nails."

Josh shot to his feet. "Can I go see him?"

Robyn offered a watery smile. "Second room on the right. He'll be the one with his ear pressed to the door."

Excitement bloomed even as his nerves frayed. Insecurity swelled. His gaze darted to Maggie.

Her eyes swam with tears even as a smile trembled on her mouth. "What are you waiting for? Go say hello to your son."

It was all the encouragement he needed. His legs wobbled as he walked the length of the hall. When he reached the door, he gave it a few soft raps. The door swung open immediately.

Will stood there, eye to eye with Josh. Blue eyes—*his*, not Ethan's—stared back at him. His cheeks were mottled pink, his hair tousled as if he'd raked his fingers through it a dozen times. He ran his palms down the sides of his pants.

Josh frowned. "You okay?"

"Did you know?"

Josh shook his head. "I thought you were my nephew."

"Your brother, Ethan—Maggie's husband? I did some research last night."

"Late husband, yes. We thought he was your biological father." Josh steeled himself for a round of questions. "Can I sit down before I keel over?"

"Uh, sure." Will stepped aside, ushering him toward his neatly made twin bed.

Josh's legs gave way. "It's not every day you find out you have a nineteen-year-old son."

Will sat beside him, seeming just as stunned as Josh felt. "It's not every day you find out your boss is your dad."

"Touché."

Will studied his face. "How old are you anyway? You don't look that old."

"Thirty-three."

"Dude, you were fourteen when I was born."

He'd done the math in a split second. Smart kid, his boy. *His boy. His son.* It would take some time to sink in. "I was sick back then— lymphoma. It's a type of cancer so I had to have chemo."

Will frowned. "Wow, you were just a kid. That's rough. I'm sorry."

"I got through it just fine. But before I had chemo, they recommended I bank some sperm in case the treatments made me sterile."

Will winced. "No offense, but I've heard enough about your sperm to last me a lifetime."

Josh chuckled. "Fair point."

"Anyway, I want to know how all this started. How did you even find out about me?"

He told her about Maggie spotting him at the carnival. "She about fainted dead away because you're the spitting image of Ethan." Josh reached for his phone. "Let me show you his picture. You won't believe it."

"I already saw him online. There's a good resemblance."

"Not the younger photos probably." Josh showed him several pictures of Ethan in his late teens and early twenties, photos he'd saved to his Favorites album after Ethan's passing.

Will studied the photos, swiping until he'd seen them all. "Wow. You weren't kidding."

Then Josh relayed the whole story, from their trip to Rock Hill to the day they'd finally found him at the carnival.

"Did you think I was your nephew then? When you hired me?"

"We didn't know for sure. But we were determined to find out. The similarity was too great to be a random fluke."

"Why didn't you just ask me? If not right away, then later after you'd hired me?"

Josh gave him a sheepish look. "I'm sorry for the subterfuge, Will. I hope you can forgive me for that. I didn't ask you questions because I didn't know anything about your family situation. What if you thought your dad was your biological father? We didn't want to blow up your homelife." Josh shot him a humorless grin. "So much for that, huh?"

"Yeah, no joke. It's been kind of hard on my mom. She's been frazzled since Maggie came by that night. But my dad . . . We're not very close. He came along when I was six, and I've always known he wasn't my biological father. Since the divorce we don't see much of each other."

"I'm sorry about that."

"I don't think I lived up to his expectations, you know? We don't have much in common. He's kind of disappointed in how I turned out or something." Will averted his eyes as he blinked back tears.

Josh's heart went out to the kid. "Believe it or not, I know what that's like. We'll have a talk about that sometime." He wrapped his arm around Will's shoulders. "For what it's worth, Will, I think you turned out pretty awesome."

Will's gaze slid hopefully to Josh. "Yeah?"

"Yeah, I really do." He pulled Will into a hug, some part of him still dazed that this amazing young man was his kid.

When Will latched on, Josh let out a sigh. His throat closed up at this unexpected blessing. He stared heavenward as his eyes filled.

Thank You.

When they parted, Josh squeezed Will's shoulder. "You know, it turns out I did end up sterile and the cryobank lost my . . . Well, we won't go there again."

Will gave a strangled laugh.

"The point is, I'd given up hope of ever having a child of my own." Josh's eyes filled with tears. "This is pretty much the best gift I ever got."

Will's lips trembled. "Thanks, man." He blotted his eyes with the heels of his hands. "Hey, you can't tell the crew I blubbered like a baby."

Josh chuckled as he dried his own eyes. "Right back atcha, kid."

Chapter 49

After Maggie returned to Fayetteville, she picked up Zoey from her friend's house and took her to the neighborhood park. As she pushed Zoey on the swing, the humidity beaded on Maggie's skin. The day was blistering hot, but she'd promised Zoey a trip to the park upon her return.

"Higher, Mommy!"

"If we go any higher, you'll have to become an astronaut."

"Astronauts have rockets and special suits and helmets."

"Then we'd better not go any higher."

"You're silly." Zoey kicked her feet out, then tucked them under her.

"Look, Mommy, there's Jada! Stop the swing. Please."

Maggie did as her daughter asked and the minute the swing stopped, Zoey hopped off and ran toward her preschool friend on the jungle gym. Maggie waved at Jada's parents but opted for a spot in the shade. She settled on a bench at the perimeter of the playground, where she could keep an eye on Zoey from the shadow of a live oak.

As Zoey and Jada got reacquainted, Maggie's mind went back to Robyn's house. To the revelation that her husband had not been unfaithful. Once again profound relief poured through her. On that two-hour drive home, she'd mentally apologized to Ethan a hundred times. How would she ever forgive herself for suspecting him of cheating?

Despite the emotional roller coaster she'd been on this summer, she couldn't bring herself to regret the journey because it had led them to Josh's son.

Josh's son.

The wonder of it stung her eyes. She was so very happy for him. He might have missed out on the boy's childhood, but he would be a great father to Will as the boy stretched his wings and came into his own. She hoped Will would be open to a relationship with him. It sounded as if he would.

She was so hopeful that Josh would have a constant, steady *someone* in his life. Not long ago she had dreamed of being that person. But just because Ethan hadn't cheated didn't mean Josh had changed. He was still that fickle guy who flittered from relationship to relationship. He might never settle down with one woman, and her heart couldn't bear another loss.

Especially the loss of *him.*

Her chest squeezed tight. She missed him so much. Seeing him today had only reminded her how much.

Her phone vibrated in her pocket, and when she checked the screen, a smile spread across her face. She accepted the call. "Hi."

"Is it okay that I called?" Josh's voice buzzed with excitement.

"I would've been upset if you hadn't. Josh, you have a son!"

His laughter was full of joy. "I know. Isn't it the craziest thing you ever heard?"

"How'd it go? What did Will say? Is he open to a relationship? Are you just now leaving?"

"Slow down there, Mags. It went great. He's always wanted to know who his biological father is, and it sounds like his relationship with his dad is strained. He wanted to know all about how we found him and I relayed the whole story."

"Was he upset that you didn't tell him?"

"Not at all. He understood."

"I'm so happy for you, Josh. I was just sitting here thinking about that. What else did he say?"

"He wanted to know everything about me and the family. He'd already done some research online. He's smart as a whip, Maggie."

"He gets it from his dad."

"I don't know about that, but I'm pretty proud of him. That's probably stupid when I had nothing to do with his upbringing."

"He's part of you, Josh. You're allowed to claim that. How long did you stay? Did you talk to Robyn again?"

"Just for a bit, mainly to reassure her. She's kind of freaked out. She's had Will to herself all these years. I'm actually just now leaving. I have you on Bluetooth." A long beat of silence followed. "I couldn't wait to call you."

The ragged edge of his voice scraped the corners of her heart. "I'm glad you did. I was dying to know how it went."

"I wanted to check on you too. You must be so relieved."

"Good news all around. Except now I feel so guilty for even questioning Ethan's fidelity."

"Me too. But be kind to yourself, okay? Give yourself a little grace here. You've been through a lot."

"Thank you for saying that." She wished it were that easy. "Well, now what? How'd you leave things with Will?"

"I made sure he was okay with me telling my family. And since we're having our annual Labor Day picnic at Mom and Dad's— you're still invited by the way—I'll tell them the news tomorrow."

That was fast. But then, why delay such good news? "That's great, Josh. They'll be so happy. So surprised."

"No doubt. And I meant what I said, Maggie . . . You're welcome to join us."

She so wanted to be with them. To be with *him*. But her heart wasn't ready for that. She was still in love with him and needed to put some boundaries in place, as hard as it might be. "This is your story, Josh. Your good news. Besides, a friend from school is having Zoey and me over for a pool party. She's looking forward to it."

Silence swelled across the distance. "I understand." His words were weighted with sadness.

She hated that she'd deflated his festive mood. "I'd like to meet Will sometime if that's okay. I mean formally."

"I'd love that. If I have my way he'll be at all the family functions from now on."

"I'm sure your parents won't settle for anything less. They'll be ecstatic."

"They will be. Will's excited to meet them too. Robyn's folks live out of state and don't make an effort to see him, so he's never had real grandparents."

Maggie thought of Brad and Becky's enthusiastic grandparenting and laughed. "He's in for a real treat then."

"That he is." His voice held a smile.

Maggie was reluctant to disconnect the call. Maybe Josh was too. She tightened her grip on the phone as if she could hold on to him for just a minute longer.

I miss you. I still love you.

She imagined him returning the sentiment. A fanciful thought. Still, her vision grew blurry and she blinked back tears.

"Well," he said at long length. "I should probably let you go. I just wanted to chat a minute."

"Thank you for calling. And good luck with your family tomorrow, though you won't need it."

"Thanks. Don't be a stranger."

"I won't. Bye, Josh."

"See ya, Maggie."

Tears pooled in her eyes again as she disconnected the call. She pressed the phone to her chest and told herself they were happy tears.

Chapter 50

*J*osh's goal was to make it through lunch before spilling the news.

But they were only halfway through the meal when his sister aimed a look his way and interrupted the conversation. "What's up with you, Josh? You've hardly said a word since you arrived."

Owen spoke around a mouthful. "And he's had a creepy smile on his face."

"Don't talk with your mouth full." Patrick pinned a napkin down as the wind tried to snatch it away.

"I don't have a creepy smile. I was going to wait until after lunch to tell you, but—"

"You and Maggie are back together!" Erin's eyes sparkled with hope. "I knew it."

"We're not, actually, but thank you for the reminder."

Her expression wilted. "Oh. Sorry."

"I so hoped she would change her mind and come today," Mom said. "I thought after you invited her yesterday she might."

"Let it be, honey," Dad said. "It'll work itself out."

Mia chimed in, "I wanna show Aunt Maggie how I can get in the ocean now."

Mom offered Mia a smile. "You can show her next time she comes, sweetheart. She'll be so proud of you."

"If anyone's interested," Josh said, "I still have some news to share."

"Go right ahead, honey," Mom said. "The floor's all yours."

Josh took a breath, his gaze sweeping around the table. He'd given a lot of thought about how he'd deliver the news and decided he'd cut right to the chase. "It's good news, but you might want to brace yourselves because it's a doozy."

Dad's eyes flared with curiosity. "What is it?"

"Tell us."

"Stop teasing already."

Josh leaned on his elbows and made eye contact with each one of them. "Mom, Dad, everyone . . . I have a son."

Dad's fork paused midair. Mom's mouth dropped open. Erin blinked. Patrick frowned in thought.

"Whoa, dude," Owen said.

Dad lowered his fork. "That's . . . that's not possible. Is it?"

"Honey . . . how can that be?"

"I know it's a lot to take in. Let me explain. I'll start at the beginning." He told them about the mystery man Maggie spotted at the carnival. "He was the spitting image of Ethan. I'll show you." He pulled up the photo Maggie had taken of Will and showed it to them. Mom gasped. Erin covered her mouth.

"The resemblance is uncanny," Dad said.

Josh took them through the ups and downs he and Maggie had experienced as they tried to figure out who Ethan's doppelganger actually was.

When he got to the part where they visited Ethan's friend in Rock Hill, his mom's eyes turned glassy. "You actually thought Ethan might still be alive? And you didn't tell us?"

"We just had to rule it out, and we didn't want to put you guys through that."

He told them about finally finding Will working at the carnival and about adding him to his crew. Told them about the DNA test he'd taken weeks ago. Along the way they stopped him for questions.

"This was going on all summer?" Erin said. "I could've helped you guys."

"We didn't want to get your hopes up. It was hard enough having our own hopes up." He turned to his parents. "And we didn't want to ruin your big trip. We knew you'd fly home."

"Who did you think he was, once you knew he wasn't Ethan?" Mom asked.

Dad gave Josh a knowing look. But there was no reason to go into that part of it. "We thought he must be Ethan's. Given Will's age, he would've conceived him when he was away for his first year of college."

"Ethan was with Maggie then," Mom said. "He never would've cheated on her. He loved her to pieces."

Josh shrugged. "We just didn't know what else to believe."

"This doesn't explain how he's your son," Dad said.

"I'm getting to that. So yesterday I got a call from Will's mom, asking if I could come over and talk. Maggie was there. She told us that Will was conceived through artificial insemination and later found out the cryobank had accidentally switched up the sperm samples."

Mom gaped. "Yours?"

"Mine."

"What's sperm, Mommy?"

All eyes darted to Mia.

Erin cleared her throat. "Um, that's a good question, sweetheart. We'll talk about it later." She shifted her attention to her son. "Owen, can you take your sister inside, please?"

"Oh, man."

"Now, please."

He got up. "Come on, Mia. We're going inside."

"I'm not finished eating."

"We're gonna have a great big piece of apple pie—with all the ice cream you want."

"Yippee!"

Owen shot his mom a disgruntled look before he slid inside the house, but Erin was too involved in the revelation to notice.

Josh handed Mom and Dad the DNA results he'd printed off this morning. "This is from My Legacy DNA, the company where I sent my sample weeks ago. These are my matches."

"'Parent/child.'" Dad's voice was full of wonder.

Mom covered her mouth as she met Josh's gaze. Tears pooled in her eyes. "It's really true? You have a son?" She jumped up, dashed around the table. "You have a son!"

Josh stood and enveloped her in his arms. "I do, Mom. And he's pretty amazing."

"Oh, honey, it's a miracle. A precious miracle."

"It is that." Josh's voice wobbled.

"This is unbelievable," Erin said.

"I talked to him for a long time yesterday. He's such a good kid: kind, helpful, hardworking, and so smart. He was very curious about me, about all of you."

Mom turned loose of Josh and wiped her face. "Well, we need to have him over. We need to meet him. Can you call him?"

"*Now?* Mom . . . don't you want to let this sit a minute? Take some time to digest it?"

"What's to digest? We have another grandson. We've already missed nineteen years of his life and we'll not waste another minute."

Dad flashed Josh a grin. "What she said."

Erin nodded emphatically. "The sooner the better."

"No time like the present," Patrick added.

From the other side of the screen door, Owen smirked. "'Bout time I had a male cousin around here."

Josh breathed a laugh. Well, Will might as well know what he was in for. "All right then. Guess I'll give him a call."

Will put the mower back in the shed, thoughts of a cool shower drawing him toward the house. Of all the days to mow, he'd picked the one with hades-like temperatures. But it was a holiday and he had to take advantage of his day off. Plus, he'd wanted to stay busy and mowing was good thinking time. He had a lot to ponder—he'd already reviewed yesterday a million times.

Over the past twenty-four hours, he'd spent hours chatting with Addison on the phone. She'd been amazed to learn that their boss was his father. She'd helped Will sort out his feelings.

After he grabbed a shower he dressed in casual clothes. Mom was baking—cinnamon rolls, judging by the delicious scent wafting through the house—a sure sign she was troubled. And likely still feeling terrible about the way she'd handled Maggie's first visit. He should probably put her out of her misery.

"Something smells good," he said as he entered the kitchen.

She pulled a pan from the oven and his mouth salivated at the sight of the golden-brown, pecan-glazed rolls. "You're just in time."

It really didn't matter that lunch had only been an hour ago. "Bring it on." He sat at the island and watched Mom sweep around the kitchen. She was always busy, his mom. She'd worked two jobs since the divorce and never complained.

She served up a roll on a small plate and set a fork and napkin beside it.

"Thanks, Mom." Josh dug in, savoring the sweet and yeasty combination. He didn't come up for air until he was finished.

"Is Addison coming over today?"

"No, she's got plans with her family."

Mom turned off the tap and leaned against the counter. She studied him for a long moment. "How are you doing with all this? Are you okay? You've been kind of quiet."

"I'm good. Just taking it all in, I guess." He glanced at the cupcakes sitting in a carrier and a fresh loaf of bread nestled inside a paper bag. "I'm not sure about you, though. You've been baking up a storm."

Her eyes turned down at the corners. "I just want you to be okay, honey."

"Mom, I *am* okay. I finally got to meet my biological father and he's awesome. Are you worried about, I don't know, losing me or something? 'Cause you don't have to. You'll always be my mom."

Her eyes teared up. "Thank you for saying that, honey. I am kind of used to having you to myself. I guess I'll have to learn to share."

"You're the one who taught me that particular skill, so I'm sure you're up to the task."

She approached the island and grabbed his hands. "I can handle anything as long as I know we'll be all right."

"Aw, don't get all sloppy on me."

"I can't help it. You're my baby and—"

"I always will be. I know, I know." He gave her hands a squeeze as his thoughts sobered. "You don't have to worry about us, Mom.

We're good. I understand why you got so rattled when Maggie came knocking. And you eventually told us the truth. That took courage."

"I'm planning to call your dad tonight and tell him the news." They'd decided she should be the one to do it.

"I wonder how he'll take it."

"I don't know—but that's not your problem."

Maybe he'd be relieved. He hadn't seemed very interested in parenting since he left. And his version of parenting only made Will feel misunderstood and insecure. "It's kind of a sticky situation."

"Speaking of sticky." Mom winced as she pulled her hands from his. "Did you even use that fork I gave you?"

Will smirked, then licked his fingers for good measure. His phone vibrated in his pocket—and he did use his napkin before withdrawing it. He wasn't an animal.

The name on the screen made his heart skip a beat. "It's Josh."

Mom offered a smile, then went to the sink to wash her hands.

His nerves jittered. It was just Captain Josh. *Your biological father.* He accepted the call. "Hey, how's it going?"

"I was just gonna ask you that."

Will smiled at the familiar voice. "Going well. Mowed the lawn for Mom and I just helped myself to one of her fresh cinnamon rolls."

"Sounds great." A pause ensued. "Hope you don't mind my calling. I was, um, wondering if you had plans this afternoon."

His chest lightened. "Not really. Why?"

"Well, I'm at my parents' house—most of the family is actually here—and I just told them about you. They're beyond excited to meet you and wondered if you'd want to come over now. I know this is quick, so if you need some time to—"

"I'd love to." Will couldn't help the smile that spread across his face.

"You sure? There's no pressure." Josh lowered his voice. "My family can be kind of a lot."

Will chuckled. He was just excited to have a big family. Grandparents. And cousins! He apparently had three of them. "I'm stoked to meet them. Can you text me the address?"

"I'll do it right now."

"Then I'll be right over."

He disconnected the call and jumped from the stool, energy zinging through his veins. He was about to meet his extended family. "Josh told his family about me. They want to meet me."

Mom dried her hands on a towel, beaming. "Of course they do. They're gonna love you."

"I sure hope so." Will swiped his keys from the counter and his gaze caught on the cinnamon rolls. "Can I bring a roll for Josh?"

Mom's expression softened. "You can take the whole batch for his family. Let me find a nice plate to put them on."

Chapter 51

*M*aggie dashed from her car to the office building, clutching her coat against the blustery forty-degree evening. As usual she approached Harvest Counseling with mixed feelings and a pack of Kleenex.

She stepped inside the office, relieved to escape the cold but trepidatious about the upcoming session. Maggie had been meeting with Miss Allison weekly for three months now. The sessions were in equal parts painful and enlightening.

She was helping Maggie set boundaries—or at least attempt them—with her mother. Helping Maggie unpack the abandonment issues caused by her father's sudden and permanent departure from her life—and exacerbated by the loss of her husband. Also, they were tackling the insecurities leveled upon her by her mother.

In short, Miss Allison had her work cut out for her, as did Maggie. But already she saw improvements. Setting boundaries hadn't yet changed her mom's behavior, but it did allow Maggie to draw a line in the sand and feel justified in following through with the consequences. It gave her some measure of control rather than allowing her mother to steamroll and disrespect her, which had only left Maggie feeling flustered and wounded. It remained to be seen whether the boundaries and consequences would effect a change in Mom. But Maggie already felt less encumbered by their interactions.

After she signed in she took a seat in the small lobby. She had a busy evening ahead with papers to grade and tomorrow's lesson plan to review. She'd been more or less going through the motions at school. There were only two more days before Thanksgiving break, and she was anticipating it as much as her students were.

Another part of her dreaded the holiday. She was heading back to Seabrook for the first time since the meeting with Robyn. Maggie feared her feelings for Josh hadn't waned. Seeing him would be difficult.

The door to the office opened and Miss Allison aimed a smile her way. "Hi, Maggie. Come on back."

"Hello."

Maggie followed the petite midforties woman down the short hall. She wore her red hair in short waves and dressed in colors that flattered her fair skin tone. Tonight she wore a moss-green sweater that matched her eyes.

Miss Allison ushered her into the office that always smelled pleasantly of a flower meadow due to the candles she burned.

Allison Brevard was a woman with keen eyes, excellent listening skills, and uncanny insight. Given all the sharing Maggie had done, she was pretty sure Miss Allison now knew more about her than anyone on the planet—perhaps more than Maggie herself.

It had been scary, making herself so vulnerable, but also incredibly helpful because the woman had a gift. And she was so very careful with Maggie's feelings.

Miss Allison settled in her armchair and Maggie took her usual seat on the sofa.

After a few pleasantries the therapist dove right in. "Well, tell me how the past week has gone with your mother."

"Much the same. She brought up Dr. Derrick again and I reminded her of the boundary. She got very angry and accused me of trying to control her. Then I told her if she was going to speak with disrespect I was going to hang up. So I did."

"And since then?"

Maggie gave a mirthless grin. "She's giving me the silent treatment."

"And how are you dealing with that?"

"I'm trying not to let it bother me."

Miss Allison encouraged Maggie and reminded her not to give in to her mother's manipulations. To keep the big picture in mind instead of getting tangled in the weeds of her mother's tactics.

After they covered that topic, the woman asked how Maggie's homework had gone.

"Pretty good. I wrote seven pages." She was journaling about her abandonment issues. Each week Miss Allison gave her a prompt and Maggie completed the homework. It was difficult work that often left her in tears, but it was also a safe outlet she'd found cathartic.

"That's a lot. As you delved into your relationship with Ethan in light of your abandonment issues, did you discover anything new?"

"I already told you how difficult it was to trust him in the beginning. How insecure I felt. How much I feared being left behind. I realized as I was writing that I felt deserted when he left for college and again when he left for the military. Then of course when he died, I felt abandoned all over again—permanently this time."

"That's perfectly natural even for someone without those issues. But they would've hit you particularly hard."

"When I was writing I remembered how Ethan would sometimes get annoyed with the way Josh and I were together."

"What do you mean, 'the way you were together'?"

"Well, not like Ethan was jealous or anything. I didn't view Josh that way and I think Ethan knew that. But it was so easy being with Josh—and I think he sensed that."

"Why do you think that is?"

She lifted a shoulder. "I could be myself with him."

Miss Allison tilted her head, letting the silence draw out.

Maggie considered her words. Thought back to those days, full of laughter and ease. A light bulb went off. "I guess I could be myself with him because it didn't feel risky." Maggie paused, reflected on that thought. "Ethan used to ask me why I acted differently with Josh than with him. He once said I seemed happier when I was around Josh."

"Were you?"

Was she? She thought back. "I think I was just relaxed with him, and maybe that made me happy. I guess it came as a relief to be who I was."

"You weren't who you were with Ethan?"

"I think I was still trying to figure out who I was. My mom's criticism went bone-deep, and with Ethan, maybe I was afraid to be myself because what if I showed him who I was and he left me, just like my dad?"

Maggie bolted back against the sofa, breathless. Was that what had happened? Was that true?

It sure feels true.

Miss Allison smiled gently. "Aha?"

Maggie took a moment to let the realization sink in. Blinked back tears. "That one took me by surprise."

"How does it make you feel, that realization?"

"Kind of bad that I didn't show my true self to Ethan. But also excited to understand what must've been going on inside me. It makes perfect sense."

"It does. When the first man you love leaves you, you're bound to be afraid it'll happen again. Children often think it's their fault, something they did. But as an adult you can see now it had nothing to do with you."

"I know that up here." She pointed to her head. Her heart was another matter.

"Going into your relationship with Ethan, you had a lot of self-doubt and trust issues as a result of your mom's and dad's actions. Don't forget to give yourself some grace. From everything you've told me about Ethan, he would've been the first person to tell you that."

Maggie went soft inside. "You're right. For someone who came from such a normal family, he was very understanding about my hang-ups. He wasn't perfect, but he was patient with me." She thought of all those months he'd hung in there while she panicked about getting engaged. They went a few rounds about it because she'd already delayed it until they both graduated. Trusting him with her heart had been so hard, though that was no fault of his. And what had she done in return? Held back a part of herself.

"I wish I'd been able to give him my true self. He deserved that."

"From what you say, he seemed pretty happy with the Maggie he knew."

"That's true." She'd been very blessed to have him in her life for as long as she did. He'd been an amazing man. A wonderful husband.

"Have you been in communication with Josh lately?"

Maggie's heart took a tumble at the shift in topics. Strangely enough she was more comfortable talking about her deceased husband. In earlier sessions she'd relayed everything that had happened over the summer. "Just a few texts here and there. I'll be seeing him over Thanksgiving."

Miss Allison's gaze flicked to the clock. "We're almost out of time, but one last thought. I know you're apprehensive about a romantic relationship with a man you describe as fickle. But the ability to be your authentic self with someone is a rare gift. Maybe you can find your way back to that friendship you once had with him." The woman smiled warmly as she came to her feet. "Just something to think about until next time."

"Sure." But as Maggie followed her from the office, a band tightened around her heart. After what she and Josh had shared, the way she felt in his arms, the love that filled her tattered heart . . . she didn't think she could ever be satisfied with mere friendship where Josh was concerned.

Chapter 52

$\mathcal{M}$aggie made it to the Food Lion with thirty minutes to spare. Becky had texted her a few minutes ago and asked her to grab some whipped cream on the way over.

Her nerves had begun clamoring the second she crossed the bridge to Seabrook. She was about to see Josh for the first time in nearly three months. She probably should've turned down the Reynoldses' invitation to Thanksgiving dinner, but she missed them. Missed Josh. And she couldn't deprive Brad and Becky of seeing Ethan's only child. They hadn't seen Zoey since their last trip to Fayetteville over a month ago, and holidays were always hard on them all.

Maggie opened the car's back door and Zoey clambered out. She'd put her daughter's hair in two pigtails, and Zoey chose her pink dress with the tulle skirt because Papaw said she looked like a princess in it.

"Can we get Lucky Charms, Mommy?"

"I'm sure Mamaw stocked up on all your favorites, sweetheart." They were spending two nights. "And Aunt Erin made dirt pudding just for you."

"Yum! Can I eat it first?"

"You have to eat your supper first. But you like turkey and mashed potatoes, and the green beans are the good kind."

"With bacon and crunchies on top?"

"With bacon and crunchies on top."

"I love Thanksgiving!"

Maggie chuckled. "Me too."

The grocery doors slid open, welcoming them inside. The store bustled with last-minute shoppers. She waved to a familiar cashier, then made her way back to the frozen section.

"Ice cream!" Zoey said.

"Mamaw already has ice cream. I'll bet she even has rainbow sherbet."

"My favorite!"

As they progressed down the aisle, Maggie spotted stacked tubs of butter pecan ice cream behind the frosty glass. Her heart gave a soft squeeze at the reminder of Ethan. She said a prayer for the family, that the holiday wouldn't be painful for them. That perhaps Will's presence might serve as a distraction.

This would be her first time meeting the young man, outside of that quick encounter at the carnival. That night seemed so long ago. The entire family already loved him, and if he was anything like Josh, Maggie was certain to love him too.

She slowed at the whipped cream section and reached for the door handle just as another shopper reached for the one beside it. Maggie's glance turned into a double take.

Samantha.

She hadn't seen Josh's ex-wife since the divorce. Before she could decide what to do, the woman recognized her. She was as beautiful as ever, the rich curtain of mahogany hair framing her pixie face. Maggie had always envied her petite build and delicate features—but those features were less than welcoming today.

"Well, Samantha, hello. Fancy running into you here."

Samantha offered a brittle smile. "Maggie."

"Um, it's been a while. How are you?"

"Well, honestly, I've been better." A gush of arctic air escaped as Samantha pulled open the door.

"I'm sorry to hear that." Once upon a time Samantha had been warm toward her. They'd been fairly close. She'd changed in the latter part of her marriage to Josh, grown distant and cold.

"Divorce tends to take its toll."

"Yes, it does. I was sorry to hear about you and Josh."

"Were you now." Samantha grabbed a tub of Cool Whip.

Maggie frowned at her glib tone. "I always thought you guys were great together. You seemed happy."

"I thought so too. Which was why it came as such a shock to discover he was in love with someone else and had been since long before me."

Maggie sucked in a breath. *"What?"*

"Oh, come now, Maggie. You can't be that surprised. You of all people, the object of his affection. I never even stood a chance."

The object of his . . . Maggie shook her head. "Oh, Samantha. You're mistaken."

"When your husband confesses, under the influence of dental sedation, that he's been in love with his sister-in-law since he was a teenager . . . well, it makes things pretty clear."

Since he was a . . . Maggie's mind whirled back in time. When she'd met Josh they became fast friends, sure, but that was all. There were never those kinds of feelings, not back then. She was two years older than him—an enormous gap at that age. "No, that's not possible. He was just drugged and talking out of his mind."

Samantha shoved the door closed. "Save it, Maggie, okay? He confessed the truth later when he was stone-cold sober. I always knew there was something between the two of you. He denied it. Should've trusted my instincts and saved myself a whole bunch of trouble."

She turned away and was gone before Maggie could even string together a coherent thought. What had just happened? Samantha's words reverberated in her head.

"Since he was a teenager . . . He confessed the truth."

Could Samantha be right? Josh had mentioned having feelings for her for a *while*. She assumed he meant sometime around that first kiss a couple years ago. But had it actually been longer than that? Much longer?

"Mommy, aren't you gonna get the whoop cream?"

Her daughter's voice jerked her back to the present. Maggie opened the freezer door and stared mindlessly at the options. She needed to give Samantha time to exit the store. She couldn't face her again. The woman had basically blamed the demise of her marriage on *Maggie*.

A moment later she grabbed two large tubs of whipped cream and took her time heading to the front of the store. She approached the register only when she was sure Samantha was nowhere in sight.

In a daze she waited in line and checked out, responding to Zoey's questions and comments robotically.

At the car she opened the door for Zoey, who clambered in and buckled up. Then Maggie got into the driver's seat and tossed her purse and grocery bag on the passenger side.

Gripping the steering wheel, she thought back to those early years as a teenager. All the games and goofing off and hanging out with Erin, Josh, and Ethan. Through Josh's illness. Was there any evidence Josh had felt more than friendship for her? What about later, after Ethan went off to college? She depended on Erin and Josh for support, for things to do so she wouldn't have to sit at home missing her boyfriend.

She shook her head. Josh had given her no indication of romantic feelings. He'd dated practically everything in a skirt!

And then later, her engagement, the wedding. Josh was Ethan's best man. He planned the bachelor trip to Raleigh, stood beside Ethan while he pledged his life to Maggie, and gave a beautiful, heartfelt toast at the reception.

Had Maggie been completely clueless? Could the whole family have been so clueless? Perhaps Ethan had picked up on it. Maybe that was why he'd questioned her about her relationship with Josh.

Early on Josh had truly seen who she was and, according to Samantha, loved her. Another thought crowded in: Had all the women he'd dated merely been stand-ins for the woman he couldn't have? If Josh's feelings for Maggie went back that far, she must've broken his heart in a million different ways.

Pain unfurled in her chest. He'd driven to Fayetteville so many times during that first year after Ethan's death. He held her, cried with her over the loss of his brother. He walked Zoey for hours. He waited almost three years to kiss her, and when he did, Maggie let him believe she was thinking of Ethan.

Her eyes stung with tears.

"Why aren't we going, Mommy?"

Zoey's voice startled Maggie from her thoughts. How long had she been sitting here? She started the car and a country tune provided background noise for her earth-shattering thoughts. In a daze she pulled from the parking space.

If what Samantha said was true, no wonder his relationships were short-term. No wonder his marriage didn't last. Maybe he wasn't romantically restless after all. Maybe he'd just been in love with Maggie this whole time.

Her thoughts weighed heavily as she stopped at a red light. The song on the radio faded out and a tender guitar riff took its place. The poignant words of "In Case You Didn't Know" filtered through the car.

Her chest tightened at the familiar melody. The last time she'd heard the song she was in Josh's arms, swaying to the music, feeling all the things he made her feel. She was thinking about his fickle heart and regretting that she'd been in denial about her feelings for so long. She was realizing how badly she must've hurt him.

He gazed at her with such care and affection. *"It'll be okay, Mags. I'm not gonna let anything bad happen to you."*

She pressed a fist to her heart. He'd always been thinking of her, taking care of her. When she needed someone, he was the first person she called because she knew he'd be there. He listened, he understood, he loved her *for who she was* and had for a long, long time.

Her pulse thrummed in her ears, and her breaths came quick and shallow as her vision went blurry.

A horn tooted and she blinked. Green light.

With renewed energy and purpose she shifted her foot to the gas and accelerated.

Chapter 53

*J*osh was watching for Maggie out the beach house window. He realized that might have seemed pathetic, but really he just needed to clear the air before she stepped into the madhouse that was his parents' Thanksgiving.

A bit of smoke hung in the air—spilled grease apparently. In the kitchen Mom fussed over the turkey and nearby Dad stood on a chair waving a towel in front of the smoke detector. Patrick and Owen pretended to help in the kitchen while sneaking peeks at the Cowboys game blaring in the living room. Since it was seventy and sunny, Erin and Will set the tables on the deck, their chatter carrying through the screen door. Mia ran from room to room in a pink tutu, waving a magic wand, its pink ribbons fluttering alongside her.

He was usually immune to the chaos, but today it was plucking at his last nerve because, Maggie. No doubt seeing her would pick off the scab he'd been growing for almost three months. But he could do this—fake it. He'd done it a million times before, hadn't he?

He just needed a moment with her to set the tone. To show her he could be casual-friend Josh. Brother-in-law Josh. Return to their old ways and get their footing back before she reentered their family. Before she met his boy. He needed to set his mind at ease—and hers too. She was no doubt worried about how this might go. Worried about how he was doing. He'd reassure her all was well—then they could all relax and enjoy the day.

Ha.

Like it or not, this would be his future, since moving from Seabrook was no longer an option. He'd missed Will's entire childhood. There was no way he was missing another day. Even if it meant having his heart wrenched apart every time he saw Maggie.

The hum of a car's engine sounded, drawing his focus down to the drive. Maggie pulled in, edging up to Will's bumper. Josh's heart rocked in his chest as he headed toward the front door. He slipped outside, made his way down the steps, and caught sight of Maggie opening the back door for Zoey.

Maggie was beautiful in a casual sage-green dress that fluttered around her long legs. Some of her hair was pulled back into a clip and the shimmering waves ruffled down her back. He'd thought maybe he'd grow used to that dull ache in his chest, but nope.

Zoey jumped from the vehicle, scooted around her mother, and caught sight of him at the bottom of the steps. "Uncle Josh!" She ran straight into his arms.

"Hey, Cupcake." He swooped her up, tightening his arms around her. Man, he'd missed the kid. "Long time no see. Did you behave on the drive down?"

"I wrote a book for Mia. I know all my letters now."

"That's because you're so smart."

"It's Thanksgiving and Aunt Erin made dirt pudding just for me, but I have to eat my mashed potatoes and turkey first."

He tweaked her nose. "You like mashed potatoes and turkey, silly."

"Yeah, but I like dirt pudding better."

He chuckled. "Can't blame you there, kid."

"Hi," Maggie said as she approached.

His laughter faded as the soft tone of her voice warmed him through. "Hey." His gaze homed in on her bloodshot eyes. The pinkened tip of her nose. He recognized the signs of a recent crying jag and frowned.

Zoey wiggled from his arms. "I'm gonna go see Mamaw and Papaw."

He set her down and took the grocery bag from Maggie. "Here, honey, run this inside. We'll be in in a minute."

"Okay!" Zoey grabbed the bag and dashed up the steps.

Josh focused on Maggie's expression. The tentative smile didn't fool him one bit. "What's wrong? What happened?"

Her smile wobbled. "Nothing. I'm fine."

"You've been crying."

She gave up all pretense. "I, uh, ran into Samantha at the grocery store."

"*Samantha?*" His ex-wife was capable of delivering quite the tongue-lashing, not that *he* hadn't deserved it. But Maggie sure didn't. The thought of her dressing Maggie down in public made him see red. "What did she do? What did she say to you?"

Maggie glanced over his shoulder toward the beach. "Um, can we maybe take a quick walk on the beach?"

"Sure." This wasn't exactly the conversation he'd anticipated, but it needed to be had. They headed down the walkway between the homes. "Was she mean to you?"

"No. Well, she wasn't exactly nice, but that's not why I'm upset."

"What is it then?"

She was quiet as they took the few steps to the boardwalk that led over the sand dunes. When they reached the top she touched his arm, stopping him.

He made a study of her face. Eyes that flicked away. Tension straining the line of her forehead. Teeth clamping the soft flesh of her lower lip.

And he suddenly knew what Samantha had said. He could even imagine exactly how she'd said it. Hadn't she uttered such things to him a hundred times during the downward spiral of their marriage? *"You're disgusting. You're in love with your brother's wife. You've been sniffing after her this whole time! You should be ashamed of yourself."* That sneer on her face. That look of contempt. He'd deserved all of it.

And now Maggie knew his terrible secret. She must think he was an awful person. And an awful brother. Heat flushed his face. His heart slammed his rib cage. He scratched his neck.

But there was no avoiding this. It was happening, right now, and he might as well own up to it. His gaze skittered to her eyes and found them searching his face.

"Is it true?" she said softly.

Wary, he nodded. Scanned her face for traces of loathing. Disgust. Contempt.

But he found none of that. She didn't seem to be mad or horrified. Didn't seem to hate him. Instead she was gazing at him like . . . like maybe she loved him anyway. She palmed his cheek, her touch so soft he could've wept. The weight of guilt fell off him like broken shackles.

She leaned closer, brushed his lips with hers. His arms went around her and she slid into his embrace, arms snaking around his shoulders. He tilted his head and went for broke. To have her back in his arms was heaven. Especially because she knew the truth and didn't hold it against him. What a sweet release.

He lost himself in the kiss, which went on long enough to steal his breath and stir his blood. But as his brain surfaced, reality came with it. They had some talking to do. He eased away, framed her face with his hands just to make sure she didn't go far.

"How long?" she whispered.

He stared into those doe eyes. "Since the first time I saw you in the kitchen, sitting at the island with Erin, eating grapes."

Her eyes twinkled. "That's very specific."

"I can still see you like it was yesterday in that white top, cutouts on the shoulders. You wore a white choker necklace made of ribbon and dangly silver earrings. And your laughter . . . the sound of it made my heart skip a beat. I'd never felt anything like it."

Maggie shook her head. "I didn't know. I didn't have any idea. I remember meeting you. You hung out in the kitchen with us for a while, but you were so quiet. I thought you were shy."

"I was nervous. You made me tongue-tied."

"But you were always so good with girls!"

"What can I say? Love slammed into me pretty hard." Remembering what happened next, his smile wilted. "Then Ethan came around and I noticed the way your eyes lit up when you saw him."

She winced. "Oh, Josh."

"I was too young for you and I knew it. It took about two minutes for you guys to hook up."

"I'm sorry. That must've been painful to watch."

Nothing like teenage heartbreak. Except when those same feelings followed you into your twenties and beyond. "I thought it would pass. I'd had crushes before and they were fleeting. But this was different. This was love."

"Nobody knew?"

"I was embarrassed at first. You viewed me as Erin and Ethan's kid brother. I could see that. Then as we grew up and your relationship with Ethan became serious—permanent—I felt like a dog. I harbored feelings for my brother's wife. Feelings I would've done anything to eradicate. God knows I tried my best."

Maggie smirked. "You sure did."

His gaze sharpened on her. Was that jealousy flaring in her eyes? Well, what about that? "Every woman fell short, way short, because none of them were you."

Her face softened. She turned his hand, pressed a kiss to his palm. "Speaking of all your conquests . . . Now's probably the time to admit the real reason I called things off between us."

The *real* reason? He searched her face.

"I was scared to death you'd never be able to commit to me."

He couldn't help it—he burst out laughing. "Oh, that's rich."

"*What?* You dated every woman in Seabrook for, like, two seconds each."

He nailed her with a look. "Because I couldn't have *you.*"

"Well, I didn't know that then." The sheepish look on her face tugged at his heart.

"It's okay. I guess it must've seemed like I had massive commitment issues." He kissed her forehead as his laughter died off. "I did make my marriage work, for a while anyway. I really thought I might be able to make a life with Samantha. I did love her at one time, though not the same way I love you. It was . . . love *lite*, I guess you could say. I hoped it would grow into more. Thought that as it did, my feelings for you would surely subside.

"But they never did and I felt terrible about that. I was swamped with guilt. First because Ethan was my brother and then because the woman I really loved wasn't my wife. All that guilt caused me to put up walls with Samantha—took me a while to see that—and it caused a lot of insecurity on her end. Then she found out how I felt about you." He shook his head. "There was no coming back from that."

"I'm sorry."

"Not your fault. You didn't do anything wrong."

"You couldn't help how you felt, Josh. You kept it inside. You never acted on it."

"Till a few years ago." He gave a wry laugh, remembering the playful moment that turned serious on her living room couch. "That kiss rocked me back on my heels."

"You and me both."

"You didn't admit it to me, though. You let me believe you were thinking of Ethan. And when we finally got together this summer—even though it wasn't for long—I loved every minute of being with you. I always felt a little second best to Ethan, but this summer I thought if I could just have *you*, I could live with playing second fiddle to my brother where you're concerned."

Maggie's eyes went glassy. "Oh, Josh, that's not the case at all."

"You don't have to say that, honey. I know he'll always be your first love."

Maggie shook her head, an adamant look coming over her features. "You don't understand. You're not my second choice, Josh—you're the first man to love me for who I truly am."

He blinked, trying to absorb the words.

"Counseling has been very enlightening on several fronts. Among other things, I've learned I was afraid to be myself with Ethan—but never with you. I was myself with you and you loved me anyway. You have no idea how precious that is to me."

Was that true? She seemed so certain. He wasn't in competition with his brother: She would always love Ethan, as she should. But the revelation soothed some wounded part of him. "You're perfect the way you are."

"Perfect for you." Her smile trembled. "Everything you've been through all these years . . . It must've been so hard for you. I hate that I caused you so much pain."

His thumbs swept across her cheeks. "It was hard. But I'd go through it all over again if it ends with you in my arms. I love you, Maggie."

"I love you too." She brushed his lips with hers. "You've always been there for me, always loved me just the way I am, flaws and all. I'm yours, Josh, if you'll have me."

He took her mouth in a kiss that left no doubt about his answer. It betrayed all the love, all the passion he felt for her. He couldn't believe she was finally his. He was never going to let her go.

When they broke apart, she beamed. "I haven't even said hi to your family."

"Might as well do that now." He jerked his head toward the beach house, where his entire family gawked from the deck.

She burst out laughing. Gave a wave.

They whooped and hollered.

Owen jabbed his fist in the air. "Way to go, Uncle Josh!"

Josh laughed, taking her hand. "I think our private little interlude is officially over."

Maggie fell in step beside him. "Just as well. Isn't it about time you introduced me to your son?"

Epilogue

The gondola climbed slowly, the wheel lifting them above the fray. Above the shouts of carnies, the trill of a game, the squeals, and the peals of laughter. All of it faded as Maggie and Josh rose into the night. Off to the side waves rolled onto the beach with their steady rhythm, and the moon hung overhead, casting a silvery light on the water.

The May wind tugged at Maggie's hair and she captured it in her hand. Leaned into Josh's side, getting cozy. "It's such a beautiful night."

"Um, have I ever told you I'm not altogether comfortable with heights?"

She lifted her head. "Really? Didn't you go paragliding after you graduated from high school?"

"That was eighteen-year-old Josh. Thirty-four-year-old Josh likes something a little more substantial than air beneath him."

"Are you gonna be okay?"

"I'll be fine. Just feeling a little jittery—and not enjoying the view quite as much as you."

"You should've said something earlier. We didn't have to ride."

"I wanted to be brave for Zoey."

Maggie smiled. "That's very sweet." She zeroed in on the gondola just ahead of them, now sweeping downward. Will sat beside Zoey, his arm flung around her shoulders. "I wonder how she's doing."

Just then her daughter turned, the top of her head barely visible over Will's arm. "Mommy, I'm doing it! I'm riding the Ferris wheel!"

"I see you! You're so brave, honey." Maggie smiled as Will's arm tightened protectively around her daughter. "He's really good with her."

"He sure does love her. And she's pretty smitten with him too."

Josh groaned as they swooped down toward the ground.

She set her hand on his thigh—and her diamond solitaire caught under the carnival lights, glittering. Two days after Thanksgiving Josh had proposed on the beach in what would forever be the most romantic moment of her life. It had been a short engagement—Josh had already waited so long, Maggie saw no reason to make him wait any longer.

They'd married on New Year's Eve in a private ceremony officiated by Patrick. Will and Big D stood with Josh, and Erin and Zoey attended Maggie. Her mother had been invited but, still in a snit about Dr. Derrick, chose not to attend. Maggie was okay with that. The wedding was drama free, a lovely affair, full of meaning and poignant moments. Josh gazed at her throughout the ceremony, eyes shimmering with unshed tears. Just the memory of it made her heart swell.

"I guess we're going around again," Josh said as the gondola swept past the exit stairs and started back up.

"We can ask to get off anytime, you know."

"If Zoey can do it, so can I."

She patted his leg. "All right, tough guy. Have it your way."

When they neared the top again, Will shouted back to them. "Hey, look over there!"

"There's fireworks, Josh!" Zoey called. "They're big! Do you see them?"

A red starburst bloomed over the water, accompanied by a deep boom.

"I see them," Josh called.

Since the wedding, Zoey had taken to calling him *Josh*, just like Will. After all, he was her stepfather now. Will came over to the house at least once a week to hang out, have supper. Sometimes they included his mom or Addison—they were such a cute couple. Will and Josh played basketball together regularly, sometimes with Brad, who was no match for his son or grandson.

While Will might have inherited Ethan's looks, he'd taken after his father in the athletic department. He'd also inherited Josh's little eyebrow hitch—a fact Maggie loved more than she could say.

According to Will, the man who'd raised him hadn't seen him much since learning about his biological father. But apparently that wasn't much of a change. Maggie still held out hope the man would come around in time.

In the spring Will had finally agreed to let Josh supplement his college costs, eliminating the need for school loans. Will still insisted on paying what he could. He worked for Josh part-time during the school year and planned to work full-time again this summer.

Maggie glanced at Josh. "How you doing over there?"

"Is it almost over?"

She homed in on his face, which seemed relaxed enough. He might be a little wobbly, but he was mostly messing with her. "Maybe I can distract you from your fear."

He flashed a grin her way, eyes gleaming, his phobia apparently forgotten. "Now we're talking."

"Wow, that was easy enough." She pretended to think. "Hmm, distractions . . . Well, let's see. Katherine called today. A cute two-story bungalow east of the state park just went on the market. There's an open house on Sunday afternoon." They'd been living at his place since the wedding but agreed they needed a bedroom for Will.

He gave her a wry look. "That's great, but not really the kind of distraction I had in mind."

She played clueless. "Oh, well, I also got a new client today—two actually—twin brothers. They're on the swim team at school and want to train with me this summer."

"Hey, that's great news. Your roster's really filling up. Before you know it you'll have a waiting list."

After she'd gotten engaged, Maggie gave her notice at school. She'd miss her students, but she was ready for a new chapter. Swimming lessons were a natural fit and there seemed to be a need for instructors on the island. Ever since she'd moved back to Seabrook, she'd been building a clientele for her new business, the Mobile Mermaid, which she'd kicked off in April. Their new house would either be equipped with a pool or have the space to install one.

Josh nudged her. "Still not quite the distraction I was hoping for."

"Really? Jeez. I'm running out of ideas over here."

"Maybe I can help you out." He turned her face toward his and kissed her. His mouth moved slowly, reverently, taking its sweet time. His lips parted hers and he went to work, kindling a familiar fire inside her. Oh, the man was good.

She set her hand on his neck, where his pulse thrummed steadily against the soft flesh of her palm. She forgot about distractions and gondolas and other people. Her world shrank to the two of them, to the love that burned for him, the desire that built for him every time he touched her.

"Ew, they're kissing again!"

Zoey's voice and subsequent giggle dragged Maggie from that dreamy cocoon. The gondola swayed to a stop as Maggie opened her eyes to find they were midway down.

Will regarded them over his shoulder. *Really, guys?*

Josh shrugged, then tightened his arm around her shoulders and whispered in her ear. "Now that's what I call a distraction."

She gave him a coy look. "To be continued . . ."

"Yes, ma'am," he said with enthusiasm.

As the gondola steadied, Maggie's gaze drifted around the carnival below. The rides, food stands, game alley. Her thoughts went back to last summer. To that first sighting of Ethan's look-alike just over there. It had been such a shock. But look where it had ended up. Look where *they* had ended up.

"This is where it all began," Josh said as if reading her mind.

"It seems so long ago, doesn't it?"

He gave her a squeeze. "It was quite the summer. You found my son. Saw him and wouldn't let it go. Did I ever thank you for that?"

"Several times. And you didn't let it go either. We found him together." She squeezed his hand. "And then we found each other."

Josh had been right there through every twist and turn. More recently he'd been a great support as she'd shifted careers—her biggest cheerleader. And he always gave good advice when it came to her mother, with whom she now maintained a more distant relationship. He encouraged her to keep her boundaries in place. Listened when guilt swamped her. She'd continued counseling with Miss Allison remotely, but Maggie sensed she would soon be ready to fly on her own.

Well, not entirely on her own.

She glanced at Josh as the ride swooped them downward. He stared off into the distance, a furtive smile lingering on his lips. "What's that grin all about?"

He peered at her, his eyes going worn-denim soft as the moment drew out. "I was just thinking that I've never been this happy before. I love you, Mags, and I love doing life with you."

He did know how to make her light up inside. "I love you too. Every day with you, with our new little family, is a blessing from above."

The ride swung to a stop, and the carny opened their door and freed them from the safety bar. Then they stepped out into the night together, hand in hand, ready for whatever came next.

Acknowledgments

*B*ringing a book to market takes a lot of effort from many different people. I'm so incredibly blessed to partner with the fabulous team at HarperCollins Christian Fiction, led by publisher Amanda Bostic: Patrick Aprea, Savannah Breedlove, Kimberly Carlton, Caitlin Halstead, Margaret Kercher, Becky Monds, Kerri Potts, Nekasha Pratt, Taylor Ward, and Laura Wheeler.

Not to mention all the wonderful sales reps and amazing people in the rights department—special shout-out to Robert Downs!

Thanks especially to my editor, Kimberly Carlton. Your incredible insight and inspiration help me take the story deeper, and for that I am so grateful! Thanks also to my line editor, Julee Schwarzburg, whose attention to detail makes me look like a better writer than I really am.

Author Colleen Coble is my first reader and sister of my heart. Thank you, friend! This writing journey has been ever so much more fun because of you.

I'm grateful to my agent, Karen Solem, who's somehow able to make sense of the legal garble of contracts and, even more amazing, help me understand it.

To my husband, Kevin, who has supported my dreams in every way possible—I'm so grateful! To all our kiddos: Justin and Hannah,

339

ACKNOWLEDGMENTS

Chad and Taylor, Trevor and Babette, and our four beautiful grand-children. Every stage of parenthood has been a grand adventure, and I look forward to all the wonderful memories we have yet to make!

A hearty thank-you to all the booksellers who make room on their shelves for my books—I'm deeply indebted! And to all the book bloggers and reviewers, whose passion for fiction is contagious—thank you!

Lastly, thank you, friends, for letting me share this story with you. I wouldn't be doing this without you. Your notes, posts, and reviews keep me going on the days when writing doesn't flow so easily. I appreciate your support more than you know.

I enjoy connecting with friends on my Facebook page: www.facebook.com/authordenisehunter. Please pop over and say hello. Visit my website at www.DeniseHunterBooks.com or just drop me a note at Deniseahunter@comcast.net. I'd love to hear from you!

Discussion Questions

1. Which character did you most identify with? Why?

2. When Maggie first stumbled upon the mystery man at the carnival, who did you suspect he might be? Would you have been able to let it go? Or would you, like Maggie and Josh, have had to find out who he was?

3. Did Maggie and Josh's quest for the truth take you where you expected to go? Discuss.

4. Maggie had been dealing with her mother's narcissism all her life. Discuss some of the ramifications of that and how her mother's behavior played into Maggie's self-worth. What advice would you give Maggie regarding her mother?

5. Josh carried his unrequited love for Maggie for years. Was it wrong for him to have married Samantha? Should he have handled his feelings differently?

6. Will always felt the deficit of not knowing his biological father even though he had a father in his life. How did his relationship with that father leave you feeling?

7. Josh had always felt second best next to Ethan, especially where his father was concerned. Discuss how his childhood illness played a role in that. Discuss how Josh might be able to help Will in this area.

8. Maggie was reluctant to believe Ethan had an affair with Robyn. Did you feel the evidence supported his guilt, or did you feel there must be another reason Will bore such a close resemblance to Ethan?

9. Josh's ex-wife was understandably bitter about his long-standing feelings for Maggie. Discuss how her harsh words deepened his shame and how that ultimately impacted his relationship with Maggie. Have you ever dealt with shame? What advice would you have given Josh?

10. Discuss the ways Maggie's abandonment issues, which stemmed from her father's desertion, impacted her relationship with her husband. Have you faced abandonment issues? If so, what have you found helpful in overcoming them?

About the Author

Photo by Salve Ragonton

Denise Hunter is the internationally published, bestselling author of more than forty books, three of which have been adapted into original Hallmark Channel movies. She has won the Holt Medallion Award, the Reader's Choice Award, the Carol Award, and the Foreword Book of the Year Award and is also a RITA finalist. When Denise isn't orchestrating love lives on the written page, she enjoys traveling with her family, drinking chai lattes, and playing drums. Denise makes her home in Indiana, where she and her husband raised three boys and are now enjoying an empty nest and four beautiful grandchildren.

DeniseHunterBooks.com
Facebook: @AuthorDeniseHunter
X: @DeniseAHunter
Instagram: @deniseahunter